Praise for *Me and Johnny Blue*

"*Me and Johnny Blue* is old-fashioned storytelling raised to the level of home-grown art, told in an American language that is almost gone."
> —Loren D. Estleman, four-time Spur Award–winning author of *Wh... ...rt*

"Wildly comic and darkly compell..."
> —Robert Olen Butler, Pulit...
> of *A Good Scent from...*

"Real cowboys never lie... usually only to make a g... rollicking big windy has o... ...s of truth, but not enough to keep it from ... very funny."
> —Elmer Kelton, six-time Spur Award–winning author of *The Good Old Boys*

"*Me and Johnny Blue* is a tragicomedy with the humor transcendent. It is an original, imaginative work. A delight. Do not miss this one."
> —Max Evans, Spur Award–winning author of *The Rounders*

"Take a pair of pugnacious cowboys who never saw trouble they didn't like, mix them with a fiendish villain and his diabolical filibusters, and the result is comic delight. Joseph West brings to this engaging novel an encyclopedic knowledge of the West. He keeps the body count sufficient to satisfy gluttons, frosts his cake with bawds, throws a few wolfers, a boxer, and a patent-medicine huckster into the pot, rings in all the Western legends worth recounting, and seasons the stew with smiles."
> —Richard S. Wheeler, Spur Award–winning author of *Sierra*

The Silver Arrowhead

JOSEPH A. WEST

A SIGNET BOOK

SIGNET
Published by New American Library, a division of
Penguin Putnam Inc., 375 Hudson Street,
New York, New York 10014, U.S.A.
Penguin Books Ltd, 80 Strand,
London WC2R 0RL, England
Penguin Books Australia Ltd, Ringwood,
Victoria, Australia
Penguin Books Canada Ltd, 10 Alcorn Avenue,
Toronto, Ontario, Canada M4V 3B2
Penguin Books (N.Z.) Ltd, 182–190 Wairau Road,
Auckland 10, New Zealand

Penguin Books Ltd, Registered Offices:
Harmondsworth, Middlesex, England

First published by Signet, an imprint of New American Library,
a division of Penguin Putnam Inc.

First Printing, April 2002
10 9 8 7 6 5 4 3 2 1

For my daughter Alexandria . . .
Shaolin-Kempo karate black belt,
sword fighter and perfect young lady.

ONE

"Oh my God!"

Those whispered words fled like desperate fugitives from the trembling lips of my employer as he first beheld Crow Creek, a faded, ramshackle cow town huddled on the prairie close to the foothills of the Rocky Mountains.

Chester Wong and I had come to save a client from the hangman's noose, yet even that lofty purpose could not compensate the great and brilliant detective for this devastating introduction to the Montana cattle country.

As for myself, being just twenty and of a somewhat adventurous nature, the little town with its single muddy street filled me with a tingling excitement.

Crow Creek had been built by hard-drinking track-layers and tough ranchers, and in the olden days it had boasted a dozen saloons and several bawdy houses before anyone thought to build a church. False-fronted buildings, shacks, and a sprawl of corrals and feed sheds where the cattlemen put their herds while waiting shipment east all rubbed shoulders with the railroad.

Even at this early hour of the morning the bustling

street was filled with cowboys in wide hats and high-heeled boots, thick-shouldered hardrock miners, grave and bearded farmers, and smartly dressed townspeople. Wagons jostled in the narrow thorough-fare and red-faced drivers yelled, "'Way there!" and "Pull aside, damn ye!" and cursed villainously both at their fellow drivers and their white-eyed mules.

As far as I could see, burdened down as I was with my employer's valise, carpet bag, and satchel con-taining his latest book manuscript—in addition to my own small suitcase and, of course, the precious Dragon Box—the town consisted of a general store, a two-story hotel, a saloon, a restaurant with a badly lettered sign outside that said MA'S KITCHEN, a livery stable, a bank, and the sheriff's office.

All these buildings were much weathered, their clapboard planks curling outward here and there, re-vealing bent and rusty iron nails. On one side of these structures were some boarded-up tar-paper shacks, and beyond the shacks, shaded by tall cottonwoods growing along the creek that gave the town its name, stood a dozen or more white-painted gingerbread houses, each on a five-acre lot, their fronts bordered by neat picket fences. The other side of town ended abruptly with the general store, and beyond that there was only the open prairie, a sea of rippling buffalo grass stretching all the way to the pine and aspen-covered foothills of the mountains.

"This," said my aghast employer," is the low-rent district of hell."

Unlike myself—loaded down as I was with lug-gage—that great mind of Mr. Wong's, the nemesis of archcriminals from San Francisco to Boston, had to remain unfettered at all times, thus he carried only his cane, the silver handle of which was cunningly wrought into the shape of a Chinese dragon, its eyes two glittering red rubies.

My employer, guardian, and mentor transferred the cane from his right hand to his left, and his now unencumbered digits clutched the front of his chest. "Chance, what have we done?" he gasped.

Indeed, as I stated earlier, we had come to save an innocent man from the noose, but my employer's face, round as the moon and red as an apple, with eyes of periwinkle blue, betrayed not the determination and resolution one might expect but only the most manifest horror.

That fall of 1908, Chester Wong was in the prime of life, being somewhere in his mid-forties and of a most robust constitution that never admitted even a single day of illness. He was of short stature, and somewhat portly in physique, being just a shade over five-foot-five, tipping the scales at around three hundred and fifty pounds. His belly was very large—owing in most part to his great fondness for food—but he had small, well-formed feet that carried his girth admirably. His hair was sleek and black as a raven's wing, brushed straight back from a high, intelligent forehead. Over-all he was, despite his lack of height, a most imposing and noble figure.

Unlike myself—I am one hundred percent Chinese-American—Mr. Wong's mother was Irish, his father a recent immigrant from Canton—and the great detective was possessed of all of the virtues and none of the vices of both these ancient cultures, including a bent for philosophy and a gift of the blarney that could charm the birds off the trees. But if he had a vice—and I whisper this only in the strictest confidence—it was an unfortunate tendency toward gluttony. Even that soaring intellect succumbed regularly to the baser instincts of a growling belly.

And he was vain, yes. But his vanity was of a pure sort, the vanity of a great thinker who had outwitted some of the most brilliant criminal minds in the world and was thus supremely confident of his superior intellectual powers and took great and justifiable pride in them. The lord Buddha tells us ego and vanity are impure desires that cloud the mind, but surely my employer had avoided such a trap, because his wonderful intellect remained intact, his wisdom famous. Indeed, many men can utter words of wisdom, few can practice it themselves.

Chester Wong was one of those few.

"Bacon and beans," quoth my employer, despair cracking his voice like ice on a winter pond.

"What did you say, sir?" I asked, struggling with my heavy burdens along the station platform to his side.

"Bacon and beans, Chance, that's all they eat out here on the far side of nowhere. I shall starve to death for sure." Mr. Wong beat his breast and made a dramatic show of fainting away. Behind us the mighty locomotive that brought us here hissed and steamed on the track like a teakettle on the hob, and my employer now cast a longing glance in that direction.

"Thaddeus Brent has a sin to answer for," sighed that great detective, "bringing us to such a benighted place."

Mr. Brent was an old and distinguished lawyer in

New York City, an ancient, wizened little man who handled Mr. Wong's finances and affairs. Those who wished my employer to embark on a case sent their requests in writing to Mr. Brent who—if he thought the matter offered a possibility of challenging detective work—made the necessary arrangements and passed the details on to Mr. Wong.

And indeed, that's how our present client in Crow Creek had recruited our services.

An advertisement for our agency, and I say "our" because in my own humble and amateurish way I tried to help as much as I could, appeared weekly in the Eastern newspapers of the more respectable sort, stating simply:

PRIVATE INVESTIGATIONS
DISCREET   REASONABLE RATES
NO CASE TOO LARGE OR TOO SMALL

The ad gave Mr. Brent's name and address, since Mr. Wong and I had none. We were, as the Scotland Yard detectives say, "of no fixed abode," traveling around the country, and indeed the world, as my employer's whims and restless, seeking nature dictated.

Happily, Mr. Wong was of independent means. His father, a gold miner, had left him a considerable fortune that Mr. Brent invested wisely, allowing my employer to live off the interest while the principal remained untouched, and indeed had grown apace since his parent's demise some ten years earlier.

Mr. Wong tore his eyes from the locomotive and vented a drawn-out and anguished sigh. "Chance, there's nothing else for it but to proceed at all possible

speed and dispose of this case in short order. Then"—
he smiled for the first time that morning—"we can return to civilization. A great Chinese philosopher once
wrote that the bravest sight in the world is to see a
great man struggle against adversity. Behold that
sight now, child. And learn."

Modestly, my eyes downcast as befits someone of
my lowly station in life, I replied that I was indeed
honored to witness such a notable and, yes, noble
event.

"As you should be, child," returned Mr. Wong.
"Now, our first stop is—and I use the term very
loosely—the hotel."

My employer's method of locomotion was most
peculiar and one of great dignity and purpose. He'd
point his mighty belly at the destination of his choice,
propel that prodigious protrusion resolutely forward,
then allow his short and sturdy legs to catch up as
best they could. He now proceeded in this stately
manner, waving his cane at passersby like a
broadsword while declaring in a loud voice, "Clear
the way there, clear the way."

Small and slight as I was, and burdened down with
our baggage, I struggled after him. But on more than
one occasion, to my shame, Mr. Wong, had perforce to
glance over his shoulder and declare in exasperation:
"Come along, Chance. Don't dawdle, child. The habit
of tardiness is first a cobweb, later a cable."

How I would have managed to cross that bustling
and crowded street without mishap I do not know,
had not a voice at my shoulder declared: "Need some
help, little lady?"

I turned my head and beheld a tall and lanky cowboy, his horse's hairy chin resting on his shoulder. He was about my own age with brown, lively eyes, an amused smile playing on his lips. His huge, wide-brimmed hat was pushed so far back on his head—revealing a thick shock of curly yellow hair—I declare I thought it would fall off at any moment. He sported a large and gallant mustache the sight of which, I must confess, made my heart go all aflutter.

Ahead of me, Mr. Wong was setting a fine pace, parting the crowd as Moses parted the waters, and, left far behind, I confess I was uncertain as how to proceed, so this gallant and timely offer of assistance was most welcome.

"I'd be most grateful, sir," I said.

"Hey, don't call me sir, and you a little Chinee gal no bigger'n a nubbin'," the cowboy grinned.

"The name's Gary Finucane, though most folks around here call me the Teton Kid, or just Kid for short. This here"—he slapped his horse affectionately on the nose—"is Big Boy, or just Boy for short."

"Well, I'm pleased to meet you both." Weighed down with luggage as I was, I nevertheless managed to drop a little curtsy. "My name is Last Chance Lee."

"That's a dilly of a name, an' it suits you perfect, seein' as how you're pretty as a speckled pup under a wagon an' all."

I felt my face flush. I knew men had begun to look at me in a certain way, but this was the first time one of them had come right out in the open and said I was pretty, Mr. Wong being of a serious nature and above all such frivolities.

In those days I stood a shade under five feet and was very slender as most American women of Chinese descent are. That morning I wore a straight black skirt to my ankles, a pink-and-white striped blouse with the puffed sleeves that were then in fashion, and I'd piled my long hair up under a straw boater, its crown circled by a gay red ribbon.

My employer paid me a clothing allowance that was, to say the least, less than adequate. But by sewing most of my own clothes I managed to make do, though shoes, hats, and hose were always a problem. Those I could not make.

I had recently raised this very subject with Mr. Wong, but he'd sternly replied: "Chance, the great Confucius once wrote that outside show is a poor substitute for inner worth. Always remember that."

And thus chastened by that towering intellect, I had not broached the subject of my allowance since.

"Let's get all that stuff on ol' Boy here," the Teton Kid said, taking the valise from my hand. One by one, the rest of the luggage followed, stashed in various places around Boy's saddle—all but the Dragon Box, which I kept close to hand.

"What you got there?" the young cowboy asked.

I replied: "This is a box much cherished by my employer, Mr. Wong. I am charged to never let it out of my sight."

The Kid laughed. "That where the old guy keeps his money?"

I merely smiled in reply, and the cowboy didn't press the matter. He placed his spurred and booted foot in the stirrup and swung easily onto the horse's back. Then he reached down and effortlessly lifted me into the saddle.

"But we're only crossing the road to the hotel," I protested.

The Kid laughed, showing strong teeth of remarkable whiteness. "A cowboy never walks where he can ride. Even across a road."

I must confess, I found the experience most enjoyable. The young man smelled of horse and woodsmoke and harsh lye soap, a not altogether unpleasant combination.

As his steady mount picked its way toward my employer, who was waiting impatiently on the boardwalk outside the hotel, I glanced at the sky. Iron-gray clouds were piling up like vast mountains and in the distance I detected the distant rumble of thunder.

Following my glance, the cowboy observed gravely: "Big storm's comin'. Means we'll have a sight of thunder and rain. An' that's good, because the range could sure use a good duck drencher."

The Teton Kid suddenly stopped his horse in the middle of the street and swept off his sombrero, and I immediately saw why. A funeral procession, preceded by a man of somber mien in a frock coat and tall hat, was marching solemnly toward us, beating slowly on a black-draped bass drum. After the drummer came the hearse, drawn by four mules covered to their hooves in dusky mourning cloths of the darkest velvet.

The melancholy and hollow BOOM . . . BOOM . . . BOOM of the drum echoed the roll of the gathering thunder, the soft clop, clop of the mules' feet and the rumble of the steel-shod hearse wheels providing an eerie counterpoint.

Behind the hearse strode a preacher dressed all in

black, his white hair falling to his shoulders, his eyes burning in his pale face like hot coals. He had a huge Bible pressed against his chest and he cried fervently: "Help us, Jesus! Jesus save us!"

At his heels came the bereaved, a plump woman in widow's weeds supported by a couple of stalwart matrons. The woman pressed a lace handkerchief to her eyes and wailed in unison with the preacher: "Oh sweet Jesus! Oh my Jesus!"

At regular intervals the widow's supporting women raised their eyes to heaven and joined in the lament: "Hallelujah! Save us, sweet Jesus!"

"That," said my young cowboy friend as the melancholy procession slowly rolled past, "is Old Man Johnson. He had the rheumatisms an' was took a couple of days ago. His widow there owns Ma's restaurant and she makes the best apple pie in Montana. 'Course," he added, settling his hat back on his head, "that's when she ain't grievin' or nothin'."

I don't know if it was the dreariness of the funeral procession, the casket jiggling back and forth with the motion of the carriage as if the white-faced man inside was struggling to break free, or the ominously approaching thunderstorm—but I suddenly felt a strange sense of unease. It seemed to come from Crow Creek itself, as though the whole town was on edge, holding its breath . . . waiting for something dreadful to happen.

Apart from the Kid, that irrepressible cowboy, I noticed no smiles on the features of the people in the street. They looked gray and drawn, going about their business like automatons, expressionless, just so many painted eyes on wooden faces.

According to the letter we'd received from Mr. Wong's client, a senseless and savage murder had been committed in the hills to the west of Crow Creek, and the alleged killer now awaited trial in the town jail.

Was it because the townspeople believed they harbored a deranged assassin in their midst that they acted so strangely?

Or was my sense of foreboding a portent of things to come, not of events present and past?

I had no time to ponder these questions just then, because at that moment occurred a most distressing event that served to plunge my employer into an even blacker mood, if that were possible.

As I approached the boardwalk on the Kid's horse, I beheld a small and ragged dog, full of fleas and mischief, explore with his nose the immaculate drape of the great detective's pants over his spats and patent leather shoes.

Who can fathom the mind of a dog? Certainly this little fellow, through a thought process I can't even imagine, apparently decided that Mr. Wong's expensive gray broadcloth was the perfect place to . . . shall we say, "do his business." With a brazen disregard for my employer's reputation and lofty status, the uncaring cur cocked his leg and emitted a yellow stream against the great detective's leg!

My employer must have felt the hot splash on his ankle and lower calf, because, with a nimbleness that belied his great bulk, he hopped smartly to his left, looked down and beheld the small canine, its face full of slyness and ancient deviltry, closely studying his other leg with great determination of mind.

Mr. Wong let forth with a mighty roar of outrage and raised his cane as if to strike the offending beast. But the dog, seeing the writing on the wall and not liking what it read, tucked its tail between his legs and scuttled away with an alarmed "Yip! Yip! Yip!"

The detective ran—if that is the right word for my mentor's rather ponderous method of locomotion—after the hound but soon realized that pursuit was hopeless. He thereupon contented himself with shaking his fist at the fleeing animal, declaring darkly that if there was a God in heaven, they would meet again and then the outcome would be vastly different, to the detriment of the cur's health.

The Teton Kid reined up his horse outside the hotel and gently lowered me to the boardwalk beside my employer who was tapping his foot and trembling all over in obvious agitation.

"*Yeeeehaw!*" the Kid exclaimed delightedly. "That mutt was so ugly, somebody ought to shave his rear end an' make him walk backwards!"

But the great detective was in no mood for such levity.

"That," declared Chester Wong nodding toward the Kid's mount, "is an undignified way to travel, Chance. Remember that the young lady who constantly draws attention to herself encourages the lecher and the false suitor alike."

"I'm so sorry," I said, "but this young man offered to help, and I was a little overburdened." I waved toward the Teton Kid who was sitting his horse, an amused little smile on his face as he studied my irritated employer. "His name is—"

Mr. Wong raised his hand. "No! That is trivia,

Chance. Minutiae. The name of one of the local aborigines does not interest me at this time because it signifies nothing. My brain"—he tapped the side of his magnificent head with a forefinger—"must be kept free of all such distractions until this case on which we are now embarked is solved to my satisfaction."

Indeed, as always, the great man was right and I was wrong.

That powerful intellect had to remain completely uncluttered so that its rationality, reasoning and deductive powers could be honed to a razor-sharp edge and thus cut through to the heart of the matter at hand.

Once more I humbly apologized, a little afraid that I had perhaps, all unwittingly, become an ally of the disrespectful dog and blunted Mr. Wong's great prowess in the field of criminal detection. Somewhat mollified, my mentor told me, though rather sternly, not to let it happen again, that a mind like his was a most delicate precision instrument and could be quite unbalanced by an overload of extraneous information.

"True greatness," he said, "is to be free of all trivial thought."

As the Kid laid my luggage on the boardwalk, he smiled at my employer and said: "I know you, you're the famous detective Angela Hudson sent for all the way to New York City."

"You're singularly well informed, sir," quoth Mr. Wong brusquely. He was kicking out his right foot as he shook his pants leg, his face registering disgust not unmixed with a certain amount of despair.

"Well, it's Angela's daddy who's in jail for killing

the scientist gal who dug up that big chicken back in the hills," pursued the Kid. "That gal was right pretty, too. A mite unfriendly, but pretty."

"Chicken?" echoed my employer. "What's this about a chicken?"

"She found the chicken buried in the hills, just afore she was killed. I rode over thataway one time, an' afore she run me off, I seen this big chicken skeleton lying in a pit. Must have been twenty feet long if'n it was an inch." The young cowboy shook his head. "Darndest thing was, that chicken had the biggest teeth I ever saw in a critter, up to an' including a full-grown, daddy grizzly bear."

"Chickens . . . teeth . . . scientists . . . bears . . . I'll be the judge of what's relevant here," Mr. Wong said shortly. He waved a dismissive hand toward the Kid. "Now be off with you." He turned to me. "Chance, bring the luggage. And this time, please don't dawdle or talk to strangers."

"Only thing is," began the Teton Kid, halting my employer as he turned to walk into the hotel, "you're a mite too late."

"What do you mean, too late?" inquired my employer irritably. "Young man, Chester Wong is never too late. The sluggard does not tell the busy bee that he's tardy."

"Well, the buzz is that you're too late this time," the cowboy said dryly. "Brad Hudson hangs three days from now. He's already been found guilty."

A look of consternation crossed the face of the world's greatest detective, but he recovered quickly and said vehemently: "Then we have little time. The die is cast and speed is of the essence."

My employer pointed his belly at the door of the hotel and thrust it forward, his short legs and small feet hurrying to catch up.

I picked up the luggage, and once again burdened, made haste to follow.

"How can you work for that feller?" the Kid asked, shaking his head. "I swear he's got a fuse shorter than an ant's eyebrow."

"Mr. Wong has his peculiar little ways," I said, and gave my new cowboy friend a quick smile. "His is one of the greatest minds in the world, you know."

"You could have fooled me," said the Teton Kid as he turned his horse away from the boardwalk.

"One thing before you leave," I said quickly. "Do you believe this Brad Hudson killed that woman?"

"The jury thought so."

"But I want to know what you think."

The cowboy removed his hat and wiped the inside band with a bandanna he took from the hip pocket of his jeans. "Little lady," he said, a touch of anger honing a thin edge to his smile, "I think he's as guilty as hell, an' if he lasts till Monday without bein' lynched it will be a miracle. Look at these people, look at their faces," the Teton Kid added grimly, waving a hand toward the street. "They know what Brad Hudson done. That scientist gal was . . . ravaged, then cut up real bad with a knife. Folks around here reckon the man you've come all the way from New York to save ain't a human being, he's a wild animal."

The Kid settled his hat back on his head and tipped me a nod. "Glad I could be of service, ma'am. Now, good day to you."

As I watched the young cowboy knee his horse into

the street, I recalled with a shudder the sudden flash of hate in his eyes as he uttered Brad Hudson's name.

Why did he dislike the rancher so much?

And did he plan to be part of a lynch mob that would take the law into their own hands? As I entered the hotel lobby, these were many questions without answers, and they disturbed me terribly, adding to my dreadful sense of unease and dark foreboding.

TWO

"Two rooms," declared the hotel clerk loftily, motioning with an upraised hand, "on the *second* floor."

He said it with the slightly condescending air of a man who managed not this dark and dingy little false-fronted shack, but a hotel of many levels, where only the very best rooms were located on the *second* floor.

"That will do, I suppose," declared Chester Wong gloomily, "though I would have preferred adjoining rooms." He nodded toward me. "When one's ward is so very young, one can't be too careful. What God is to the world, guardians are to their children."

"Indeed," said the clerk, nodding sympathetically. He was a small, plump man with a neatly trimmed mustache, his hair parted in the middle and arranged on each side of his forehead in kiss curls that had been artfully pressed into place with sugar and water. "But unfortunately, the hotel is almost fully booked." The clerk leaned conspiratorially across the counter toward my employer. "Folks are in town for the hanging."

"I am aware of that," declared my employer sternly. "In fact, I am here to put a stop to it."

"You mean the hanging?" exclaimed the clerk in alarm, quite taken aback by this bold statement.

"The very same," said Chester Wong, puffing out his cheeks and shuffling his tiny feet in a display of great determination.

His face stricken, the clerk spun the registration book toward him and looked at my employer's scribbled signature. "Here," he said, glancing up after a few moments of deep study, "I know you, you're that famous detective feller they talk about all the time in the Eastern newspapers."

Again, my mentor went into a magnificent display of an almost avian nature, nodding his noble head in agreement as he smiled broadly and shuffled his feet even faster, thrusting the vast spread of his belly this way and that as he strutted for the awed clerk's benefit.

"An' you write books and stuff, don't you?"

"Famous," quoth the supreme detective, halting his spectacular exhibition long enough to hold up an imperial hand. "My works are famous all over the world."

"My employer's first important book—*The Cuisine of Central Europe, Being a Dissertation Upon the Soups, Ragouts, and Fowl of Each Region*—is currently being well received both by the critics and the public at large," I interjected.

My mentor nodded his head, as much as to say the case for his genius had been clearly put.

"He is now," I added, "hard at work on his monumental five thousand page work, *The Great Chefs of Europe from the Time of Louis XlV to the Present, Being an*

Account of Their Curious Lives and Great Culinary Creations."

"Indeed," declared Mr. Wong with feeling, "after six hundred pages I have left the Sun King in my wake and I am about to hurdle the Revolution before tackling the cooks of the mighty Napoleon. It is as Miss Lee says, a monumental work, and, let me add"—and here he sighed in a state of feigned dejection—"it is also an arduous task. I say, sir, ard-u-ous."

The clerk absorbed this information with a rapid nod of his head, and then inquired in a somewhat subservient tone if the great detective and renowned author would perhaps care to see his rooms?

Mr. Wong shook his head at him.

"I'm sure they're adequate," he said, though I saw from his sour expression that he secretly harbored no such opinion. "Just have our luggage sent up. There are important tasks at hand, namely a man's life to save, and I must be about my business."

The clerk called to a teenage boy who was slouching in a corner of the lobby. "Sammy, take this gentleman's luggage to room 204."

"He's got enough of it," the youth observed insolently. He was a dull-eyed and gangling boy, his face covered in red, angry pimples.

"Never you mind about that," countered the clerk. "Just do as you're told."

"And be careful with that satchel, it contains a manuscript of great value," cautioned my mentor anxiously.

The young man, who up close smelled like manure and moldy hay, effortlessly picked up the baggage that lay at my feet and reached for the Dragon Box. "Gimme that," he said.

I shook my head at him. "This stays with me."

"Eastern folks is so damned uppity," the teenager growled.

With an ill grace, Sammy made his way upstairs, and when he had gone Mr. Wong asked the clerk if the local constable was in town.

"If you mean Sheriff Burt Havenick, you'll likely find him in his office just down the street," the clerk replied. He studied my mentor closely. "A word of warning," he added. "Sheriff Havenick is a hard and dangerous hombre. Back in the old days when Crow Creek was booming, he killed half a dozen men, four of them right out there on Front Street. He ain't a man to be trifled with."

Once again, I felt icy fingers of dread clutch at my stomach. As I heard my mentor assure the hotel clerk that Chester Wong was not a man who dealt in trifles and would do nothing to antagonize the lawman, no matter how quick his trigger finger, I tried to analyze that feeling—and realized to my horror that it was fear!

But fear of what?

Try as I might, I could not put a shape to it. It was just a vague, formless dread, like being stalked by something monstrous on a darkened street, hearing its echoing footfalls, knowing it is coming after you, evil and invisible and patient, grinning in the gloom. With fangs . . .

Mr. Wong put his hand on my shoulder, and I declare I jumped three feet in the air!

"Chance!" declared the great detective in surprise. "Whatever's gotten into you, child?"

"Sorry," I said, feeling a blush creep into my cheeks, "I . . . I guess I was daydreaming."

"First dawdling then daydreaming," my mentor said sternly. "That's no way to behave when there's much work to be done. Remember, work keeps at bay three great evils: boredom, vice, and need." He looked at me askance. "Mind yourself, honored Keeper of the Dragon Box."

Thus chastened, I hung my head and meekly followed Mr. Wong out to the boardwalk.

The approaching thunderstorm was now a looming threat, piling up black clouds in the sky that looked like huge, curling sheets of lead. The wind had picked up as the storm grew close and a dust devil danced in the street, spiraling this way and that between the legs of horses and mules, rousting an alarmed hound dog from his place under the boardwalk before spinning out of sight down a narrow alley between the bank and the doctor's office.

An empty can tumbled end over end in the wake of the dust devil and pieces of waste paper fluttered in the air like tattered butterflies. People walked with their heads bent, covering up against the sting of blowing sand. The wind sighed and blustered around every corner, banging doors and rattling locks as if eager to come inside and work even more mischief.

I turned to watch the erratic progress of the bouncing can and saw the hotel clerk hurry outside. He glanced briefly up and down the street, then rapidly made his way across the road before disappearing down the same alley that had been taken by the dust devil.

I pointed out the clerk's furtive behavior to my employer, and for a brief moment he considered this new intelligence. Finally he said: "He's probably just gone for an early lunch, nothing more. So you see, my dear Chance, what you've told me is trivia."

"But," I protested, "the only restaurant in town is closed because of the funeral. Besides, it's on the same side of the street as the hotel."

"Triv—" Suddenly Mr. Wong was aghast. "What did you say?"

"About what?" I pushed down my skirt that kept being lifted above my ankles by the inquisitive wind.

"The restaurant."

"It's closed today. That funeral you saw was Ma's poor husband being put to rest—he had the rheumatisms, you know."

"Then it's all up with me," gasped my employer, falling against the outside wall of the sheriff's office, for we had, despite the vagaries of the wind, reached our destination. "I now know I shall starve to death." He seemed to consider other and less dire possibilities and added: "Or at least fade away to a mere walking skeleton."

"Perhaps the sheriff knows of another place we can eat," I suggested. "Perhaps the saloon."

"Perhaps," echoed my employer, though in a hopeless tone of voice. "We can but ask."

As we pushed open the warped door of the sheriff's office, I was still pondering the mysterious behavior of the hotel clerk. I believed he was hurrying to make a report to someone. But report what? Obviously that the great detective Chester Wong was in town and had vowed to free Brad Hudson from the noose.

But who would care if my employer proved the condemned man's innocence?

I believed there was only one person who had anything to fear from that eventuality—the real killer.

THREE

When we walked into the sheriff's office, a tall, wide-shouldered man rose from behind his desk. He wore a dark blue shirt and black jeans held up by a belt with a fancy silver buckle. A gun belt circled his slim hips, the mahogany grips of the huge revolver in his holster much worn from use. A sheath containing a broad-bladed knife with a staghorn handle hung on the left side of the belt, and a star cut from a silver dollar adorned the breast of his shirt.

Sheriff Burt Havenick was in his mid-forties, a long-faced man who, like the Teton Kid, still sported the full, sweeping cavalry mustache that had been popular during the wild days of the frontier. His eyes were the color of washed-out denim, revealing nothing, offering less. They were, I decided with a shudder, the cold, pitiless eyes of a killer legitimized by the star on his chest.

The office itself was small and cluttered. A gun rack containing a dozen rifles and shotguns adorned one wall, and beside it a large clock that kept time with a dignified tock, tock, tock. Some wanted posters, yellowed with age, curled away from the woodwork here and there, and a photo of some long-forgotten posse, Sheriff Havenick looking grim and determined in the middle of them, hung on the wall behind his desk.

"What can I do for you folks?" the lawman asked pleasantly enough.

His trained gunman's eyes quickly traveled from Mr. Wong to myself and back again, missing nothing. He saw a moon-faced, Oriental-looking gentleman of portly physique and a slender slip of a Chinese girl carrying a box with a dragon on the lid, and I guess he sized us up as being no possible threat.

"I," said my mentor loftily, "am Chester Wong, a detective of no small reputation. You may have heard of me."

An amused smile played around Havenick's lips. "Yeah, I've heard of you all right," he said. "You're the private dick Angela Hudson sent for all the way to New York City."

My employer, shuffled his little feet and nodded his head, making a somewhat halfhearted display, like a peacock in a box.

"Well, you're plumb too late, Mr. Wong. Brad Hudson hangs at dawn Monday morning."

"So I've heard," said my employer earnestly, "and I've come to save him from that dismal eventuality."

Havenick sat on the corner of his cluttered desk and shook his head. "You haven't a hope in hell."

"Perhaps you can tell me the circumstances of the murder?" suggested Mr. Wong.

"There ain't much to tell," Havenick countered.

"Whatever you can do to enlighten me would be appreciated," returned the great detective. "Enlightenment must come little by little, otherwise it would overwhelm the mind."

With a surge of joy, I realized for the first time that morning that Mr. Wong's powerful intellect was at last ready to deal with the case that had brought us all the way from New York to Crow Creek. The game was afoot!

"Well," said Havenick, "since the 'nineties, there have been people all over the Sun River country"—he waved a hand toward the foothills of the Lewis Range to the west—"and they've been looking for what they call dinosaurs, big lizards I guess. When they find 'em, they ship them to museums back East. There's money in it, a lot of money. Why, just a few months ago some scientist feller uncovered what he called a . . . Tyr . . . a Tyr—"

"Tyrannosaurus rex." I finished it for him.

Havenick flashed his cold smile. "Yeah, that's it. He found the monster north of the town of Jordan and the marshal there tells me it's worth a fortune, enough to keep a man in beef and beans for the rest of his life at any rate."

"Yes, yes," said my mentor impatiently. "This is all very interesting, Sheriff, but, come now, no trivia, get right to the point."

"Well, the point is," Havenick drawled, unfazed by Mr. Wong's brusque speech, adjusting the gun on his hip to a more comfortable spot, "last spring this pretty scientist gal named Victoria Grant discovered a new kind of dinosaur in the hills an' she spent all summer digging it out of the bedrock. There was a passel of museums interested in that thing, especially a big one in Boston that wanted it real bad."

"What kind of dinosaur is it?" I asked.

Havenick shrugged. "Like I said, Victoria Grant told me it was new, so it ain't any kind of dinosaur that anyone's identified afore."

"Did you see it?" I inquired.

"Of course. I rode out there a couple of times to see how the work was progressing. It's just a skeleton, and it's pretty small, maybe fifteen feet long from snout to tail, but from what I could see it was all teeth an' claws an' bad attitude." The sheriff's hand strayed to the handle of his gun, like it was a sudden comfort to him. "Little lady, it seems to me that thing up there in the hills was a killing machine that could put a real hurt on a man. The Flatheads say it was the dinosaur that done for Victoria Grant, the way she was all tore up an' all."

"Why do they say that?" I asked, and I heard a little tut-tut of impatience come from my employer.

"Because they believe the creature, whatever it is, was appointed by the Great Spirit to guard them hills until the end of time. See, the Indians believe them hills are sacred, so when Victoria Grant disturbed the monster's resting place it was a great sacrilege, an' the creature, well the Great Spirit made it rise out of the ground an' tear her all to pieces."

"Why . . . why that's horrible," I gasped, fear spiking at my stomach.

"Unfortunately," quoth my mentor, "it is also trivia." Chester Wong shuffled his feet and pointed his great belly at the sheriff like a loaded cannon. "Now, sir, if you please, let's cut right to the chase. What had my client—for indeed, Brad Hudson is my client, let there be no doubt about that—I say again, what had my client to do with all this?"

Havenick smiled, a slight twisting of the lips that didn't reach his cold eyes. "That dinosaur was found on Brad's northern range," he said. "He told Victoria Grant—she called herself *Doctor* Grant, you know."

The great detective nodded his sleek and handsome head. "Trivia. Proceed."

"Well, Brad told her the monster was his, since it was found on his range. He told Dr. Grant that her financial backers, that Boston museum I was telling you about, could have the skeleton for ten thousand dollars."

"And?" prompted my employer.

"She told him to go to hell, that it was a case of finders keepers. Besides, Victoria Grant knew that Brad had no real claim to that land because them hills is all open range, and that means federal property."

"But why would Mr. Hudson, one of the biggest and richest ranchers in the state, care about a paltry ten thousand dollars enough to kill for it?" I asked, instantly drawing an exasperated look from Mr. Wong.

Havenick shook his head at me. "Dunno," he said. "But I do know things have been pretty bad around here for the past three, four years. First a drought killed off a lot of cows, then the last couple of roundups have met low prices at the Chicago railheads. I'm told Brad was into the bank pretty heavily, just to meet his payroll and keep the Rafter H goin'."

Chester Wong sighed. "Sheriff, my ward, who is innocent in all matters of finance since she has no worries on that score, may consider ten thousand dollars a paltry sum, but I say to you, sir, it is a considerable sum, and men have killed for less."

Havenick nodded. "True. Fact is, I've done it several times for a lot less than that my own self. You're talkin' a measly fifty bucks a month an' a tin star."

The sheriff's icy eyes met mine, and I could see pride there, the pride of a slick and practiced killer who counts his victims then files them neatly in his memory, dusting them off now and then to relive the moment.

I realized in that instant that I disliked Sheriff Havenick intensely. And I feared him. This man would kill without remorse or a shred of feeling, and when called to it he'd be as sudden and deadly as a coiled cobra.

My mentor held up his hand. "When I said men had killed for less, I did not mean those words as an implication of my client's guilt. It was merely a statement of fact." The great detective shuffled his feet. "Now, sir, once more to the root of the case. A jury found Mr. Hudson guilty of a terrible crime. What other evidence was introduced at his trial?"

Havenick rose easily to his feet and walked to the potbellied stove in a corner of his office, his spurs ringing like silver bells. He lifted the coffee pot. "Sure you don't want some?"

Mr. Wong shook his head, but I said: "I'll have a cup, if you please."

I watched Havenick get another cup and pour my coffee. He wore his gun on his right, yet lifted the pot and poured the coffee with his left. It was a small thing, probably of no significance, but I stored it in my memory.

The coffee was strong and bitter, but it tasted good.

"The morning of the day Victoria Grant was murdered, she met Brad in the street, and the two quarreled," the sheriff said, resuming his perch on his desk. "Brad, who was in a mean and ugly mood, had been drinking all night with one of our local troublemakers, a rider for the Circle O by the name of Gary Finucane."

"Oh," I said, "the Teton Kid."

"You've met him?" Havenick asked in surprise.

"My ward," said Mr. Wong sternly, "is sometimes not too choosy in the company she keeps."

"Well," the sheriff said, "the Kid ain't really a bad sort when he's sober. This burgh"—he nodded toward the street—"ain't big enough to have a town drunk, so the local cowboys take it in turns."

"Ah yes, very amusing I'm sure," said Mr. Wong, smiling faintly. "Now, sir, the facts."

"The fact is, Brad Hudson told Dr. Grant that if he didn't get his ten thousand, she'd never leave this county alive. Again she told him to go to hell, and that night she was murdered."

"How was she killed?" asked the great detective, his wide, intelligent brow, the bane of the criminal class the world over, furrowed in thought.

Havenick opened his mouth to speak, then hesitated. "You might want to step outside, young lady," he said. "What I have to say ain't for the ears of the weaker sex."

"Sheriff," I retorted, an edge of anger in my voice, "despite my years, I have seen murder most foul many times in the past. Believe me, the results of violence no longer have the power to shock me."

"This is true," interjected Mr. Wong. "Chance has assisted me, albeit in a small way, on some of my most diabolical cases. She has seen bloody death in all its forms, and it holds no terrors for her."

Havenick shrugged. "Suit yourself." He paused for a moment, took a deep breath, then continued. "Victoria Grant was raped savagely, perhaps several times. She had bloody bite marks all over her neck and shoulders, like a wild animal had been at her. She'd been tore up badly by a knife. Her breasts were slashed away and her . . . her . . . female parts was all cut an' hacked to ribbons." The sheriff shuddered. "Doc Lawson said he couldn't tell if the woman was alive when the cuttin' began." He turned his frosty eyes on me and said: "I hope to hell she wasn't."

Havenick turned to my employer. "You ever seen a woman's body after Apaches have done their work, Wong?"

The great detective shook his head. "I can't say I have."

"Well, I have, back in 'eighty-two in the Sierra Madres. I was a young man then, barely out of my teens, an' scoutin' for the Army. I've never forgotten what I saw. We came across a couple of settlers, a man and wife I guess, an' the man had been tortured to death. Then they started on his woman.

"The lieutenant who led the patrol reckoned the woman had been raped by twenty, thirty bucks afore they started to cut her up. Took her, oh, maybe from sunup to sundown to die. Reason I'm tellin' you all this, Wong, is that Brad Hudson tortured Miss Grant worse than them Apache bucks did that settler woman. Much worse. Maybe Victoria Grant died a shade faster, but she died screaming in mortal agony, an' that's a natural fact."

I felt suddenly sick and put my coffee mug down on the sheriff's desk. "That's horrible," I said. "I can't believe any man in his right mind would do such a thing. He would have to be completely insane."

Havenick shrugged, his eyes hardening. "Well, it happened. An' that's why there's talk of vigilante justice in town. There's them as say we shouldn't wait until Monday, an' that's how come I'm wearin' this gun in town for the first time in three, four years. I ain't never lost a prisoner to a lynch mob afore, an' I don't aim to start now."

The lawman shook his head and contemplated first me, then my employer. "Look," he said, "Brad Hudson an' me go way back. Hell, he was a friend of mine an' he even gave me this buckle." Havenick pointed to his belt. "Had a couple of them made up special a few Christmases ago. I don't want to see him hang, but I got to tell you, after what he done to that Grant woman, well, I reckon he's got it coming."

"May I..." Chester Wong's words died in his throat and he tried again. "May I see my client?"

"Your funeral," Havenick said, rising to his feet. He nodded toward a closed door at the back of the office. "His cell is back there."

My employer and I followed the lawman to the door, which he unlocked with a ponderous iron key, and we found ourselves in a dark, narrow hallway. At first I could barely see in the windowless gloom, but Havenick lighted an oil lamp and held it at shoulder height and I beheld two iron-barred cells to my left, one used as a storeroom filled with ledgers, stacks of papers, a broom, mop and bucket, and other odds and ends, the other containing a bunk whereupon lay the recumbent figure of a large and bulky man.

"Brad," the sheriff called to the man on the bunk, "you got visitors."

The man rose slowly to his feet and shuffled, leg irons clanking, to the barred front of his cell.

Brad Hudson was unshaven, unwashed, and smelled of stale sweat. He had a heavy, jowly face with deep-set black eyes, and his shoulders under his stained shirt were thick and sloping. His huge arms and hands gave the impression of raw power. I could see determination and dominant will in this man, and knew at once how he'd been able to carve a thriving ranch out of the harsh and unforgiving Montana wilderness.

I could also see that here was a cattle baron who would kill to keep what he regarded as rightfully his.

Strangely, when he spoke his voice was light and melodious, almost shy. Pressing his face against the bars of his cell as he tried to make us out in the guttering light of the lamp, he said: "The only visitors I'm expecting are my daughter and the preacher, so who are you?"

"I," said my employer with great importance, "am Chester Wong, a private detective hired by your daughter to save you from the doleful fate that awaits you. And this"—he waved a negligent hand toward me—"is my assistant, Miss Last Chance Lee, whom I've raised since she was orphaned as a child."

Indeed, the great detective had saved me from the horrors of the orphanage when I was but eight years old, he having known my father, though but slightly, as the result of a murder case he'd investigated in San Francisco's Chinatown. My father had been of some small help to Mr. Wong, at one point saving him from an assassin's dagger, and the famous investigator, out of a sense of gratitude, had rescued me a few years later from the workhouse and raised me as his own daughter.

Over the years the bond between us remained very strong, and in many ways I considered Chester Wong not only as my guardian, but as my real father.

I had been gently raised, and therefore dropped Brad Hudson a little curtsy, telling him I was glad to meet him, even under these most melancholy of circumstances.

"I remember now," Hudson said in his soft voice, nodding toward Mr. Wong. "You're the famous private detective my daughter sent for all the way to New York City."

My mentor admitted that he was, and shuffled his feet and bobbed his head in a fine and handsome display.

"Well," began the condemned man piteously, "you're too late. They've done for me at last and I must hang."

"Not if I can help it," returned the great detective with determination.

"I'm an innocent man, Mr. Wong," Hudson continued. "They say I killed that Grant woman an' . . . an' ravaged her. Well, that ain't my way. I admit I hated her for tryin' to cheat me out of the money that was rightfully mine when she found that dinosaur on my land, but I didn't hate her enough to kill her."

Hudson slammed his open palm angrily against

the iron bars of his cell. "Besides, I wouldn't have gone at her with a knife; I'd a got me my ol' .45 an' shot the bitch."

"That don't wash, Brad," Sheriff Havenick interjected. "Them hills was full of Flatheads, they'd have come a-runnin' when they heard a gunshot. Besides, your knife, all covered in blood, was found in your barn."

"Somebody put it there, Burt, I tell you. I didn't kill that woman."

Havenick sighed. "Brad, you tole all this to the jury an' it didn't save your hide. Me, I just gotta do like I'm told, an' that's to hang you quick an' clean as I know how come Monday morning." The lawman walked across to the bars of Hudson's cell, holding the oil lamp aloft. "I got a new hemp rope that's never been used afore, an' I swear, I'll break your neck so quick, you won't even have time to realize what's happening."

The rancher dashed a tear from his eye and declared: "Thanks, Burt, you always was a good friend."

"Think nothing of it," returned the lawman. "It's the least I can do."

"You're gold dust, Burt," Hudson persisted in a heartrending voice. "Pure gold dust."

My employer, made even more impatient by this exchange, sighed and asked: "Mr. Hudson, is there anyone, anyone at all, who might have had a reason to kill Victoria Grant?"

The pathetic prisoner thought for a few moments and shook his head at the great detective. "That's the hell of the thing, Mr. Wong. The only ranny with any reason to kill her was me, an' that's a natural fact."

Havenick turned to my employer. "Miss Grant was a real eyeful, but she came and went and minded her own business an' the only man I ever saw her talk to was Brad. Oh, I guess maybe now and again one of the roosters around here could have rode into the hills an' tried to get navel to navel with her, especially since the flatbackers that used to work on the line have all been run out of Crow Creek. But a horny ranny who went out there all liquored up an' was refused would have no reason to cut her up like that, even if she told him to skedaddle."

I remembered those boarded-up tar-paper shacks on the edge of town, and deduced that was where the soiled doves had once worked and lived.

I make no judgments. Life is a struggle for all of us, and sometimes a woman has to do what she must to survive. As my headmistress at my finishing school in Boston, dear Miss Chastity Charmaine, once told me: "Chance, there's more to prostitution than just lying on your back with your thighs open. It requires great skill and knowledge to please a man.

"Still, ancient and honorable though the profession is, I would not recommend that any of my genteel young ladies cast her lot in that direction until all other avenues of honest employment or advantageous marriage have been fully explored.

"What you have between your legs is a sought-after commodity, much in demand by the opposite sex, yet, if my reading of the newspapers is correct, it might soon be replaced by newer articles of commerce like coals and oil to feed our burgeoning factories.

"I have therefore come to the conclusion, on inquiry, that the ambitious young lady of quality might do better to turn her attention in that direction."

In those days of my youth, my thoughts often strayed back to the ivy-covered walls of my dear old school, but now I reluctantly ended my nostalgic reminiscence and forced myself back to the present, turning my attention to the despairing prisoner who clutched at the bars of his cell, his knuckles white on the cold iron.

"Like I said, Mr. Wong," Brad Hudson wailed, "I'm done for. The jury found me guilty an' they'll do for me on Monday morning, an' that's as sure as shootin'."

"Be of good cheer, for I, Chester Wong, will leave no stone unturned until you are free as a bird," returned my mentor. But I thought his voice held a note of uncertainty and I began to fear that he considered the rancher, in the words of Scotland Yard, "guilty as charged." "As for juries, tush, there's foolery for you. A bunch of uneducated rubes, I'll be bound."

When I heard this defiant statement I could not help but cheer, so I let out with a hearty "Huzzah! Huzzah!"

But my guardian gave me such a look and said sternly: "Chance, really! This is most unladylike behavior. Remember, self-discipline is a golden key that unlocks a person's true potential and without it you can never be happy."

FOUR

Before we took leave of Sheriff Havenick, Mr. Wong inquired as to the location of the crime scene, intimating that he must visit the place at the earliest possible moment.

The lawman replied that it lay to the west, some three hours ride on a good horse.

"Horse!" exclaimed the great detective. "You mean horse, as in *ride* a horse?"

I must admit I was thrilled at the prospect of riding in the hills, for I am an accomplished equestrienne, a byproduct of the first-rate education my mentor had provided for me. Miss Chastity Charmaine, a stunningly beautiful woman, had many friends among the racetrack fraternity and eager trainers readily made horses available for her young ladies.

But Mr. Wong had staggered backward in alarm at the very mention of the word horse and had collapsed into a sitting position on the sheriff's desk, a stricken look on his face.

"My good sir," he protested, "although possessed of the perfect proportions of manhood, I am not physically capable of sitting on the back of an equine for three hours at a stretch. Come sir," he demanded, "you must do better."

A fleeting grin touched Havenick's thin mouth. "Well, you could always try down at the livery stable. Maybe they could rent you a buckboard."

My employer looked like he'd been slapped.

"I experienced the jolting misery of a buckboard once in the past, and it is not something I care to repeat," he said. "Come sir, let's have you think again."

The sheriff snapped his fingers. "Hey, Wong, I got it. The Spinster Rhodes has one of them newfangled Model T Ford motorcars. It was a gift from her daddy afore he kicked off last year. I bet she'd rent it out, if'n the price was right."

"At last," declared my employer in obvious relief, "a civilized means of travel. Where can this Rhodes person be located?"

"She's out there on the edge of town, the house with the blue door. See here"—the lawman studied Mr. Wong closely—"have you ever driven one of them things?"

My mentor replied loftily that he was master of all things mechanical, though in truth, I doubted that he'd ever driven a motorcar before.

I, on the other hand, had regularly taken the wheel of the yellow Oldsmobile owned by Miss Chastity Charmaine, driving her here and there when occasion demanded, and always at breakneck speed. "Remember, Chance," she once told me, "we must live our life at full throttle. If one were determined to proceed only at a slower pace, one might as well be dead. Or a nun." Thus, I believed myself to be an expert motorist, though I was sure Mr. Wong would not consent for me to take the wheel of a rented $850 automobile.

There was one other question the great detective put to Sheriff Havenick before we left his office and ventured into the thunderstorm that had now unleashed its fury over the town.

"Where," he inquired, rather timidly I thought, as though fearing to hear the reply, "can something to eat be obtained?"

"Well," the lawman replied, "Ma's Kitchen is closed on account of her recent bereavement, but I'm sure you can get something down to the saloon. Heath Wilson always has some cheese and sardellen on hand."

"Pray, what is sardellen?" I asked.

"Fish, little lady," Havenick replied, as my mentor listened attentively. "They're saltier than the seven seas an' nobody bothers to tamper with the heads, tails or innards. You slap a couple of them between slices of rye bread, an' you got yourself a mighty memorable sandwich. I mean"—and here the sheriff winked at me—"the memory of that taste will stay with you for days."

"Oh . . . my . . . God," gasped my employer with heavy emphasis on each word. "Then Wong is surely done for."

Once outside the sheriff's office, Mr. Wong and I made a dash for the hotel through teeming rain and roaring thunder—well, I dashed, and Mr. Wong proceeded at his usual dignified pace, refusing to be hurried even by the forces of nature—in order to obtain oilskins, sou'wester hats, and galoshes. This task was accomplished quickly, for Mr. Wong insists on traveling with every necessity (though, in truth, he carries none of it), and we again ventured outside.

As we stood in the meager protection of the hotel's narrow canvas awning, I turned to the great detective and said: "I don't think Mr. Hudson is guilty of this terrible crime."

For a moment there was no reply from my mentor as he contemplated the muddy street, now swept clear of traffic. I felt a pang of guilt, for I was sure his tremendous intellect was busy grappling with the intricacies of the case.

"Wha . . . what did you say?" he asked at last.

"I said, I do not believe Mr. Hudson is guilty of this crime."

"Mmm," replied my employer. "You know, I was thinking about beef right then."

"Beef?"

"Yes, prime New York roast beef, served rare, with a mountain of mashed potatoes and perhaps some baby carrots blushing meekly at the side of the plate. And a tankard of foaming nut-brown ale. And to follow, a mighty pudding of plum duff covered in yellow custard sauce." The great detective swallowed the gathering saliva in his mouth and sighed deeply. "And what do we have on offer, but sardellen," he groaned. "By all accounts, the putrid piscine of hell."

"He has kind eyes," I said.

"What?" asked Mr. Wong in great agitation of mind, the rain drumming on his hat and the shoulders of his oilskins. "Eyes, pies, plum duff . . . eh, what do you mean, child?"

"Mr. Hudson. He has kind eyes. But Sheriff Havenick has the cold eyes of a killer."

"That signifies nothing, Chance," said Mr. Wong. "I fear," he continued, "we have come to this terrible place on a fool's errand. I believe Brad Hudson is guilty of the murder of Victoria Grant and all we can do now is go through the motions of investigating the matter for his poor daughter's sake."

I wished to tell my mentor that I did not believe this was the case, but that would have been disrespectful in the extreme. As it was, any temptation I had to give word to such a thought was banished when Mr. Wong brusquely ordered me to follow him across the muddy street.

"We must talk to the local banker and ascertain the state of our client's fortune," he said, stepping off the boardwalk and aiming his great belly in the general direction of the Cattleman's Bank. "If he was not in financial difficulties, that will remove one of his motivations for murder and perhaps give us something with which to work."

The driving rain and gusting wind, coupled with the muddy conditions of the street, made the going very difficult. Mr. Wong's oilskins had been purchased at great expense from a yachting outfitter in London who supplied nautical goods to King Edward VII, and they fitted him perfectly. Alas, my own— bought at a knockdown price at a ship chandler's store of the more unsavory sort in San Francisco— were at least three sizes too large, the sleeves hanging over my hands while the bottom of the coat dragged in the mud. The sou'wester was of no better fit, the misshapen, yellow hat coming down past my ears so that I had to fold up the brim to see.

I was also burdened with the Dragon Box and kept it pressed against my side under my oilskins with my right arm, fearing that it might get wet.

As a result, my employer proceeded apace, while I once again struggled far behind.

But there was one welcome aspect to all this rain—it had driven almost everyone indoors. Only a few stalwarts still ventured into the street, bundled up in those long riding coats Western men call slickers. For now at least, there would be no more talk of lynching. It's one thing to hang a man when the weather is fair, but it's quite another to string him up in a drenching rain with lightning spiking out of the sky every couple of seconds.

"Come, Chance," said Mr. Wong, looking over his shoulder in great irritation. "I've never known anyone who dawdles quite like you."

I will never know what made me turn and glance behind me at that moment. Perhaps I felt eyes on my back, but whatever it was, I beheld a man standing in the doorway of one of the shacks I thought unoccupied, staring intently at me and my employer. He stood hipshot, leaning against the doorframe, a tall, sallow man in a knee-length frock coat and flowered vest, his lank and greasy hair falling over his shoulders. A drooping mustache adorned his upper lip, and he had great dark circles under his eyes.

I immediately recognized him as a member of the gambling fraternity, having met many of his ilk at my finishing school where, if they were riding a streak of bad luck, Miss Charmaine provided them with food, lodging, and a road stake. (I should observe here that my dear headmistress did not consider Miss Chastity Charmaine's Finishing School for Genteel Young Ladies a charitable organization. Those light-fingered gentlemen sang for their supper in that they taught us how to buck the tiger, acquainting us with the subtleties of stud poker, faro, blackjack, seven-up, three-card monte, the nutshell and thimble shuffle, chuck-a-luck, and other games of chance that Miss Charmaine considered essential to the education of the young lady of quality.)

Turning my glance from the gambler, I intended to ask Mr. Wong if he was aware of the man's sinister presence, but that great intellect seemed deep in thought as he trudged through the mire and I thought it best not to disturb his prodigious ruminations.

As it happened, when I glanced over my shoulder again, the gambler was gone, his wood-frame and tar-paper door closed against the inclement weather. But, to add more mystery to the affair, I saw the hotel clerk hurrying away from the direction of the shack, as though he might have been inside while the gambler stood at the door.

I was very disturbed as we at last reached the opposite boardwalk and made our way to the bank; I could not escape the thought that the gambler, and perhaps the hotel clerk, meant us harm. How, I did not know—though this I was to learn quite soon when both Mr. Wong and myself were thrust into the most deadly danger and had to desperately fight for our lives.

The Cattleman's Bank was an unimposing, false-fronted building with a single large window proclaiming its name in faded gold lettering and under that the words, BEN CRANWELL, PROP.

As the great detective pushed open the creaking door of the establishment and entered, a mighty crack of thunder accompanied by a sizzling lightning bolt rent the sky, and one of the two mousy, middle-aged clerks behind the counter exclaimed: "That, sir, was quite an entrance!"

Pleased by this startled observation, which he accepted as no more than his right, Mr. Wong went into full display, shuffling his tiny feet as he strutted back and forth in front of the counter and bobbing his finely modeled head.

I took this opportunity to remove my oilskins, for the interior of the bank was hot and stuffy, with water pooling on the floor from the leaky roof.

"I have come," the great detective declared at last, "to have a few words with your proprietor. I refer, sir, to none other than Mr. Cranwell himself."

In a deferential tone, the clerk returned: "I shall see if that can be done, though I must warn you that Mr. Cranwell is a busy man and seldom sees anyone during the morning hours of business."

"I believe," said Mr. Wong haughtily, "that he will see me."

"And the name is . . . ?"

The clerk's question dangled in the air, and my guardian immediately caught it and brought it to earth with a resounding, "Wong, sir! Chester Wong, lately of New York City, San Francisco, and Boston town."

Faced with such an imposing figure, the clerk gave a little bow and walked to a door to the right of the barred counter. He scratched on the door and opened it, and I caught a quick glimpse of the man inside before the door closed again.

I observed a pale man in a black coat—who had what I can only call a moth-eaten appearance—sitting behind a large oak desk. In that split second I saw him furtively shove something into a drawer and I was sure I caught the silvery sheen of a bottle.

Was this Mr. Cranwell a secret drinker? Or, more charitably, a sick man who required regular doses of medicine?

At that moment I had an answer to neither of these questions, but they were avenues of inquiry that might be worth pursuing, though just what relevance they might have to the case at hand, I did not know.

In any case, all such thoughts were banished from my mind when the door of the office opened and Ben Cranwell himself, with a cheerful smile and bright how-de-do, lifted a hinged partition at one end of the counter and ushered us into his office.

After the necessary introductions were made, the banker, who was so round-shouldered he had the look of a hunchback, waved Mr. Wong and myself into comfortable chairs in front of his desk, then settled into his own chair, a huge, high-backed affair made of mahogany and red leather.

"Mr. Wong," he said, after studying both of us for a few moments, "I've read about you, the great and famous Chinese detective. I seem to recall you were involved in a case in San Francisco last year. Opium smuggling, wasn't it?"

"That, and murder," declared Mr. Wong in the interests of accuracy. "I call it the Case of the Pirate's

Passion, and it taxed my powers of deduction to the limit, though I had"—he waved negligent fingers in my direction—"a little help from my assistant."

"Ah, just so, just so," returned the banker. "If you will forgive me saying so, Mr. Wong, you are Chinese in aspect, as is"—I felt Cranwell's too-eager eyes slide over my body like oiled hands—"this beautiful young lady. Is not detective work an unusual occupation for people of Oriental descent?"

"Not at all," replied my employer loftily, "the Chinese emperors employed detectives a thousand years ago. In the East it is considered an ancient and most honorable profession."

Cranwell turned to me and smiled. "Still, the title of assistant detective is most unusual in one so young."

"I am most unworthy of the great honor Mr. Wong has done me," I said, casting my eyes modestly downward toward the Dragon Box on my lap. "He overlooks my inexperience and graciously allows me to work at his side."

"And he has seen to it that you were gently raised," Cranwell observed. "I can see that."

"Mr. Wong, at great expense, sent me to Miss Chastity Charmaine's Finishing School for Genteel Young Ladies in Boston," I explained. "If I learned anything of gentility there, the ultimate credit must surely belong to my guardian."

My employer and mentor nodded, as if to acknowledge that the credit was indeed all his, and added: "As you probably are aware, in your line of business, Mr. Cranwell, the young are immoderately expensive to raise."

"Indeed," agreed the banker. He was replying to Mr. Wong, but his eyes were fixed on my breasts as though he was mentally stripping me naked and desired to hungrily feed on each pink nipple.

I decided then that I liked Mr. Cranwell no more than I liked the sheriff. I believed they were both pale-eyed predators who, in their different ways, would prey on those weaker than themselves. Havenick used a gun, Cranwell his money, but the result would be pretty much the same. I had thought the banker might be a secret drinker, but now as I studied the man more closely I saw that he had an unhealthy, gray pallor and his eyes looked hot and fevered. He was either a very sick man or was recovering from a serious illness.

Still, he projected an aura of raw power and great energy and had the arrogant look of a man who would reach out and grab whatever he wanted, whether it was money or a woman's body.

Finally Cranwell tore his eyes from my damp shirt-front, settled back in his chair, and said from behind steepled fingers: "Now Mr. Wong, what can I do for you? I must tell you, I know why you're in Crow Creek, and I fear you're on a fool's errand."

"I," declared the great detective loftily, "will be the judge of that. Now, a question, if you please."

"Ask away," declared Cranwell. "I'll help you any way I can."

"The question is a simple one, Mr. Cranwell. I'd like to know the state of Brad Hudson's finances at the time of the murder of Victoria Grant."

The banker nodded, as if he'd fully anticipated the query. "As you are no doubt aware, I must respect the confidentiality of my client's affairs. However, under the circumstances, I believe I can tell you that at the time of the murder of Dr. Grant, Brad was in deep financial trouble. Years of drought and poor beef prices had left him teetering on the edge of bankruptcy. As a result he owes me, I mean my bank, a considerable sum of money. I believe you'll also find he has unpaid bills at the general store and even the saloon, if the truth be known."

"But surely, if he had such money troubles, ten thousand dollars, the price my client demanded for the dinosaur fossil, could hardly have made that much of a difference?" asked Mr. Wong.

"It would have made all the difference in the world," the banker returned. "That ten thousand could have kept him going for a year, two maybe, until the good times come back, if they ever do. When he saw the money slipping away from him, he got angry. Maybe angry enough to kill."

Cranwell shook his head. "I can't figure it, though. Brad Hudson has always been kind of arrogant, the powerful rancher who cuts a wide swath and makes his mark. But he was always an honorable man and not much given to violence."

"It is written that violence is the child of pride," whispered my mentor, as though to himself. "And arrogance and pride are dastardly twins, joined at the hip."

"Perhaps so," agreed Cranwell, who had stretched forward in his chair to hear. "And if that's the case, Brad Hudson will hang for his violent deed come Monday morning."

With a deep sigh, Mr. Wong rose to his feet and I

followed. The great detective, who appeared crest-fallen, stretched out his hand. "Well, thank you for your help and forthright honesty, Mr. Cranwell," he said. "I appreciate it, sir."

The banker's hand looked as pale and limp as a dead fish, and when he turned it in my direction I pretended not to notice, busying myself with my oilskins and hat.

"If there's anything else I can do, please don't hesitate . . ." Cranwell said, his statement hanging there unfinished, weightless in the air.

"Ah," said Mr. Wong, "perhaps there is. I wish to visit the Hudson ranch later today and I have no way of knowing how to get there." The great detective shrugged apologetically. "I should have asked the sheriff, but it slipped my mind. Perhaps you could tell me how to reach the ranch if it's not too much trouble?"

Cranwell smiled broadly. "No trouble at all. In fact, I'll do better than just tell you, I'll write it down." He pulled a piece of paper from his desk drawer and began to write—like Sheriff Havenick, he used his left hand I noticed. "The trails are tricky out there and the Rafter H is well off the main road."

He finished writing and held out the paper to my employer, but the great man disdained to touch it, merely nodding in my direction. "My assistant will take care of that."

I took the paper, Cranwell's fingers brushing mine . . . and I felt my skin crawl.

Once outside again, the teeming rain looked like a gray curtain drawn across the street so that I could barely make out the hotel opposite from where we stood. Black clouds hung low in the sky and thunder rumbled, vivid streaks of lightning forking like snake tongues among the foothills of the mountains to the west of town. I breathed deeply of the fresh air, glad to be away from the stifling heat and lecherous atmosphere of the banker's office.

To my surprise, the funeral party that had passed through earlier in the morning was still huddled together in the weed-grown graveyard beyond the town limits, seemingly oblivious to both rain and thunder. The mourners stood like statues in the downpour, umbrellas blossoming above their heads like glistening mushrooms.

How long, I wondered, does it take to bury one old man?

Then, with a start, I realized it was not yet noon and that the events of the morning had transpired in just the couple of hours that had passed since we left the train.

"Very nice man," declared Mr. Wong. "And most helpful."

"Who?" I asked absently, still perplexed by the fact that time seemed to stand still in Crow Creek.

"Why Mr. Cranwell, of course," said my mentor with some irritation. "Chance, please pay attention, child."

I muttered an apology under my breath that Mr. Wong ignored. I wasn't sure he'd even heard me, no doubt because his keen mind was much occupied with weightier matters, namely the guilt or innocence of his condemned client.

"Let us now," he declared at last, pointing with his

cane, "venture across this ocean of mud the rubes around here call a road."

We stepped into the street, but stopped to allow a strikingly lovely woman to ride past on a tall bay horse. Even buttoned into a man's slicker, a battered old hat on her head, she was stunning, with the high cheekbones, swan neck, and the thrusting, impertinent breasts of the classic beauty. The woman turned and glanced at me as she trotted past and I smiled at her. But she did not return my smile, her brilliant green eyes guarded and not in the least friendly.

I had no idea who she was, but it seemed to me her aloof nature belied her dazzling looks. Truly, beauty is only skin deep.

FIVE

We had just stepped up onto the boardwalk when the door of a tar-paper shack opened and there stood the gambler who'd studied Mr. Wong and me so closely as we made our way to the bank.

"Mr. Wong!" he called, arresting our progress toward the hotel. "A word with you, sir. I have important information to impart."

"Here's an unexpected turn of events," declared the great detective in a whispered aside. He then resolutely turned toward the gambler and inquired as to his information. But that cautious cardsharp glanced up and down the street anxiously and declared in a high, nervous voice: "Not here. Quick, inside!"

The shack was just one small room, the furnishings comprised of a rumpled, unmade bed, a single rickety chair, and a dresser. The walls were covered in pages torn from the Sears Roebuck catalog, mostly scantily clad women in corsets, and I deduced that the shack had once been the home of a soiled dove. There were no windows, the work of the oldest profession usually being conducted in the dark, and the room was lit by a single, smoking oil lamp.

Oddly, in these shabby surroundings, on the wall above the bed incongruously hung a pair of crossed épées, the handguards of the swords not the usual unadorned metal bells, but of chased, openwork silver in an intricate scroll pattern, very finely executed, obviously by a master craftsman.

The épée is the largest and heaviest of the three great dueling weapons, the others being the foil and the saber. It has a wonderfully fast, *V*-cut triangular blade and I realized to my joy that the grips were made in the Italian fashion, perhaps the most comfortable and controllable of all sword handles, far surpassing the French, English, and German.

How anyone as seedy and down-at-the-heels as the gambler could have hung on to these beautifully made and expensive weapons was beyond my comprehension. Surely, I thought, he must have loved the fine blades or he'd have sold them long ago.

"Please, take off your coats," the gambler said, and as we did so, he added in his thin, whining voice: "My name is Silas Lime, Mr. Wong, a gambler by profession, though bucking an unlucky streak that's unfortunately now well into its third year."

"Yes, yes, that's all very interesting," the great detective said. "But what is it you wish to tell us?"

Lime tapped the side of his long, thin nose with his forefinger. "What I know, I know, and that will come later. But first, can I offer you a little something?"

"Food?" inquired my employer, his interest quickening.

"Alas, no," whined Silas Lime. "I refer only to a glass of something. Perhaps a little gin?"

Sorely disappointed, Mr. Wong held up his hand. "No thankee, I never touch the stuff."

"And you, young lady?" Lime whined in my direction, his whole lank and damp-looking body writhing in an effort to appear the perfect host.

I shook my head. "Sir, I don't indulge, but thank you for the most kind offer."

Truth to tell, I had imbibed often at my dear old school, Miss Chastity Charmaine kindly placing a bottle of Old Anderson's Little Brown Jug bourbon in our dorm to soothe the cramps so often associated with that troublesome time of the month with which every young lady must cope. Our dear headmistress herself drank three fingers of the best sour mash and smoked a thin, black Burmah cheroot every morning after breakfast, except on Sundays when she delayed these indulgences until after church.

"Did you know, young ladies," she once asked, blowing a cloud of fragrant smoke across the dining room table, "that the beautiful maidens of Burmah roll these cheroots on the inner portion of their naked thighs? That is why, in the opinion of more discerning gentlemen, especially those of the gambling and racing fraternities, they have such a fine, sweet flavor."

I never quite acquired my revered and lovely headmistress's taste for strong drink, though I did wholeheartedly embrace her cheroot habit, a little vice I keep from my guardian who hates all forms of smoking, calling tobacco "the noxious weed of the devil."

"Now, sir," said Mr. Wong, "let us have your information, especially if it will help free my client from the shadow of the gallows."

Silas Lime made no reply, but rustled around in a

dresser drawer until he found a stained and dirty glass into which he poured a colorless liquid from a bottle without a label. The gambler drank this draught in a gulp, followed it with another, then rasped, his dark eyes like pools of swamp mud: "Here's my information, Mr. Wong. You'd be well advised to get out of town now—or die."

My employer was taken aback to say the least. He gasped, staggered a few steps to his rear, and placed his hand on his chest. "Wha . . . what did you say?"

Lime drew himself up to his full impressive height (he stood well over six feet) and said: "Let Hudson hang. You're upsetting some people here in town, powerful people, and if you don't leave on the midnight train, neither you or the young lady here will live to catch another."

"This is an outrage," declared Mr. Wong with feeling. "I will never turn my back on a client and I will not, I repeat *not*, sir, be run out of town on a rail."

Silas Lime shrugged. "Your funeral, though for a Chinee, you sure don't have a lick of sense."

My mentor ignored this insult, and demanded: "Who are these powerful people of whom you speak? And why do they so badly want to see Brad Hudson hang?"

By way of reply, Lime ignored the great detective and walked to his side of his stained and dirty bed. He reached up and took the swords from the wall.

"Have you ever in your life seen blades as fine as these, Mr. Wong?" he asked.

The great detective shook his head. "They are épées of exceedingly fine quality," he allowed grudgingly.

"Of Italian manufacture I would say. But enough of this, I—"

"You are correct in guessing Italian," Lime interrupted. They were forged in the town of Ferrara, famous for the quality of its steel. I would say, Mr. Wong, that in all the world there are no blades finer than these."

Indeed, though it was not my place to say it, I had seen but only one sword finer, the gold-and-silver-chased épée of the fencing master at my dear old school. Monsieur Pierre Renault Gaspar de LaChance was tiny and slender and dashing, with a mustache so thin it looked like it had been drawn on his upper lip with a pencil.

He had been a noted duelist in his day in New Orleans and San Francisco and by the time he came to teach at Miss Chastity Charmaine's school for girls, he had left a trail of some eighteen or twenty skewered gentlemen behind him.

Despite his many stays in prison for homicide (and, it was whispered, though never in the presence of Miss Charmaine, dastardly piracy on the high seas), Monsieur de LaChance had lost none of his brilliance with the sword over the years.

In fact, as I recall, Miss Charmaine had once appeared—most unusually for her—at the breakfast table with her robe and abundant cornsilk hair in a state of some disarray, and, as she drank her morning bourbon and smoked her first cheroot of the day, she had occasion to comment as our conversation turned to the martial arts: "Young ladies, our Monsieur de LaChance maybe be small, but . . . ooh la-la . . . what a swordsman!"

"And what a sword!" I exclaimed, and my dear headmistress's left eyebrow lifted up into her forehead as she looked at me strangely and said: "Yes, a very fine sword, indeed."

Feeling Miss Charmaine's emerald green eyes upon me, I thought perhaps I had spoken out of turn, so I blushed and modestly lowered my gaze to the table, laying my eyelashes on my cheek. After that morning, whenever we had a fencing lesson from Monsieur de LaChance—Miss Chastity Charmaine considering mastery of the blade an essential part of every genteel young lady's education—she always contrived to have someone looking on, perhaps a pale gambler or one of the battered prizefighters of whom she was so very fond, or even a diminutive and wizened jockey.

Looking back, I suppose our headmistress wished to make sure that Monsieur de LaChance was indeed giving us the full benefit of his legendary swordsmanship.

Alas, I had been so busy woolgathering as I recalled my dear old schooldays, I was totally unprepared for what happened next.

Silas Lime suddenly tossed one of his épées to Mr. Wong and, as the great detective instinctively caught it, asked: "How are you with the blade? I, myself, am considered a master."

My mentor looked at the man in astonishment. "Why, I have no experience of the sword." He was utterly flabbergasted by Lime's rudeness and added: "I hardly think this is the time or place—"

Silas Lime screamed: *"En garde!"* and thrust.

The man was as fast as a cobra. He had made an angulated thrust, so called because the blade moves at a marked angle and follows the direction of the hand toward the target—in this case Mr. Wong's throat.

My employer, more by good luck than skill with the sword, parried clumsily, but made no attempt to riposte. "My dear sir—" he began, but Lime ignored Mr. Wong's plea and launched into a rather pretty and well-executed balestra, an attack made in two motions—jumping forward with both feet, landing simultaneously, and then lunging.

This man has some notion of sword-fighting, I thought. *And has been taught by a master of the Italian school.*

Again my employer parried, even clumsier than before, again making no attempt to riposte, and it was instantly obvious to me that this was no sporting bout but a prelude to homicide.

Silas Lime was fencing to kill.

I was by now thoroughly alarmed, and, fearing for my employer's life, I quickly laid aside the precious Dragon Box and yelled: *"Lancez-moi l'épée!"*

I am the first to admit that "Chuck me the iron!" was not the poetic language of the blade taught me by Monsieur de LaChance, but rather the crude patois of the swaggering rapier ruffian of Renaissance France. However, I was so afraid for the bumbling Mr. Wong that I was, as the romantic lady novelists say, "in extremis."

The great detective, his round face a mask of horror, half turned and threw me the épée as though the handle was suddenly red-hot.

Deftly catching the sword in midair, I parried yet another thrust aimed at Mr. Wong's throat and followed this by a riposte, using the *croise* or semi-bind.

This is very much a defensive action that engages your opponent's blade and moves it away vertically from its intended target. I did this by reversing my hand from a *quarte* parry into a *seconde* parry and finished in a low, straight thrust.

There is no lunge in this movement—I could not lunge in any case since we wore our long skirts very tight in those days—but, in essence, the *croise* is a very effective simultaneous parry and riposte rather than an attack.

Lime stamped his foot on the floor twice in an *appel*, signaling that he wished a halt in the action. "I can tell you've some little experience with the blade," he sneered. "Well, it's of no consequence. I'll kill you first, then your boss."

The oaf then launched into a false attack, a lunge made with no intention of hitting. Lime made this movement to test my defensive reaction and to finesse me into parrying and riposting so that he could parry and counter riposte and possibly deliver the killing thrust.

But I made an excellent *finta in tempo*, a stop-thrust that engaged Lime's blade and forced him backward.

That vile killer now knew I had more than a little knowledge of fencing, and we presently engaged in a *phrase d'armes*, an uninterrupted series of attacks, ripostes, and counter-ripostes as we tested each other's mettle.

The cabin was very small, and in that confined space we fenced *corps a corps*, that is, body to body, there being little room for anything else. The bright steel of our flashing, clashing blades flickered in the light of the oil lamp and the screech and clang of metal on metal was very loud within the confining walls of that tiny room.

It was becoming more and more obvious to me that Lime had been trained by a master, but in the Italian school, a flamboyant method of fencing that lacks the classic beauty and economy of movement of the French salle d'armes, the style that had been taught to me.

As our blades engaged and disengaged, I realized the gambler—as I might have expected—was a flicker. Monsieur de LaChance would not teach the flick, considering it ungentlemanly, a wide, crude, time-consuming, energy-wasting coupe that is so often the mark of the ruffian. Nevertheless, fast flicks, a sudden upward movement of the blade while the wrist is turned, knuckles pointing to the ground, can be deadly and coping with them is hard.

But I used a modified saber *quinte* to parry Lime's flicking blade, followed by an *ibroccata*, a quick thrust to his outside line, designed to skewer the shoulder.

In addition, I took Monsieur de LaChance's lessons to heart and stepped in quickly when Lime began his flick and moved his hand upward—the notorious fly-cast hand movement—and thus got under his point. This move destroys the flicker's perception of distance and they often overshoot their target, as Lime did again and again.

"Beware, Chance!" Mr. Wong cried out in anguish as Lime's flashing blade flickered just past my right ear like a serpent's tongue. "This rogue is indeed a master swordsman."

But I could see the man was getting angry at his inability to deliver a killing thrust and that meant he would become careless. I decided now was the time to use the *Botta Secreta*.

Simply put, the *Botta Secreta* is a secret attack or special hidden technique developed by individual fencing masters and known only to themselves. Monsieur de LaChance's favorite was a *Botta de tempo*, a counter-riposte used on a shaken or angry opponent, followed by a *Mandoble*, a light slash with the point delivered by a flick of the wrist.

I used an intentional threatening extension of the arm and weapon designed to provoke a response that I could counter. The ruffian did not disappoint me and countered with a *Stocatta Lunga*, a far-reaching thrust using a forward step of the leg.

I made a simple *coup d'arret*, catching and parrying Lime's blade, then I riposted with the *Botta de tempo* and quickly followed up with the *Mandoble*, opening the skin above his left eyebrow with my slash.

This *Botta Secreta* does two things: It shakes your opponent's confidence and lets him know he is mortal; it shows him his own blood; and it blinds him in one eye.

And it did all these things beautifully to Silas Lime.

The man cursed vilely and with a roar of rage took a step backward, foolishly lifting his blade as scarlet blood ran over his left eye and down his cheek in thin, skeletal fingers.

I was now thoroughly bored with this ham-handed amateur's attempts at swordsmanship and decided to end it there and then.

And it was all over in a moment.

Lime, still cursing, made a weak *radoppio*, a straight

lunge followed very quickly by a second. But I countered by making no attempt to parry the first thrust, merely swaying out of his line of attack, but parried the second, following up with fine *stocatta*, a powerful thrust made under Lime's blade.

Thus I—rather casually, yawning into the back of my left hand—ran him through.

The point of my sword penetrated the inside of the man's right forearm and the blade stuck out a good hand's breadth between the bones of the other side just below the elbow.

Silas Lime yelped in pain and his sword clanged to the wood floor of the shack. I withdrew my own crimson-stained blade from his arm and set the point against his throat.

"Who ordered you to kill Mr. Wong?" I demanded, my blade opening a thin scarlet line on his skin.

"Go to hell!" Lime gritted, his teeth clenched against the pain in his arm.

"Chance!" yelled my employer in alarm. "Don't kill the dog!"

"The choice is his," I said quietly. "Either he tells us who gave him the order to murder you or I'll push the blade through his throat."

"Go ahead, damn you," Lime said. "It will be a quicker death than the one I'd get if I squealed."

My hand tightened on the grip of the sword and the point penetrated deeper into Lime's throat. I must confess, I was angry, angry that this man had tried to kill Mr. Wong—and with him the greatest intellect the world has ever known—and equally angry that he'd tried, admittedly in a blundering and amateurish way, to kill me.

"Chance!" cried my mentor in great agitation. "Remember, child, the bravest of the brave are those who can forgive." Mr. Wong took a step toward me and gently pushed away the blade from Lime's throat. "Can't you see this man is terrified of whoever put him up to this?" he said. "We will learn nothing from him, although he has already told us much."

"Sir," I said, my eyes never wavering from Lime, "what has he told us?"

"He has told us that Brad Hudson is undoubtedly innocent of the crime for which he must hang three days hence, and that the real killer has begun to run scared."

"That may be true, sir," I said. "If that is indeed the case, the killer has already made one mistake in hiring this miserable wretch to be his paid assassin. He may yet make another."

I took a couple of steps away from the whining, sobbing Silas Lime and said to him conversationally: "Sir, you have the makings of a fair to middling swordsman, but I fear many years of hard study with a competent master still lie ahead of you."

"Go to hell," Lime said again.

I still had the iron in my hand and I threw it up in the air and caught the grip like you would a javelin. I threw the sword with all my strength and it thudded into the wall a quarter inch from Lime's left ear.

The man let out a startled yelp and dove for the ground.

"Chance," Mr. Wong said, aghast, "that was most unseemly behavior."

But I did not reply.

I mean, one can't be expected to act like a perfect young lady all the time.

"I had no idea you could use a sword like that," said my employer as we left the confines of Lime's odorous and gloomy shack and once again braved the teeming rain. "Tell me, what else did they teach you at Madame Charmaine's Finishing School for Genteel Young Ladies?"

But in reply I merely cast my eyes to the wet boardwalk and whispered demurely: "Sir, many things."

And Mr. Wong rubbed his chin pensively as he studied me closely and said: "Hmmm . . ."

SIX

Mr. Wong was now impatient to solve this case that had taken such an unexpected and dangerous turn, and as we stood outside Silas Lime's shack in the pouring rain he determined that we should at once repair to the home of the Spinster Rhodes, there to rent her Ford motorcar. "Though I fear the expense of such a venture will be ruinous," declared my employer gloomily.

Above us the clouds were piled up in tremendous black mountains and deep, iron-gray ravines, and feeble oil lamps were lit outside the saloon and hotel against the gloom, though it was still early in the day. The funeral party had finally left the cemetery and the few pines that grew there had been shaded from green to black by the relentless rain. In the distance, thunder rolled down the mountain canyons, crashing from wall to wall with the sound of a gigantic bass drum. Vivid white lightning forked from peak to peak and struck the slopes, the thundering echoes rolling across the flat grasslands until they bombarded the town like artillery shells, shaking the wooden buildings and rattling the glass in the windows like loose teeth.

There was no one abroad in the street that was now just a sea of thick and glutinous mud.

Once again dressed in my oversized oilskins, the Dragon Box safely tucked inside, I trudged behind Mr. Wong and made bold as to comment as we neared Miss Rhodes' home that the thunder was growing in intensity.

"That is not thunder," commented my employer testily, "but the rumbling of my empty stomach." He stopped, rain pounding on his shoulders and sou'ester, and pulled up the skin on the back of his hand a quarter inch. "Look, Chance," he declared in alarm, "loose skin. It's just as I feared, I'm already wasting away."

We reached the spinster's home without incident, climbed the stairs of her porch, and knocked on the door, which was wood on the bottom, an idyllic pastoral scene featuring sheep and maidens in etched glass on the top.

After a few moments' delay, the door was opened by a very large and pleasant-faced woman who regarded us curiously—unexpectedly seeing two Oriental-appearing people at one's front door in the middle of a thunderstorm can be unsettling, I suppose. But after a moment's hesitation she smiled broadly and said: "Oh, come in out of the rain. Please do."

Once inside her home, comfortably furnished though rather heavy on floral decoration, she politely urged us to remove our oilskins and only then inquired: "And what can I do for you?"

But Mr. Wong's head was tilted back, his nostrils quivering, and he half turned to me and in an awed stage whisper announced: "Baked meat."

Indeed, though I do not eat animal flesh of any kind, there was a most wonderful smell coming from the kitchen that suggested braised beef, gravy, and golden brown pastry.

The great detective, now divested of his oilskins and galoshes, recovered quickly from his transport of delight and introduced us both, and told Miss Rhodes that we had come—if, on inquiry, the price was right—to rent for a couple of days her fine Ford motorcar.

"A man's life is at stake, dear Miss Rhodes," quoth my mentor loftily, "and speedy transportation is essential to the success of our venture." He then outlined our purpose in coming to Crow Creek, and again emphasized our great need for a mechanized method of transportation.

But Miss Rhodes, who appeared pound for pound a match for my employer and was of much the same height, declared that she was but a poor spinster woman with no husband to advise her on such matters. Furthermore, even as she spoke, she declared she was all atremble at the thought that Mr. Wong, a great and famous detective and man of the world, would take advantage of her feminine weakness and perhaps pay much less for the rent of the automobile than fairness demanded.

"The motorcar was a gift from my late father, you see, and I fear its upkeep and maintenance has been a heavy burden to me ever since," she concluded with much feeling.

"Be assured," declared the great man earnestly, "that you are in safe hands. It has never been said that Chester Wong, in any way, shape, or form, ever took unfair advantage of the weaker sex. My name may be Wong, but, dear lady, I am not Wong by nature."

After this pretty speech, my guardian went into a most wonderful display, performing a high-stepping strut up and down Miss Rhodes' parlor—the better to show off his expensive suiting and small feet—as he nodded his sleek and handsome head this way and that, and all this to the accompaniment of the crashing thunderstorm raging outside.

I could see that, despite her misgivings, Miss Rhodes was impressed, because her face, round and red-cheeked as a late-summer apple, was aglow with delight and her cornflower-blue eyes followed my employer's every move.

Perforce, Mr. Wong's elaborate perambulations ended when he stopped and closely regarded a framed photograph hanging on the wall and inquired: "Is it . . . could this be . . . but surely this is you, dear lady?"

Miss Rhodes blushed and admitted that the photo was none other than herself. "It was taken some years ago when I was much slimmer, of course."

"Then, judging by your costume, you trod the boards," declared the great detective with that keen perception that had made him famous throughout the civilized world.

"In an amateurish way," admitted Miss Rhodes humbly. "I was a member of a dancing troupe that performed all over the West. Even," she added with a touch of latent pride, "in Kansas City."

Mr. Wong turned to the rotund lady and delightedly laid his hands on his chest. "But I, too, am a dancer of some note," he declared vehemently. "Miss

Rhodes, we must, without a single moment's delay, cut a rug!"

"Lord bless you, sir," protested the spinster, "but it's been many a long year—"

"Nonsense, dear lady. As a wise Chinese philosopher once said, 'The dance, once learned, is never forgotten.'"

"But I fear I have indeed forgotten all the steps," quavered Miss Rhodes in great agitation. "I never kept up my practice, you see."

"I believe you will do wonderfully," assured my employer. "If ever I set eyes on a natural dancer, dear lady, it is you."

The great detective then approached Miss Rhodes with great solemnity, and, despite her squeals of protest, made a gracious little bow and took her plump white hand in his. "Now," he said, "let us trip the light fantastic."

Once in the middle of the parlor floor, Mr. Wong looked at the rug under his feet and asked: "May I?"

The spinster giggled and replied: "Please do. Suit yourself."

"Chance," ordered my employer, "the rug, if you please."

I did as I was told and rolled up the rug, pushing it out of the way.

"Are you, dear Miss Rhodes, familiar with the melodies of Mr. George M. Cohan?" inquired my mentor once my task was accomplished.

"Oh yes," returned that lady, still clinging to Mr. Wong's hand for support, both physical and moral.

"Then we will dance to 'I'm a Yankee Doodle Dandy,' one of that composer's greatest hits," said Mr. Wong.

"Chance and I had the great pleasure of seeing and hearing the piece performed when we attended the Liberty Theater in New York in . . . in . . . ah, let me see . . ."

"November seventh, 1904." I supplied the date.

"Yes, exactly, in 1904. Now, Chance—" my employer nodded toward the upright piano that had pride of place in the parlor, its legs modestly covered by hand-embroidered white bloomers—"music, if you please."

I was quite an accomplished pianist, having been taught the art at my dear old school by one of Miss Chastity Charmaine's associates, a gentleman of color by the name of Ragtime Charlie Crumm. Years before he came to teach at our school, Mr. Crumm had been the pianist at an establishment on the San Francisco waterfront owned by our dear headmistress. Even then, Miss Charmaine had a number of genteel and pretty ladies in her care, guiding the destinies of the young having always been her great vocation in life.

I struck up "I'm a Yankee Doodle Dandy," and no sooner had the opening chords begun than my employer and Miss Rhodes launched into a spirited and delightful dance, part cakewalk, part soft shoe, part tap, and part everything else they decided to throw into the mix.

Miss Rhodes held out her pinafore with both hands in the manner of a ball gown, and Mr. Wong, being the more talented hoofer of the two, led the movements, calling out instructions to the spinster as they stepped ever so lightly across the floor.

I'm a Yankee Doodle dandy . . .
"And left, Miss Rhodes, if you please."
Yankee Doodle do or die . . .
"And back, Miss Rhodes. Oh, my!"
A real live nephew of my Uncle Sam's . . .
"Step to the right, Miss Rhodes."
Born on the Fourth of July . . .
"And twirl, Miss Rhodes."
I've got a Yankee Doodle sweetheart . . .
"And to the left. Aaah yes!"
"She's my Yankee Doodle joy . . ."
"Shuffle, Miss Rhodes, shuffle!"
Yankee Doodle came to London just to ride the ponies . . .
"And tap, tap, tap, my dear."
I am the Yankee Doodle,
I am the Yankee Doodle,
I am the Yankee Doodle Boy.

As I glanced over my shoulder as the performance came to a close, I was struck by the elephantine elegance and solemn dignity of my mentor and his partner. There must have been close to seven hundred pounds of dancer on that floor, yet their steps landed so gently, their feet made no more sound than April rain on a river.

Amid the final chords of Mr. Cohan's masterpiece, Miss Rhodes spun giddily from Mr. Wong's left arm and landed with a thud in her armchair, her legs flying into the air, displaying a snow-white and generous expanse of bloomer.

"Lordy, I haven't had so much fun in years!" she exclaimed, regaining a more dignified position and fanning her flushed face with her pinafore. "Mr. Wong, I declare, you are a one."

My employer, no less flushed than his partner, placed his right hand on his breast and, his periwinkle blue eyes shining, said: "Miss Rhodes, I have never before enjoyed such a delightful dancing partner."

"Thankee," returned Miss Rhodes bashfully, "but perhaps if I was thinner . . ."

"Nonsense!" returned Mr. Wong irritably. "My dear, it is only the insufferable arrogance of the skinny that makes them believe they have inherited the earth."

Here both my mentor and Miss Rhodes turned and regarded me with ill-concealed suspicion, and I, in turn, felt my face flush as I lowered my eyes to the floor.

"I don't know if you feel like it after such an exertion, Mr. Wong," Miss Rhodes said after critically scrutinizing my slimness for a few moments. "But perhaps you'd like a little something to eat?"

"Not so much as a single bite," declared my mentor, holding up his hand. "That would be an unfair imposition."

"Oh just a light little something. Please do."

"Well," said the great detective, his sensitive nose quivering as wonderful odors wafted from the kitchen, "perhaps just the merest crumb or two."

"Being a poor spinster woman with no husband to support me, I can't offer much," Miss Rhodes complained, her voice breaking ever so slightly. "But I do have some parched peas and a little corn bread."

Mr. Wong's face took on a stricken look. "Parched

peas and . . . and . . ." his voice trailed off into a strangled whisper. "Corn bread," he managed at last.

"And Arbuckle coffee, but made with yesterday's grounds, I'm afraid," added Miss Rhodes.

Mr. Wong took a deep breath, kneeled beside Miss Rhodes' chair and took her fat little hand in his own.

"My dear lady," he began, "look at yourself. What do you see?"

The spinster did as she was told, lowering her head and regarding herself critically. "I see a poor single lady, thrown out into the world to survive as best she can," she said, somewhat inadequately I thought.

"That is not what I see," returned Mr. Wong. "I see a woman cast in the massy mold of female perfection. I see the rare beauty that the dexterous dauber Peter Paul Rubens placed on canvas, preserving in all its fleshy magnificence the image of voluptuous feminine charms that ring like a clarion call down through the ages."

Warming to his subject, my employer continued (did I not tell you he had a gift of the blarney?): "Not for Rubens, nor for I, the skinny, half-starved waifs that now appear in the pages of the Sears Roebuck catalog. Nay, I say, but for Rubens, and for me, women with flesh on their bones. With hips! With bosoms! My dear lady . . . with great . . . thunderous . . . thighs!"

"Eeek!" screamed Miss Rhodes in horror, covering her face with her pinafore. "Say no more, kind sir. I am quite undone."

But my mentor, his nose lifted in the air as he urgently checked on the progress of the baking meat, was not so easily deterred.

"Thou Junoesque charmer, was not thy face the face that launched the thousand ships, was it not thy hips that tumbled the mighty walls of Troy? Please, come from behind your pinafore that I may make acquaintance anew with your beauty."

"I won't," squealed Miss Rhodes, drumming her feet on the floor. "I won't come out until you stop talking them pretties."

With a frustrated sigh the great detective continued: "My point is, dear and lovely lady, that your wonderful proportions, that bosom, those hips, were not gained on a diet of parched peas and corn bread. I suggest beef as their wellspring, madam. Good, honest, American beef!"

After a few moments, Miss Rhodes lowered a corner of her pinafore and said quickly, "I have a pie," before quickly replacing it again.

"What?" asked my employer.

"I have a pie," declared the spinster just as quickly a second time, a single blue eye peeking out for a fraction of a second from the merest corner of her pinafore.

"Then," thundered Mr. Wong, "for God's sake let's have at it!"

"Will you stop talking them pretties?" inquired Miss Rhodes timorously from behind her pinafore.

"I will do my best to contain myself," pledged my employer. "Though, I must admit, it will be most difficult."

A few moments later, the spinster, her pinafore still covering her face, disappeared into the kitchen and later emerged with a pie as large around as a cartwheel, a wisp of steam rising from a hole in the center of the golden crust.

"Oh . . ." gasped Mr. Wong like Sir Galahad beholding the Holy Grail, "my . . . God."

"This way," said Miss Rhodes, inclining her head. "Into the dining room."

As she placed the pie in the center of a large, oaken table I could see the spinster's mind working feverishly to explain the sudden appearance of her culinary masterpiece. "I . . . I baked this for some orphans that came through town," she stammered. "But . . . but they all left and I clean forgot about it. Still, we can't let it go to waste, can we?"

"What . . ." croaked my mentor, so overcome he couldn't continue. He sat in silence for a few moments closely regarding the pie, perhaps fearing that it was a mirage that would soon disappear from sight, then managed: "What, dear lady, is in this wonderful creation?"

"I'll not lie to you, Mr. Wong," declared the spinster. "It is beef, sir. Good American beef."

"Beef," echoed Mr. Wong.

"And sausage, sir."

"Sausage," groaned Mr. Wong. "Pray tell me, pork or beef?"

"Both, sir. And a hint of kidney."

"Both," repeated my mentor, rapturously. "And kidney."

"Let me get us some plates," said Miss Rhodes.

"No!" exclaimed the great detective. Not for a single second did he take his eyes off the pie. "Two spoons, ma'am, and nothing else. Miss Rhodes, I implore you, make . . . 'em . . . big . . . 'uns."

"And you, young lady?" inquired the spinster.

"If it please you," I said, "parched peas and a little corn bread would be wonderful."

Miss Rhodes left and returned in moments with two large silver spoons, a round of corn bread, some yellow butter in a crock, some parched peas on a plate, and a jug of apple cider with three cups.

The peas had been boiled with mustard greens, and I smelled a hint of salt pork. This I ignored, being very hungry, and eagerly spread butter on my bread and picked up the fork Miss Rhodes had thoughtfully provided.

She and Mr. Wong sat on either side of the table, their great spoons poised for action.

"Now?" asked the great man in an awed whisper, removing his coat and hanging it over the back of his chair.

"Now," nodded Miss Rhodes.

And they set to with a will.

Thirty minutes later the mighty pie was gone and a perspiring Mr. Wong sat back in his chair, patting his great stomach in postprandial ecstasy.

"That," he gasped, "was a memorable pie."

Miss Rhodes, just as surfeited, managed to incline her head toward the empty dish. "Lordy, we didn't finish it all at last," she said, observing a solitary crumb of pastry and an atom of bone lying forlornly at the bottom of the trencher.

She tried to sit upright, failed, tried again, then decided to speak from where she was, slumped against the back of her chair. "I suppose," she managed weakly, "you now wish to speak business, Mr. Wong?"

"Later, dear lady," replied my employer, holding up his hand. "For now, a place to lie down. I pray you."

"Alas, there is only my bed," said Miss Rhodes. "But such a resting place would not, I fear, be seemly. I could be quite undone."

"Despair not, dear lady," quoth my mentor earnestly. "We will be chaste. I say again, ma'am, we will be chaste."

"In that case . . ." began Miss Rhodes uncertainly.

"Just point the way," gasped Mr. Wong, rising unsteadily to his feet. "An hour of rest, I think. Perhaps two."

"But, sir, we must visit the Hudson ranch," I protested. "And the scene of the crime."

By way of reply, my employer placed his cupped hand to his ear and said, "Harken, Chance, to the fury of the storm. I fear, we can go nowhere until it has abated."

"But sir—"

"When I awaken, Chance. Remember, what is life but a series of awakenings? That is how we progress."

My mentor turned to Miss Rhodes and held out his crooked elbow. "If you will take my arm, dear lady, you can perhaps show me the way."

The spinster took Mr. Wong's arm and together they walked, or rather staggered, to the bedroom where stood a massive brass bedstead, its stout legs as sturdy as the pair that held up Miss Rhodes herself.

Without a word, both collapsed onto the bed— which shrieked loudly in protest—and within a few moments they were sound asleep, mouths open as they snored in surfeited bliss.

There was a woolen blanket lying over a chair and I covered the sleepers with it, then tiptoed back to the parlor.

I was pleased that Mr. Wong was taking a well-deserved rest so that, even for an hour or so, the tumultuous machinations of his amazing brain could be stilled.

To my delight, Miss Rhodes owned an extensive collection of dime novels. Mr. Wong frowned on these as cheap trash and would never let me read one. But, since he was sound asleep, I chose *The Life and Trial of Frank James* published by the Wide Awake Library in New York and settled down in Miss Rhodes' easy chair to enjoy the story of the great Robin Hood of the West. So engrossed was I in the tale of Mr. James' derring-do and the adventures of his gallant but doomed brother Jesse, I hardly noticed as day shaded into early evening and the thunderstorm continued to rage with unabated fury.

I had just completed the novel when I heard the bed squeak noisily and I hurriedly returned Mr. James to his accustomed place on Miss Rhodes' bookshelf.

A few moments later my employer appeared at the parlor door and immediately took me to task. "Last Chance," he said, peering at me through the gathering gloom, his use of my full name betraying his irritation, "why did you let me sleep so long?"

"Sir, you seemed most fatigued from the exertions of your . . . dance . . . and I thought it best to let you slumber," I replied.

"Then I fear we have lost a day," sighed the great detective. "Child, one thing we do not have is time. There is, I have now concluded, an innocent man's life at stake and your constant dawdling has cut our available time from three days to just two."

I would have liked to have pointed out that we had just survived a clumsy attempt to kill us both, so believing in Brad Hudson's innocence required no great stretch of the intellect. But, being a well-brought-up young lady, I bit my tongue, lowered my eyes, and apologized to my mentor most humbly.

"Well," said Mr. Wong somewhat mollified, "dawdling is a trait of the young that can be corrected through constant instruction and example. We will therefore," he continued, "repair to our hotel and seek an early night, the better to be on the trail to the murder scene at first light tomorrow morning."

My employer sought a mirror that hung on the parlor wall and smoothed back his sleek hair, adjusted his tie, and walked toward the kitchen to retrieve his coat. "Wake Miss Rhodes, if you will, so that our business here can be concluded," he ordered, and I hastened to obey.

Groggy as she was from sleep and a surfeit of meat pie, Miss Rhodes struck a shrewd bargain for the rent of her motorcar, an expense my stricken employer whispered "would prove most ruinous."

We agreed to return before dawn the next morning and pick up the Model T from the small barn that stood beside Miss Rhodes' home and where, she assured us, there was a plentiful supply of gasoline in cans, brought in by freight train to Crow Creek at great expense.

As the spinster let us out her front door, Mr. Wong bowed and gallantly kissed her hand and that lady let out a small shriek of surprise and delight.

"Your cooking, dear Miss Rhodes, is surpassed only by your beauty and your gracefulness at the dance," declared the great detective sincerely as he straightened up and gazed soulfully into the spinster's eyes, the lady's hard bargaining forgiven, if not forgotten.

But Miss Rhodes' only reply was to wail: "Lawks! There you go, talking them pretties again!" And she covered her face with her pinafore as she closed the door and left us to the driving rain and the fury of the storm.

SEVEN

Huddled in our oilskins, we made our way to the hotel, though I looked to the right and left and often over my shoulder, fearing that another attempt might, at any moment, be made on our lives. This, of course, made Mr. Wong irritably accuse me of dawdling and he was in ill humor by the time we pushed open the hotel door against the gusting wind and struggled inside.

The clerk was not at his post and we retrieved our keys from the rack behind the desk and made our way upstairs.

"I will have my repeater watch beside my bedside so that I can awaken early," Mr. Wong said as we stood at his door. "There can," he added ominously, "be no more dawdling or sleeping late." With a promise to hammer on my door before daybreak, my employer bade me a gruff good night and entered his room. I walked farther up the hallway and did the same.

My room was about what you'd expect of a Montana cow town, a brass bed, a dresser with a jug of water, basin and towel, and—such unexpected luxury!—an oval, full-length mirror.

I lit the oil lamp that stood on a small table beside the bed and suddenly realized I was very tired. The events of the day, including my desperate sword fight with Silas Lime, had fatigued me more than I'd realized.

I quickly stripped off my clothes and gave myself an all-over sponge bath. I brushed my long hair until it fell straight and glossy black over my shoulders, then studied my naked reflection in the mirror.

As always, I looked at myself most critically, concluding yet again that my breasts were a little too small, my hips a little too wide, my mouth too full and generous and my eyes too dark and large, giving me the look of a perpetually startled fawn.

With a deep sigh I turned from the mirror and retrieved my dressing gown from my valise. It was one of my few luxuries, a robe of the finest watered pink silk, purchased for me by Mr. Wong from a rather mean-tempered merchant in Shanghai, embroidered all over with lotus blossoms and hummingbirds.

I love the feel of silk against my skin—it makes me feel rich, though I am poor—and this time when I studied myself in the mirror, I thought the vivid pink robe made me look quite pretty. Call it woman's intuition, or the instinct for self-preservation, but the events of the day induced me to place the back of one of the two wooden chairs in the room under the handle of the door. An attempt had already been made on my life, and I had to take care.

I reached into my valise and selected a black Burmah cheroot from the small cedar box I keep for that purpose and flared a match with my thumbnail, a little trick I'd learned from my dear headmistress. I lit the cigar, opened the window and pulled the remaining chair over so that I could watch the street. And there I sat, the fragrant blue smoke from the cheroot tying lacy bows above my head as I looked off into the night.

The tempest, far from abating, had increased in intensity. Rain angled into the street, forming huge puddles in the mud and lightning forked across the sky, illuminating the interior of the dark clouds for a split second so they glowed like tarnished silver. Thunder growled and cracked sullenly overhead and I felt the hotel shake, the printed admonition, DID YOU WRITE TO MOTHER? hanging in a frame above the bed rattling against the wall.

A few oil lamps dotted here and there along the empty street guttered in the wind, casting pale orange circles of light that danced on the boardwalk. A tinny player piano in the saloon cranked out the grand old tune of "She is More to be Pitied Than Censured" by Mr. William Gray, the wind catching the notes and scattering them in the darkness like fluttering moths.

The robe had slipped away from my thighs, and as I smoked I enjoyed the coolness of the breeze on my skin and softly sang the chorus of the song that had been so much loved by dear Miss Chastity Charmaine, especially on those evenings when the whiskey melancholy hung heavily upon her:

> *She is more to be pitied than censured,*
> *She is more to be helped than despised.*
> *She is only a lassie who ventured,*
> *On life's stormy path ill advised.*

Do not scorn her with words fierce and bitter,
Do not laugh at her shame and downfall.
For a moment just stop and consider,
That a man was the cause of it all.

As the player piano and I came to a halt, I reached up and dashed a budding tear from my eye and, in a somewhat disconsolate frame of mind, considered the events of the day and their implications.

That Brad Hudson was innocent of the murder of Victoria Grant I had no doubt. I believed the real killer had paid Silas Lime to kill Mr. Wong and myself, but so far, my only suspect was Sheriff Burt Havenick, though as to what his motives were, I could not even guess.

Victoria Grant had been stabbed horribly and viciously raped. Did Havenick look like a man who was capable of such insane savagery?

I shook my head. Cold-eyed killer that he was, I could not bring myself to believe he could commit such a terrible crime.

Then who?

I had no answer, but took some solace in the fact that the great intellect of Mr. Wong's had no doubt already considered that same question and had reached a brilliant conclusion that he might impart to me very soon.

Yet I could not shake the feeling that there was a terrifying evil at work here, hanging over Crow Creek like an ominous dark shadow. There had been evil in the way Victoria Grant had been murdered—and, I believed, even stark, raving madness.

Still, there is a Hindu proverb that says evil is a

screen which hides the truth, and we had little time to penetrate that screen and reach the truth that lay behind it. I was determined that Mr. Hudson would not hang for a murder he did not commit.

A sudden spike of fear froze me to my chair for a moment. Stealthy, almost silent steps in the hallway outside were approaching my room. I rose slowly and got the precious Dragon Box from the dresser and clutched it close to my fluttering breast.

The steps stopped, started again, as though someone was studying room numbers.

My breath came in short little gasps and I thought about calling out for Mr. Wong. But I knew the great detective would be meditating in the lotus position at this hour, thumbs to the tips of his forefingers, attempting to reach that state of enlightenment the lord Buddha tells us is essential if we wish to break the eternal cycle of death and rebirth.

Even if I screamed, which I very much felt like doing, my employer would be oblivious of all sounds but the gentle rustle of his own wonderful mind.

The doorknob turned, then turned again.

"Who is there?" I asked, hearing my voice quaver.

A muffled curse, then the footsteps receded.

I ran to the window and looked outside, but saw only the wind and rain and the empty street. A shadow moved around the corner of one of the buildings opposite the hotel and stopped. A few moments passed and the shadow stealthily moved again, slowly solidifying into the shape of a ragged, slat-ribbed coyote, poor thing. The animal made to cross the street, then stopped, its nose held high as it tested the wind. Instantly the coyote's head snapped downward, this time trusting to its keen eyes. It saw something near the hotel and yelped in sudden alarm, running away in terror with its tail tucked between its legs.

The coyote had seen someone—or some *thing*—that had scared it badly, and my guess was the person who had tried the door of my room.

Had the coyote sensed the presence of evil, and fled from it as all wild animals will do?

I shuddered and regained my seat, determined to finish my cheroot since seeking my bed in my present state of alarm was, at least for a while, out of the question.

A few minutes passed without further incident, then above the clamor of the storm, I heard a terrible, shrieking scream that echoed through the night.

Sitting bolt upright in my chair, I thought at first that someone had awakened from a nightmare and had cried out in terror.

But moments later, Sheriff Havenick, huddled into a rain-soaked slicker, water pounding on the rim of his hat, went splashing at a run down the middle of the street with a rifle in his hands—away from the source of the outcry!

"Here," someone yelled from the direction of the saloon, "that won't do! Who has been murdered in Crow Creek?"

I watched Havenick until he was swallowed by the darkness, and soon there was no sound but the angry snake hiss of the rain.

Rising, I pitched my cigar stub into the street and closed the window.

Later, lying in bed, my heart still beat to the same

tempo as the kettledrum rattle of the relentless rain on the window and sleep eluded me.

I believed the chair I'd placed against the door had saved my life, and that both myself and Mr. Wong were in the most desperate peril. I reached out and hugged the precious Dragon Box to my breast, gaining comfort from its warm presence.

And thus, after a long while of uneasy wakefulness, I drifted off to sleep as the storm rampaged outside and lightning flashed white in my room, casting the shadow of the window on the wall behind my head . . . a stark black cross hanging above my bed as though marking a tomb.

EIGHT

I was already awake and dressed when Mr. Wong rapped on my door an hour before daybreak. Since we were traveling light, my wardrobe choices were limited. I wore a suede skirt, split for riding, half boots with a low heel, and a blue wool shirt, soft and much faded from repeated washings. Since I had no hat but the little straw boater, I pulled back my hair and tied it with a bright yellow ribbon.

When I opened the door Mr. Wong stood there impatiently consulting his watch. "My, how you dawdle, child," he sighed.

He then instructed me to bring my oilskins since the weather was still inclement, noting that the thunderstorm had passed but the sky had settled into a sullen gray with a fine drizzle.

"We will," said my mentor, "repair to Ma's Kitchen for breakfast, since I have ascertained that the establishment of that bereaved lady is now open for business, though I greatly fear that after yesterday's memorable repast I have but little appetite."

I thought about telling my employer about the events of the previous evening, but decided against it.

That fine intellect had quite enough to deal with at present without me adding a further burden.

Ma's Kitchen was a cheerful place, bright with oil lamps and redolent of fried bacon and hot coffee. To my surprise, the Teton Kid already sat at a table, a cup of coffee in his hands, and he smiled pleasantly at me as I entered, and tipped his hat.

I dropped the cowboy a little curtsy and smiled in return, but Mr. Wong merely glanced irritably in the Kid's direction and made no attempt to greet him.

"And what can I get you nice people?"

As her name implied, Ma was a motherly-looking woman with a good-humored face framed by a halo of pure white hair.

I made bold as to offer her my condolences, which she accepted graciously, adding: "My husband was a man, no better and no worse than any other, but we'd been together for fifty years and had grown close."

These pleasantries were now put aside as Ma poured us coffee and then inquired of the great detective what he wished for breakfast.

"Not," quoth my employer, "a single morsel. I pray you, dear lady, let the coffee suffice."

"And you, young lady?"

Ma studied me for a while, shrewdly guessed the extent of my appetite and added: "I've got some nice hot buttermilk biscuits and honey, if you like."

"Oh, yes please," I replied.

Ma turned to get my order, but Mr. Wong halted her progress toward the kitchen. "Ah . . . on second thought, perhaps I should partake of a little something just to keep my strength up, for I fear I have a strenuous day ahead."

"Whatever you like," said Ma.

"Just a beefsteak, dear lady," said Mr. Wong, "and perhaps half a dozen scrambled eggs. Oh, yes, and some of those"—here he halted, before adding with due reverence—"hot buttermilk biscuits."

Across the dining room the Kid was working on another cup of coffee. He rolled a cigarette, studying us from under his hat brim.

"I guess you folks will be leaving today," he drawled.

"Then you guess wrongly, sir," said Mr. Wong. "My work here is not finished."

The Teton Kid considered this, then said: "Another murder in town last night."

"Who?" I asked in alarm, remembering that terrible scream echoing in the midst of the storm and the sheriff's pell-mell dash through the mud and rain.

The Kid shrugged. "Gambler feller by the name of Lime. Been hangin' around town for a while, down on his luck." He smiled. "His luck sure ran out for good last night."

I felt a momentary pang of horror. A thrust through the forearm should not prove fatal . . . but there is always the possibility of hemorrhage. A man can bleed to death if a major artery is cut.

"How—" I began, but choked on the word. I tried again. "How did it happen?"

The Kid shrugged and lighted his smoke. "Someone stuck him with a sword of all things. Right through the back. I hear it went all the way to the hilt and was sticking out the front of his vest." The Kid shuddered. "Settin' here, studyin' on it some, I reckon I'd rather be plugged any day." A surge of relief flowed through me. I wasn't the murderer of Silas Lime!

Ma brought us our food and for a while we ate in silence, Mr. Wong complaining that his lack of appetite compelled him to do nothing more than nibble around the edges of his plate, though his steak was already gone and his pile of eggs much diminished—to say nothing of the several biscuits that had already found their way down his throat.

I had just finished my first biscuit and was spreading honey on another when the restaurant door swung open and Sheriff Havenick walked inside, a blustery gust of rain following him.

The Teton Kid smiled cheerfully. "Mornin', Sheriff."

Havenick growled something sour under his breath and sat down beside my employer. "Wong, you can forget this Brad Hudson nonsense. I know he's guilty, you know he's guilty, and now I've got a real murder for you to investigate."

"We heard," said my employer. "I take it you're referring to the death of Mr. Silas Lime."

Havenick was taken aback. "How do you know?"

Mr. Wong nodded his head in the direction of the Teton Kid.

"I should've guessed," the sheriff said, turning in his seat, a scowl on his face. "There's some leaky mouthed folks around here who could talk the hide off a longhorn steer."

The Kid was not offended, his face cool, quiet and thoughtful. "Word gets around, Burt. Hard to keep something like that secret."

For some reason Havenick was mad clean through.

"Kid, ain't you got a job to do, an' shouldn't you be doin' it?"

The Teton Kid rose to his feet, smiling easily. "Matter of fact, I'm just leaving, heading back to the Circle O." The Kid tipped his hat in my direction. "You, little lady, have been a sweet distraction, but all good things must come to an end." He then walked outside, Havenick watching him go with ill-concealed irritation.

"That damn Kid talks too much," he said.

"Nevertheless, he did you a service by informing me of this latest murder," said Mr. Wong. "And although I don't agree with you that the case against Brad Hudson is, as they say, cut and dried, I'll assist you with this new homicide in any way I can."

Havenick circled a cup of coffee with his big hands and briefly explained how he'd been making his rounds of the town when he'd heard a terrible cry of pain and terror in the night.

"By the time I got to Lime's shack, it was all over," he said, his voice low and strange. "I ran for Doc Lawson, but I knew the man was already dead. You don't recover from a wound like that." So that was why I'd seen the sheriff run away from the scene of the crime. That is, if he was telling the truth. What better way for a cold-blooded assassin to cover up his guilt than by running helter-skelter through the night for help?

"Funny thing is, Lime had another wound." Havenick grabbed his right forearm. "Right here. It was bandaged and there was dried blood, so it wasn't done by the killer."

"I'm afraid I did that," I said quietly.

"You *what*?"

"If you will permit me, Sheriff," Mr. Wong interjected. "Silas Lime tried to murder us yesterday, and only my assistant's timely action saved us."

"Why wasn't I informed of this?" Havenick asked suspiciously.

"We planned to tell you right after breakfast," my employer lied smoothly. And I now believed, like me, the great detective had deduced that the sheriff could be the killer of Victoria Grant.

"All right, tell me now," Havenick said shortly.

"If you will permit me, sir," I said to Mr. Wong, and the great man graciously inclined his head.

As Havenick studied me closely, as briefly as possible I told him what had happened in Lime's shack and described our desperate sword fight. When I came to the part about putting the épée to Lime's throat in an effort to get him to tell us who'd hired him to kill us, I watched Havenick's reaction. But the sheriff didn't flinch.

"Talk is, Lime had killed men with the sword," he said. "I hear tell he'd been a duelist of some kind an' was considered an expert with the blade."

"He wasn't," I said. "At least, not where I come from."

Havenick rubbed his blue chin and his eyes suddenly became flat and hard. "I don't want you two to make any plans to leave town. After the hanging Monday morning, we'll talk about this some more."

"Listen, Sheriff," Mr. Wong said angrily, "someone hired Lime to kill us. We had nothing to do with his murder."

"Maybe, maybe not," the sheriff said. "As to what you're telling me, I don't think anybody hired anybody. Lime probably had an accomplice and didn't want to reveal his identity is all. You know, honor among thieves an' all that." Havenick waved a hand in our direction. "Look at you, a couple of prosperous pilgrims from back East ripe for the picking. A man as broke and desperate as Silas Lime might figger to kill you both, take what you have, then dump your bodies under cover of night. I don't know if that's a natural fact, but if you two are as innocent of his murder as you say you are, then it's a possibility.

"The way things are in town, he knew no one would lose any sleep if you two vanished and it would be days before they'd even think to start lookin'. By that time Lime and his compadre would be long gone."

"You know everyone in town, Sheriff," I said archly. "Who might this accomplice be?"

Havenick shook his head and flashed his thin smile. "Little lady, all kinds of frontier trash, saddle bums, bunco artists, dance hall loungers, an' sich drift in and out of Crow Creek. I can't be expected to keep track of them all."

"Then, since we are now under a cloud of suspicion, I suppose you no longer wish us to visit the scene of the crime?" asked my employer.

The sheriff shrugged. "I don't guess it can do any harm. Finish your breakfast an' let's go."

"Is . . . is the body still there?" I asked.

Havenick nodded. "Sure it is. Unless"—he smiled humorlessly—"dead men can walk."

I had lost my appetite for my second biscuit, but Mr. Wong scraped his plate clean with gusto, then we struggled into our oilskins and followed the sheriff outside.

The dull gray dawn was washing out shadows from the corners of the buildings and alleys, and down by the corrals and feed sheds alongside the railroad, a small herd was bawling miserably in the drizzling rain. To the west, the mountain peaks were covered in clouds that shrouded the tall timber and even reached the aspen growing on their lower slopes. The crows that nested in the cottonwoods by the creek flapped their sodden wings and cawed dismal complaints to each other about the weather as they perched together, huddling hunch-shouldered on the bare branches.

A few people were abroad in the street, mostly matronly housewives lifting their feet high to negotiate the deep mud as they frowned at a red-faced farmer who was cussing a blue streak and kicking the wheel of his bogged-down wagon. He then cracked a whip over his mule's head, interrupting his swearing only long enough to yell, "Hup, Daisy!" and "Damn ye for a bullheaded, two-bit nag."

The poor animal strained gallantly against her collar in a vain bid to move the wagon, but I decided the best four-tree horse team in all of creation couldn't have budged it.

We left the cussing farmer behind and reached Silas Lime's shack. The sheriff opened the door and in the rectangle of light that fell across the floor I saw the gambler's body lying on its right side, the sword hilt sticking out of his back.

Unlike a bullet, the sword sheds little blood, and

only a small dark pool stained the floor under Lime's chest where the blade protruded a good two feet.

"He sure lit a shuck for the pearly gates in a big hurry," Havenick said, prodding the dead man's body with his toe. "Poor son of a bitch didn't even see it coming."

"Look at his face," I said to the sheriff.

"Huh?"

"There's a look of surprise on his face," I explained. "This man turned his back on somebody and didn't expect to be killed."

Havenick shrugged. "Death surprises most people. Dying ain't an easy thing. Come to that, neither is living."

Mr. Wong looked around the gloomy little shack, then said: "There's nothing to be learned here, Sheriff. And I fear we can't waste any more time while my client still faces the gallows."

"Oh yeah?" Havenick growled sourly. "Well, like I said already, you two stay close. I don't want you to pull up your picket pins an' drift. This thing ain't over."

"Sheriff," my employer returned haughtily, "we have no intention of leaving. At least not until Brad Hudson is a free man and the real murderer is brought to justice."

Again I looked for a reaction from Havenick, but the man's face was impassive, his blue eyes steely. "You just pay real close mind to me and do as I say."

The sheriff's words lay across my consciousness flat and hard as stepping stones.

This was the voice of the gunman.

The harsh voice of the killer.

*   *   *

I breathed deeply of the fresh air when we left Silas Lime's claustrophobic cabin, disturbed by this new turn of events. Obviously the man who'd hired the gambler to kill us had silenced him. Lime died because he knew too much.

"Forward, Chance, and don't dawdle," commanded Mr. Wong, indicating with his cane even as he pointed his great belly in the direction of the spinster Rhodes' house.

He thrust that mighty protuberance into motion and his short, sturdy legs hurried to catch up. Thankfully there was boardwalk much of the way to the spinster's home, and we had only a short section of muddy street to traverse before arriving at her front gate. Miss Rhodes had told us that the car was in the barn and that we should take it without awakening her because she was a heavy sleeper and was seldom astir before the noon hour.

"I have a rather delicate constitution," she'd complained plaintively, "and therefore require much rest."

The Model T was indeed in the barn and seemed quite new. But it was covered all over in white chicken droppings and spiderwebs and its canvas top was holed in several places.

Mr. Wong, who is quite unreasonably fastidious in these matters, threw up his hands in horror. "Chance, I can't sit in that . . . that . . ." He searched for a word and finished rather lamely: "Mess!"

"Just a moment, sir, " I said. "I believe I can clean it."

I found an old piece of sacking and wiped off both

seats, the steering wheel, and the dashboard. When I'd finished the automobile looked fairly presentable, and Mr. Wong, with a deep sigh, deigned to step up to take his place behind the wheel. Alas, it soon became apparent to me that my mentor's portly physique was quite unsuited to that position since the wheel gouged into his belly and would have made driving impossible.

With another deep sigh, my employer extricated himself from behind the wheel, and said, "Chance, I've decided, on consideration, to let you drive."

"Thank you, sir," I said humbly. "It is a great pleasure of mine."

"Think nothing of it, child," Mr. Wong said affably, waving his cane. "I try to indulge the young as much as I can. Now," he added brusquely, "crank the handle and get her started."

Easier said than done.

The Model T apparently hadn't been driven in some time and refused to start, despite the fact that I cranked and cranked until I felt perspiration trickle down my back and my arm fell against my side like a chunk of lead.

Disturbed by this unfortunate turn of events, my employer ran this way and that in great agitation, clucking indignantly that Miss Rhodes had deceived him into paying a large sum for the rental of a motor-car that, no matter from which angle you looked at the situation, would not motor.

"A man's life is at stake, and we are held hostage by this infernal machine!" he wailed.

"Please, sir, " I said, my voice trembling from exhaustion, "I think I heard the engine cough the last time I tried. I believe it will start with a few more turns."

"Then get to cranking, Chance, for heaven's sake," declared my employer with considerable irritation. "Don't dawdle so, child."

Tired as I was, I cranked the handle again. Nothing. I tried again. This time the motor coughed feebly and a cloud of black smoke shot out of the exhaust.

"Oh jolly good," declared Mr. Wong, clapping his hands together. "Now try again, Chance, and this time put some snap into it."

I pushed back the brim of my sou'ester and wiped perspiration from my brow with a trembling hand. I cranked the car again. Nothing. I tried once more and—success! The machine roared into life and I quickly ran to the steering wheel and adjusted the throttle.

"Please, sir," I said, "I believe we can now get underway."

"And about time, too," declared my mentor sternly.

Mr. Wong, with great dignity and sense of purpose, took his seat beside me and I drove the Model T out of the barn, turning on to the main road out of town.

At first, because of the heavy mud, the automobile made hard work of the task, but after we'd cleared the outskirts of town the going became firmer and the automobile clattered along at a brisk clip.

As I told you earlier, my dear headmistress, Miss Chastity Charmaine, insisted that I drive her at the fastest possible pace, even to church on Sunday, but Mr. Wong did not share her love for speed.

"I believe you should slow down this vehicle, Chance," he said as he watched the grass on each side of the trail whiz past. "As a great Chinese philosopher once said, 'Slow and steady wins the race.' "

I throttled the car back until my employer, with a nod of his head, indicated that we had reached the velocity he desired. "This," he said, "is quite fast enough."

In truth, we were driving so slow I believed a turtle could have overtaken us, but at least our reduced speed meant that the drenching rain didn't pour so hard through the gaping holes in the canvas roof.

After an hour of driving on a road that seemed to be either clinging mud or a rock-strewn obstacle course, I remembered that Ben Cranwell, the little hunchbacked banker, had written out instructions on how to get to the Hudson ranch. He'd also kindly indicated the position of the dinosaur dig and a few other features, and I consulted his notes as I drove.

"How far?" inquired Mr. Wong impatiently. "Are we there yet?"

"Soon," I said. "If Mr. Cranwell's directions are correct, we should see the hill around the next bend of the trail." I nodded toward high bluffs of tumbled volcanic rock that rose on each side of the road, their jagged crests dotted here and there by a few stunted pine and aspen.

"Not too soon for me," sighed my employer above the roar of the engine. "I think I like automobiles even less than I do buckboards."

I turned around the bend of the trail, my tires throwing up great gobs of mud, and sure enough, as Mr. Cranwell had indicated, a low hill lay to our left, a pair of flapping tents clinging precariously to its slope.

"That, sir," I said, "is the scene of Victoria Grant's murder."

The gallant little car chugged up the gradual rise of the hill quite easily and we stopped just short of the tents.

I hadn't noticed her before, but a young, red-haired woman was bent over a bare patch of hillside, a trowel-like tool in her hand. As we braked to a halt she rose, brushed a fallen lock of hair from her face, and studied us closely. For a moment I felt a jolt of superstitious fear.

Could this beautiful creature be Victoria Grant, the woman who was long dead and buried? Was I seeing her ghost?

But all such thoughts were dispelled when the lady strode purposefully toward us and stopped beside the Model T, her eyes puzzled and wary. "What do you want?" she asked brusquely. "This is private property."

Now I recognized her as the aloof woman who had ridden past us in the street and had not returned my smile.

Mr. Wong climbed out of the car and immediately displayed his fine manners and good breeding, strutting this way and that as he introduced himself and recounted the reason for our being in Crow Creek.

The woman had listened in attentive silence, now she said bitterly: "Brad Hudson murdered Victoria and he'll hang for it the day after tomorrow. Your being here, Mister . . . Mister . . ."

"Wong," I supplied the name.

". . . won't make a bit of difference. The whole town knows he's guilty, and I know he's guilty."

"And you are . . . ?" my employer dangled his half-finished sentence in front of the woman like a baited hook.

"Dr. Charity Hamilton," she replied. "I was Victoria's assistant."

The great detective was about to say more, but Charity turned and called out over her shoulder:

"Hey, Schramm, get out here!"

The flap of one of the tents opened and a tall, thin man stepped into view, his hands dangling from the too-short sleeves of his brown corduroy coat like great meat hooks. His black hair was long, falling limp to his shoulders, and he sported a ragged goatee.

"Ah, visitors," Schramm smiled. "How very nice."

The man walked toward us, lanky and stooped, and all I could see in his face as he grew closer was avarice, greed, and when he looked at me, the twisted smirk and raised eyebrow of a dawning lust.

"This is so nice," Schramm said, extending his hand to Mr. Wong. "My name is Jeremiah Schramm, of the Maine Schramms, don't you know, but much more recently of the Boston Museum of Prehistoric Antiquities." He waved a hand, taking in the tents and hillside. "We financed this expedition."

"How de do?" replied Mr. Wong affably. He took Schramm's hand then introduced me: "Last Chance Lee, my valued assistant."

I was forced to take Schramm's huge hand. I expected steel in his grip, but instead felt only clammy softness.

"Now, what can I do for you both?" he asked pleasantly enough.

But before either of us could reply, Charity Hamilton told him why we were there and our purpose in coming to Crow Creek.

"How exciting," declared Schramm, nodding and bowing from the waist so that he looked like a child's bobbing toy. "I've never met a real-life detective before." The man winked at me. "I suppose you want me to 'spill the beans,' as you sleuths say?"

"Sir," I said, "anything you can tell us about the circumstances surrounding Victoria Grant's death would be most helpful."

"But of course," Schramm smiled, "but first you must see our star attraction."

"Schramm, I really don't think that's necessary," Charity snapped.

Schramm ignored her. "Sadly, that is also the spot where poor Victoria was so horribly murdered. So, we kill two birds with one stone."

As Schramm turned and walked away, Mr. Wong and myself stood as though rooted to the ground. But the man glanced over his shoulder, crooked his finger at us, and said lightly: "Come, come, there's much to see."

We stirred ourselves and followed Schramm up the hill, coming upon a pit about twenty feet in length and maybe fifteen across. The pit was about three feet deep and had once been deeper but the heavy rains had washed muddy detritus into it from higher up the hillside and broken down the steep sides.

"Well, what do you think?" Schramm asked proudly, inclining his head toward the skeleton of the creature that lay at the bottom of the dig.

"In God's name, what is that?" gasped my employer.

"That," replied Schramm, "is one of the greatest paleontological finds of the new century. It is enough to ensure Victoria Grant's place in the history books, even if she was an unprofessional crackpot."

"That, Schramm, is a matter of opinion," Charity returned, her dislike and contempt for the man palpable. "*Doctor* Grant was one of the world's leading paleontologists."

"*That*, my dear, is a matter of opinion," Schramm said smugly. "As to her being a crackpot, that is a matter of fact."

Charity opened her mouth to say something else, but I headed off trouble at the pass, as they say in the West, by asking: "What kind of animal is that?"

The creature in the pit, though reduced to a stony skeleton over millions of years, had been small, no more than six feet tall and perhaps eight feet long, including its long, whiplike tail. But the jaws of its skull were lined with two rows of savage teeth and on each of its legs, just above the three-toed foot, it bore a vicious, curved claw.

"That is one of the deadliest predators to ever stalk the earth," Schramm said. "It is an advanced, binocular-visioned dinosaur with a remarkably large brain. Called a 'raptor,' it probably hunted in packs. It was intelligent, quick and active, and a born killer." The man turned to me and smiled thinly. "Do you know what would happen to you, young lady, if you had the misfortune to meet such a creature?"

My ill-fitting sou'ester had worked itself over my eyes, and I pushed it back and shuddered: "I'd rather not think about it."

Schramm ignored this and, with more than a touch

of insensitive arrogance, continued: "It would use the claws on you, not the teeth, at least not at first. The small front legs would grasp your shoulders to hold you fast, then the hind legs would come up, all the way to your pretty little throat. Then it would slash downward with the powerful claws, first one, then the other, instantly opening you up like a gutted doe. After that the teeth would come into play, plunging into your body while you yet breathed, seeking the tastier morsels, the liver, heart and lungs, tearing—"

"Enough, Mr. Schramm, if you please," interrupted Mr. Wong loudly, holding up his dragon-topped cane in an attitude of command. "I can see you are scaring my assistant, and I think your case for the savagery of this beast has already been well presented."

In truth, I was fascinated by the fierce creature.

"A question, Mr. Schramm, if you please," said Mr. Wong. "Can you show me the exact spot where Dr. Grant was murdered?"

Schramm smiled thinly. "Why, right down there." He indicated with a nod of his head. "She cashed in her chips right alongside her greatest discovery."

"Schramm," Charity said, her beautiful face white with anger, "you're a pig."

The man took the insult in stride. "Maybe so," he shrugged, "but I call a spade a spade. I'm an outspoken man by nature."

I let that strange reference pass, and asked: "Sir, you called Miss Grant a crackpot. Were there others who thought so?"

The man laughed, a high-pitched cackle a full octave higher than his normal speaking voice. "Why, young lady, she was the most hated woman in America."

"Aha," declared my mentor, "here's fine information. There's no trivia here. Was she hated enough that someone would want her dead?" he demanded shrewdly.

"Of course," Schramm replied, "and not just for being a woman in a man's profession, but because of her idiotic theories. Mr. Wong, her colleagues roundly despised her."

"What were those theories?" I asked.

"Oh, she believed that dinosaurs were warm-blooded, that was just one of her idiocies. She also wrote in a scientific journal of the more sensational sort that the entire dinosaur species was wiped out sixty million years ago by some catastrophic event. She had the temerity to suggest a meteor from outer space could have thrown so much debris into the atmosphere that the world was plunged into a dark winter that lasted for decades."

"Dr. Grant believed the dinosaurs could not adapt to these changing conditions and became extinct," Charity said. "I happen to agree with her."

"Then you're as crazy as she is," Schramm snorted, a faint anger growing in his eyes.

"Sir, what is so wrong with such opinions?" I asked, drawing an exasperated look from Mr. Wong. "I must admit, they seem perfectly reasonable to me."

"Ah, forgive me," Schramm said, sarcasm edging his voice. "I had no idea you were an expert in such matters."

"I'm sorry, sir," I returned. "I speak only as a layman."

Somewhat mollified, Schramm smiled and said: "It is my opinion and the opinion of the Boston Museum

of Prehistoric Antiquities, that the dinosaurs, large—
let me emphasize this—cold-blooded lizards, were
destroyed by the great flood, say around 4000 B.C., as
the Holy Bible tells us. It stands to reason that such
large and"—he nodded toward the pit—"savage creatures could, under no circumstances, be admitted to
the Ark.

"That," Schramm concluded, "is mainstream opinion, the belief of most respected paleontologists now
working in the field. Victoria Grant chose to ignore
this and ride the winds of infamy, but instead she
reaped the whirlwind of terrible death."

Schramm looked up at the iron gray sky and whispered: "It was a reckoning."

I glanced at Charity Hamilton. She stood white-
lipped and angry enough to kill.

"Ask Schramm where he was when Victoria was
murdered," she said truculently, all her rage suddenly
ready to vent itself.

"Yes," said Mr. Wong sagely, "that's a good point.
Where were you, Mr. Schramm?"

"In the hills, riding," Schramm replied, waving a
hand toward the distant mountains. "There are other
finds to be made in western Montana, maybe as important as this one." The man looked Charity right in
the eye and his gaze was steady and untroubled. "All
that came out in court, my dear. You know that."

"Lies are told every day," Charity said flatly, her
very body posture a challenge.

"Do you mean to imply—"

"Miss Hamilton," I interrupted, "where were you
when Dr. Grant was murdered?"

"It's *Doctor* Hamilton, and I was on my way into town to fetch the sheriff."

"I don't understand."

"It's quite simple, really. I was also out scouting the hills—we sometimes rent horses from the livery stable in town—and as I rode back to camp Victoria ran toward me, waving her arms, screaming at me to get the sheriff."

"Did she indicate why?" I asked.

Charity shook her head at me. "No, she didn't. But Victoria saw something out here, something that scared her badly. I asked her what was wrong, but she just yelled at me for asking too many questions and told me to bring Sheriff Havenick."

The woman's shoulders slumped. "When I got to Crow Creek, the sheriff wasn't there. But some of the men from the town rode out here with me and . . . and when we got here, Victoria was already dead."

Charity hesitated, as though trying to draw on some inner strength, then she continued: "She . . . she was lying at the bottom of the pit. She was naked and . . . her body was covered in blood. Her legs had been forced apart and her face . . . her face bore a look of horror I'll never forget as long as I live."

The beautiful paleontologist shuddered. "Victoria's eyes were wide open, still terrified, even in death, and she was not a woman who scared easily."

She turned to Mr. Wong, and the great detective's face, experienced as he was in such matters, was pale from the horror of Charity's story. "If Brad Hudson did all that to her, he was out of his mind, insane with rage and hate. Mr. Wong, Victoria wasn't just raped and murdered, she was devoured by a wild animal."

I gave an involuntary gasp of fear, just as thunder rolled across the sky and the rain increased in intensity. Charity's red hair was plastered over her forehead and the man's shirt and blue jeans she wore clung like a second skin to her remarkably voluptuous body.

"Dr. Hamilton," said Mr. Wong, as that great and unique mind began to grapple with the facts of the case, "could there have been a rejected lover in the picture? Perhaps someone from her past?"

Charity shook her head at him, her chin lifted defiantly. "Victoria had no lovers in her past. I was her lover, and the only one she ever had."

My employer seemed nonplussed by this statement, but not I. At my dear old school I'd been long familiar with the love between women that dare not speak its name. Often in the night, I'd lie awake in the dormitory, drowsily aware of giggles and soft sighs and muffled murmurs in the darkness, the insistent creak of a bed, the silken whisper of hands caressing skin. Dear Miss Chastity Charmaine, who knew of course that such things happen, even among the most genteel young ladies, never took the lovers to task.

"I, who have been judged so often and so unjustly myself, will not judge others," she once said at the breakfast table. "I neither condemn nor condone. Such a love exists, therefore I accept its existence."

And at once two pretty young ladies of gentle birth farther down the table lifted their coffee cups to their faces to conceal their blushes and giggled.

But Charity was not blushing nor giggling as she made her relationship with the dead woman known.

And it was Schramm who broke the silence that followed, grinning maliciously as he said: "And that's another reason why Victoria's male colleagues hated her so much. She was such a lovely woman, and they thought, 'What a damnable waste!'"

"As I told you already, Schramm," Charity said, her anger bubbling over, "you're a pig."

Once again, the man was not in the slightest bit upset, merely bowing in Dr. Hamilton's direction. "Charmed I'm sure, dear lady."

Mr. Wong, the heavy rain battering his sou'ester hat and the shoulders of his oilskins, said firmly and definitely: "There's no more to be learned here, so it's time for me to take my leave. And I suggest everyone seek shelter from the rain."

"Please, sir," I said. "I would like to climb into the pit. There might be a clue."

"A *whaaat*?" asked my employer, aghast.

"A clue, sir."

"Chance, do you think I am Dr. Doyle's detective that I should be concerned with"—he shook his head in exasperation—"clues?"

My mentor could not bring himself to utter the name Sherlock Holmes, referring to him only as "Dr. Doyle's detective," and then in a most slighting manner. It was Mr. Wong's great fear that Mr. Holmes' fictitious exploits might overshadow his own very real work in the field of criminal investigation.

"Sir," I said in a wheedling tone, "I know you've already brilliantly deduced that the recent rains will have covered up any cl . . . ah . . . traces that may have been left by the killer. Yet I believe a perusal of the pit might be most appropriate at this time."

"You have stated my deduction correctly," agreed

Mr. Wong, seemingly pleased by my praise. "Very well, investigate the pit if you must, but don't dawdle, child. And don't expect *clues* to be scattered around quite as conveniently as they always seem to be for Dr. Doyle's detective."

Before my employer could change his mind, I jumped down into the pit, not an easy task in my oversized oilskins, and made a quick study of the dig. Detritus from the hillside, mostly mud and fist-sized chunks of rock, had drifted into the pit, so that the cut opposite from where I stood was quite covered over, only an inch or two of Victoria Grant's original wall showing above the debris. It seemed to me that not all the drift into the pit had been caused by erosion. There was evidence that more dirt had been introduced and a shovel used to tamp it down hard, perhaps to create a makeshift dam to stop further sediment from reaching the skeleton of the dinosaur.

I walked over to the heaped dirt and dug into it with the toe of my boot. I didn't really expect to find anything, nor did I.

Mr. Wong, in a state of some agitation, walked to the edge of the pit, flanked by Charity and Schramm, and urged me to climb out at once. "You're wasting your time, Chance," he said. "There's nothing to be found there."

I was about to clamber out of the dig when something caught my eye where I'd dug into the earthen dam with my boot. Keeping my eye on the object, I walked over and picked it up. It was small, silvery, and covered in mud. I rubbed away some of the clinging dirt with my thumb and gradually made out a small, silver triangular shape.

"What do you have there?" Schramm asked, looking at me intently.

I shook my head at him. "I don't know. I think it's an arrowhead."

"Chance," declared my employer wearily, waving his cane in a circular motion, "at one time this was all Indian country. An arrowhead is not unusual." He reached out his hand. "Come, let me assist you."

I took Mr. Wong's hand, and, with surprising strength, he pulled me out of the pit.

"Look," I said to him when I was once again standing beside him. "It seems to be made of silver."

My employer glanced at the arrowhead with a marked lack of curiosity. "Trivia, Chance," he said. "This case will not be solved and our client freed by finding clues. It will be solved"—he tapped his temple with his right forefinger—"by my powers of deduction."

Mr. Wong was, in all probability, correct. Still, I carefully reached under my oilskins and pushed the arrowhead deep into my skirt pocket. It might warrant further investigation.

When I looked up, Jeremiah Schramm was studying me out of the corner of his eye, as though he was noting closely where I'd put the arrowhead and was storing the information away for future use.

My employer bowed to Schramm and Dr. Hamilton. "I will now take my leave, and I thank you both. You've been very helpful. However, Dr. Hamilton, I must warn you . . . that . . . I . . . ."

The great detective's voice trailed off into a

stunned silence. He was looking over Charity's shoulder toward the crest of the hill and I followed his gaze. A man on a paint pony, a Winchester rifle across his saddle horn, was coming down the slope at a steady canter.

Charity turned and looked over her shoulder. "Oh, that's Ghost Bear," she said, annoyed. "He's a Flathead and he made a lot of trouble for Victoria over the raptor."

The Indian reined up his horse a few feet from Schramm and Charity, and the paleontologist asked him in obvious irritation: "What do you want, Ghost Bear?"

I must admit, I thought the Flathead a fine figure of a man. He wore two thick braids that fell to his wide, muscular shoulders. His face was very dark from sun and wind and his expressive hazel eyes showed more green than brown. He wore a bright yellow slicker against the rain and a wide-brimmed sombrero decorated by a single feather that slanted upward from the beadwork band.

"Woman, it is time you leave," Ghost Bear said. "There is great evil here in this place." He looked around him.

"There is no evil here," Charity said irritably. "As Dr. Grant already told you, Ghost Bear, there are only a few old bones and a hole in the ground."

"Other red-haired woman die here. You die here, too. Pretty damn soon, I think."

"Now see here . . . um . . . Ghost Bear, are you threatening this woman?" asked Mr. Wong with a great display of determination.

The rain dripped off the Indian's hat brim as he

shook his head. "I no kill." He pointed to the pit with his rifle. "He kill like he killed other woman. He rip her apart with his great claws for disturbing his rest."

Ghost Bear waved his rifle. "All these hills are sacred to Flathead. The Great Spirit appointed dragon creature to guard hills for Indian for all time, as long as the wind blows and the rain falls." He looked directly at Charity Hamilton. "You cover animal with dirt and leave, then you no die. You stay, and great animal kill you." He stared at her, his eyes suddenly hard. "Or the Flathead kill you."

Charity stood her ground, unafraid. "Don't threaten me, Ghost Bear. I'll leave only when the skeleton is safely on its way to the museum in Boston. I owe that much to Victoria."

"Fool," Ghost Bear snapped angrily. "Then you surely will die like Vic-to-ria."

The Flathead turned his horse and galloped back up the slope, scattering a covey of quail from a stand of pine and brush. He didn't look back.

"Dr. Hamilton," Mr. Wong said when the Indian was gone, "I very much fear for your life. I urge you to come back to town with us and stay there, at least until the real killer of Dr. Grant is found."

Charity shook her head at him. "Mr. Wong, the killer has already been found. He now sits in the jail in Crow Creek and will hang come Monday morning. As to being in danger, I can look out for myself. Besides, Schramm may be a pig, but he has a British Bulldog revolver in his tent."

Schramm made another of his mocking little bows. "At your service, Dr. Hamilton. I'm always the white knight ready to come to the aid of a lady in distress."

"Go to hell," Charity snapped, and strode to .her tent, throwing the flap wide and vanishing inside.

Jeremiah Schramm watched her go, a strange, vindictive look in his eye, and I suddenly feared for Charity's life. She was a woman alone out here in this wilderness, and vulnerable.

"I do wish Dr. Hamilton would have agreed to come back to town with us," I said to my employer as we walked back to the automobile.

But Mr. Wong shrugged. "She's a grown woman and must do as she pleases. Besides, Mr. Schramm has a revolver."

But even as I turned the Model T on the hillside, my guardian hanging on for dear life as we leaned over at an alarming angle, I could not shake the feeling that Charity Hamilton was in terrible danger. Not from the fanged and clawed thing in the pit, but from enemies much more human and just as savage.

NINE

We drove off the hill, to Mr. Wong's visible relief, and rejoined the main trail, a steady curtain of lashing rain angling across the wind-tossed prairie grass. I felt the little Ford shudder as the wind did its best to blow us off the trail and, despite the canvas cover, rain pelted off our oilskins and drove, stinging, into our faces.

The sun of the hot summer had scorched the prairie to a dull brown color. Railroad tracks, flanked by telegraph poles, cut across the grass in the distance, shining like a slim rapier blade. The mountain peaks to the west were blotted out by low, sullen clouds that now moved like gray ghosts among the aspen growing on their lower slopes and here and there I could make out deep buffalo wallows, made by animals that were now only a distant memory.

"Consult Mr. Cranwell's directions, Chance," ordered Mr. Wong, stirring from a deep reverie that had kept me in silence, since I feared to disturb the machinations of that magnificent intellect. "We do not wish to miss the trail to the Hudson ranch."

"I believe it cuts off to the south about a mile from

here," I said. "We'll see a stand of pine and a ruined cabin just before our turn."

Once again, Mr. Wong lapsed into silence, and I had no doubt he was pondering the many intricacies of the case we seemed no closer to solving than we did when we first stepped off the train.

"I do hope," said my employer after a few moments, "that Miss Hudson offers us a little something. A light breakfast is all very well and good, but it does leave one hungry for a decent lunch."

I considered a beefsteak and half a dozen eggs anything but light, but then I did not have to nourish a powerful brain like Mr. Wong's that needed constant sustenance to keep it functioning at full capacity.

We found the road to the ranch just as Mr. Cranwell had described it, parallel lines of wagon tracks that had been cut thorough a saddleback hill before curving alongside a shallow creek bed lined with ancient cottonwoods.

Another ten minutes and we had the ranch in sight, a cluster of low frame buildings surrounded by corrals, barns, and a blacksmith's shop. The main ranch house was back under the arching limbs of a huge oak, and a stream, fed from somewhere in the mountains, ran across the front of the property. A sturdy wooden bridge had been laid across the cut banks, allowing for the safe passage of both wagons and horsemen.

I drove the little Ford over the bridge and braked to a halt outside the ranch house. Almost immediately the door swung open and a tall, wide-shouldered man who looked to be in his early forties walked outside, jammed his hat on his head, and studied us with more than passing interest.

The man wore faded blue jeans and a butternut-colored wool shirt. His face, burned to the color of old saddle leather by the sun, seemed good-humored and intelligent, but his eyes above his fine cavalry mustache were hard and steel-gray, and the gun he wore on his hip was as much a part of him as his boots and hat.

As he strolled, relaxed but ready toward us, he carried his head in a way that suggested pride not unmixed with a degree of arrogance, the same attitude I'd already noted in Sheriff Havenick. I was familiar with men like this and had grown to know some of them quite well.

My dear headmistress, Miss Chastity Charmaine, was a woman who was generous to a fault. Yet, she never forgot a favor she'd done for anyone, and had a habit of calling them in, even years after the event.

It was her opinion, from experience, that the world was a dangerous and uncertain place and that any young lady of quality should be expert in the use of small arms, the better to discourage the would-be ravisher and unwanted suitor alike.

For that reason, we were well schooled in the use of firearms, especially the Winchester rifle, Colt revolver, and the belly gun, notably the .41 caliber Derringer, a personal favorite of our headmistress and a weapon she wore tucked into a frilly garter on her right thigh.

Since Miss Charmaine believed that nothing was too good for her young ladies, she called in her old favors and we were taught the use of arms by some of the very best shootists in the country, including Mr.

Bat Masterson, then employed as a sports columnist on *The Morning Telegraph* in New York, and Mr. Buckskin Frank Leslie, who was currently appearing as a rough rider in Buffalo Bill's Wild West Show and had, alas, spent some years in the penitentiary.

It was Miss Chastity Charmaine's desire, most earnestly communicated to the student body, that Mr. Masterson and Mr. Leslie be given the honorary title of professor, and must be addressed only by that title.

Both these very careful gentlemen, and several others who came and went at various times, were a strange blend of pride, arrogance, and self-effacing humor, just as this man who was confronting us now appeared to be.

"Step down," he told us, his right hand never far from the worn walnut butt of his revolver.

We did as we were told and Mr. Wong introduced us both, declaring that he'd come to see Miss Hudson who had engaged our services.

The tall man stepped back out of the rain under the protection of a wooden awning over the ranch house door.

"Miss Hudson ain't seeing anybody today," the man said. "My name's Matt Jerrell and I'm the foreman of the Rafter H. You got any questions, you can address them to me."

"That I will not do," declared my employer defiantly. "Miss Hudson is paying my fee, and my business is with her."

"Mister," Jerrell said, his voice suddenly harsh, "you heard my name. Doesn't it mean anything to you?"

Mr. Wong shook his head. "No sir, it doesn't. And why should it?"

Jerrell looked at my employer, his hard eyes level and cold. "A few years back it meant something, here an' all the way back to Texas. It meant Matt Jerrell is not a man to be trifled with. I told you Angela isn't seeing anyone, an' that's how it stands." He nodded toward the Model T. "Now get back into that rig an' light a shuck outta here afore I fergit you're just a pilgrim an' a dumb Chinaman who don't know no better."

"Sir," said Mr. Wong, drawing himself up to his full height as he puffed out his chest and made a fine display of wounded pride, stabbing his cane in Jerrell's direction, "I may be quite Oriental in appearance, but I can assure you I'm as American as you are, and, being American, I will not be intimidated by any . . . any . . . Chance, help me?"

"Two-bit gunman," I supplied, recalling my conversations with Mr. Masterson on that very matter, since he had made the unwelcome acquaintance of many such during his time on the frontier.

"Yes," exclaimed Mr. Wong, "any two-bit gunman!"

"Mister," Jerrell said, his voice very flat, "there ain't a man alive who can say that to me."

Before, the ranch foreman seemed relaxed, almost indolent. Now, behind a curtain of rain falling from the awning over his head, he was coiled and ready, his hand very close to his gun.

"Them was war words," Jerrell said huskily. "This here hoedown is now over. You head back to that auto-mobile or, I swear, I'll put a bullet into you right where you stand."

I thought of the Dragon Box under my oilskins. But it was so far out of reach my mentor would be dead before I could open it.

"'Ware, sir," I whispered urgently. "I think he means it."

"Then be damned to you, sir," quoth Mr. Wong, his magnificent head held high in a gallant gesture of defiance. "I've come to see Miss Hudson and I will not move from this spot until I've spoken to her."

"Chinaman," Jerrell said, "you just signed your own death warrant."

The foreman's revolver slicked out of the holster in a movement too fast to follow and he hammered off two quick shots. I stood stunned, almost deafened by the roar of the six-gun, as two spurts of rain and mud kicked up just inches from the toes of Mr. Wong's galoshes.

"That was just a warning," I heard Jerrell say, his voice sounding like it came from the end of a long tunnel. "Next time I aim three feet higher."

"Matt, what are you doing?" A very pretty blond woman stood at the door of the ranch house, her face horrified. "Are you trying to kill this man?"

Jerrell smiled thinly. "Nah, Angela, jest scarin' this here Chinaman into salvation an' a Sunday school is all."

"Put that gun away!" Angela ordered. She turned to my mentor. "I'm so sorry, you must be Mr. Chester Wong."

"Indeed I am, dear lady," replied my employer, his face a little pale. "I came here to talk to you about your poor father and"—he shrugged, adding apologetically—"my fee. That is, until I was accosted by this assassin."

Angela Hudson smiled. "Matt means well, but sometimes his methods are a little, well, old-fashioned."

"I just don't want anybody bothering you, Angela," the foreman said, and I detected real tenderness in his voice. "Seems to me you've been hurt enough already."

For a moment, Angela's eyes misted, then she clapped her hands and exclaimed: "Goodness gracious, where are my manners? Please, Mr. Wong and Miss . . . Miss—"

I gave her my name.

"Ah yes, of course, Miss Lee, please come inside out of the rain."

My employer followed Angela into the ranch house as Matt Jerrell stepped aside to let them pass.

"You, too, little lady," he said to me.

I walked to where Jerrell stood in the doorway and stopped.

"Mr. Jerrell," I smiled sweetly, looking up at him, "had your aim been three feet higher, you would not have lived another second to boast of it."

The tall foreman was shocked. "Whaaa . . . ?" he gasped.

"In the words of a learned professor at my dear old school, I would have ventilated your brisket pretty damn quick."

Under the surprised gaze of Jerrell, I dropped my eyes modestly to the ground and, without another word, followed the others into the ranch house. The tall foreman continued to stare after me, his manly jaw dropped to his chest.

"I'm afraid I've wasted your time," Angela Hudson was saying to my employer as I entered. "The trial . . . well, the trial convinced me of Dad's guilt." Her eyes searched Mr. Wong's face. "How could he have done such a hateful thing?"

"Miss Hudson, a wise Chinese philosopher once said that hatred is a madness of the heart. Indeed, the man who murdered Dr. Grant is truly mad." Mr. Wong studied Angela closely. "You believe we have come here on a wild goose chase?"

The woman nodded. "I'm afraid so."

Like the immaculate cabin itself, with its scrubbed flagstones and well-chosen furniture, Angela Hudson was very pretty in a frilly, very feminine way. She wore a pink cotton dress printed all over with little white flowers that left her shapely shoulders bare with just a suggestion of deep cleavage, and silver bracelets encircled both her small wrists.

But there was a jarring note—a yellowing purple bruise around her left eye and paler smudges on her throat. Her slender arms were also covered in fading welts and I noticed what looked like bite marks on her shoulders.

"Mr. Wong," she said, "I want you to stop your investigation immediately."

"That might not be so easy," replied my employer, his eyes puzzled and wary. "You see an attempt has already been made on my life, and I believe the real killer of Dr. Grant was behind it."

"Who tried to kill you?" Matt Jerrell asked from the

doorway. He glanced at me quickly. "An' if you're talking about me, I wasn't really tryin'."

"No, not you," said Mr. Wong irritably. "A man by the name of Silas Lime."

"He's trash," Jerrell said. "He'd kill you for five dollars. No one needed to put him up to it."

"Well, someone did, because Mr. Lime is now also dead, killed I believe by his disappointed employer." Mr. Wong shrugged. "A quick sword thrust through the back."

"Good riddance," Jerrell said. "He'd done his own share of killin', that one. They say he done some of it his own self with a sword."

Mr. Wong nodded. "Mr. Lime lived by the sword and he died by the sword."

"All that don't prove a thing," Jerrell said. "One of his compadres could've stuck him. He was always hanging out with trash just as low as hisself."

My employer nodded. "That is always a possibility."

"Please, no more talk of killing," Angela said, her face pale. "Mr. Wong, we were about to eat, would you care to join us?"

"Not so much as a single crust of bread, dear lady," replied my mentor, throwing his hands up in horror. "My appetite is delicate in the extreme. It is a very uncertain thing."

"Oh, I'm sorry to hear that." Angela rose from her chair with an air of finality. "Well, if you will submit your bill before you leave town, I'll see that it's paid, though it may take me a few weeks."

Alarmed by this sudden and unexpected turn of events, my horrified employer tried his utmost to backtrack. "Um . . . on second thought, perhaps we shouldn't leave so hastily, for we have a long journey ahead," he said. "Under those circumstances, perhaps it might be wise to partake of just a little something . . ."

"Of course," Angela smiled. "We have a very good Chinese cook, you know. His name is Chang."

A few minutes later, the aforementioned Chang appeared, bearing platters of food. He was all Chinese and wore the round hat and long pigtail I hadn't seen since we were last in San Francisco.

"You, missy," he said to me. "You too thin. You eat now." He laid plates in front of me and Angela.

"You, too, Miss Angela. Chang cook, you eat. You get nice and fat and attract very good husband."

Laying another plate in front of Mr. Wong, Chang glanced at his great belly and snapped: "You no need eat. Go six, seven months without eating, and still be fat."

My employer spluttered his indignation, but Angela laughed musically and said: "Ignore Chang, Mr. Wong. He's a bit outspoken by times."

"A great Chinese philosopher once said that only the vulgar take delight in the supposed faults of great men," said my mentor, eyeing Chang coldly.

"Other Chinese philosopher say that secret to long life is to eat but little grub," returned Chang, grinning.

How all this would have ended I do not know, had not Angela chased the little man back to the kitchen and, with much pleading, urged the irritated Mr. Wong to fill his plate.

My employer's ill humor vanished in an instant as he beheld the table in front of him groaning under the weight of platters of steak, venison, mashed potatoes, and beans swimming in pork fat.

He and Jerrell set to with a will, but Angela looked at the food then suddenly stood up, put her hand to her mouth, and ran for the back door of the cabin.

As the men sat in a stunned silence, I followed Angela outside and found her retching convulsively a few yards short of the outhouse.

When she finally straightened up, her face white, I took a handkerchief from the pocket of my oilskins and wiped the corners of her mouth. "How far along are you?" I asked.

Angela looked at me. "I guess it's getting obvious, huh?" she asked.

I nodded. "This was pretty obvious."

"Three months. Maybe a bit longer."

"Is Matt Jerrell the father?"

Angela shook her head at me. "I can't tell you who the father is."

"Who did that to you?" I pointed to the bruise on her eye and the others on her neck and shoulders. "And that? Was it Jerrell?"

"No!" the young woman exclaimed. "Matt's good to me. He's kind and gentle in his own rough-hewn way. The man who did this to me . . . he . . . he'd kill me if he found out I'd told you."

"Who is it, Angela?"

"Leave," she pleaded, tears starting in her eyes. "He doesn't want you here. Leave Crow Creek tonight, before it's too late. He'll destroy you if you stay."

"Give me his name, Angela," I said firmly. "I'll make sure he doesn't harm you, or your baby."

The young woman shook her head violently. "I'll never tell." She turned her tear-stained face to mine. "You see, I need him. I need him more than I've ever needed anyone in my life."

We returned to a somewhat strained lunch during which my employer ate mightily but in silence (I was sure he was deep in serious thought about this strange case, since to a great mind like his, the whole universe surrenders, even at table).

"Ah, Miss Hudson," declared Mr. Wong, pushing his plate away from him at last. "I was just thinking that I detected a hint of sage in the venison. And perhaps just a soupçon of rosemary?"

"Chang has a heavy hand with spices," Angela replied absently. "It's something he learned while working as a ranch cook in Texas."

"Then he is to be complimented," returned my employer, daintily dabbing at his mouth with his napkin. "Though I fear along the way he has also picked up the manners of Texas."

I caught Angela's eye and realized she was very tired, her duties as a hostess very much in conflict with the desire of a pregnant woman to lie down and rest.

I rose to my feet and turning to Mr. Wong said: "Sir, I think it's time we made our way back to town. The rain could considerably delay our return."

"Ah yes," replied my mentor, "duty before everything, and now it calls in the voice of my young assistant."

He rose with some difficulty—for indeed he had eaten many steaks and perhaps half a deer—and bowed to Angela. "Dear lady, you are a sweet distraction, but a detective's life is one of endless purpose. In short, to unlearn what has been learned and to"—here he tapped his temple—"remember what has been forgotten."

"Then forget this case," Angela pleaded. "Mr. Wong, if you persist it will be the death of you."

But my employer would not be so easily turned aside.

"Miss Hudson," he said with considerable sincerity, "if I do not persist, your father will hang on Monday morning. Do you really want that to happen?"

Angela bit her lip. She laid her hand on Mr. Wong's arm. "Please, just . . . just go away from here."

"That," declared my employer, "I cannot and will not do. The chase is on and the hounds are in full hue and cry."

"Then," said Angela, tears in her eyes, "we, every single one of us here, could be dead before my father walks to the scaffold."

TEN

As Mr. Wong and I climbed into the Model T the afternoon was shading into evening and the rain clouds had parted, their edges touched by the red glow of the setting sun. From somewhere in the oaks a jay noisily celebrated the end of the downpour and the swollen stream chuckled as it rushed headlong under the little wooden bridge.

Matt Jerrell, tall and grim-faced, came out of the ranch house and walked up to the automobile. "You two see that sheriff in town, you give him a message from me," he said, his voice flat and level, as though he was trying hard to control his anger. "You tell him to stop comin' around here an' botherin' Angela. You tell him that."

Mr. Wong nodded. "It's a strange message, but I'll pass it on to Mr. Havenick."

"One more thing," Jerrell said, laying his hand on the worn butt of his revolver. "You tell him that if he don't stop comin' around, I'll be callin' on him." Jerrell nodded, as though he'd just made up his mind about something. "Yeah, you tell him that."

The moon had begun his climb into the darkening sky as I turned the Model T off the Rafter H trail and onto the main road back to town. The surrounding prairie was dark, silvered by the rising moon, the buffalo wallows pools of deep shadow. Here and there shallow hills rose on each side of the road, many of them crowned with jumbled glacier rocks, triangular wedges of inky blackness in their clefts and folds.

The gallant little Ford's headlights did little to illuminate the trail ahead, but the moonlight more than compensated for their failings, and the carriage lamps on either side of the hood were cheerful beacons of brightness against the gathering gloom of the evening.

As I drove I thought about Angela Hudson and the mysterious man who terrified her so. That she feared for her life and the life of her unborn child was obvious, and she was scared so badly that she was willing to see her own father hang from the gallows rather than reveal his identity. Who could have such a horrific hold over her? Sheriff Havenick, that cold-eyed killer? Was he the father of her child? Was it Havenick who wanted Mr. Wong and me dead and out of the way? Or was it someone else, someone much more evil and sinister? Someone, I shuddered at the thought, who might well be completely insane.

Out of the corner of my eye, I could see that my employer was in obvious distress, fidgeting in his seat as he ran a finger around the inside of his shirt collar. With a pang of compassion, I realized the hopelessness of this case was getting to him. Even that great mind, renowned throughout the civilized world for its analytical powers, was starting to buckle under the strain.

"Oh, it's no good, Chance," Mr. Wong declared in

exasperation. "You must stop and let me relieve myself. I swear, that blasted cowboy coffee goes right through me."

I eased the Ford over to the side of the road, and my mentor moved to his right as he fumbled in great haste for the door handle.

BLAM! BLAM!

A bullet shattered one of the Ford's headlights and another missed Mr. Wong's head by a fraction, nicking his earlobe as it zipped past with the sound of an angry bee.

My employer clapped his hand to his injured ear, then pulled it away, gasping in horror as he saw blood on his palm. "Chance," he wailed, "I've been shot!"

"Sir!" I yelled. "Out of the car!"

BOOM! BOOM!

Two more rounds in quick succession hit the Ford, one of them striking the left carriage lamp before it ricocheted away into the darkness with an angry whine!

"Out, sir!" I screamed, pushing my mentor out of the door so that he rolled in an undignified heap into the mud.

"Really, Chance, this is most—"

I dived on top of Mr. Wong, eliciting a surprised "Oof!" as I landed on his large and swollen stomach.

"Chance, are you trying to kill me, child?" groaned my employer as I rolled off of him and huddled behind the running board of the car.

"No, sir," I replied, "but someone is."

A quick succession of shots hit the car and kicked up fountains of mud around us.

"The person who laid this ambuscade," I said anxiously, "is a fine marksman and he'll soon have the range."

"Open the Dragon Box, Chance," Mr. Wong demanded impatiently. "That is an order."

"I'm sorry, sir," I said, "it's in the back seat of the car and I dare not raise up to reach it."

"That is most careless and inconsiderate," declared my employer angrily. "And it may cost us our lives in the end."

I felt my cheeks burn with shame. "Sir, this forgetful one is most unworthy to be your assistant."

Whatever my employer said next was lost in the crash of a rifle as more bullets ripped through the thin metal of the Ford. One round narrowly missed my right thigh, plowing into the mud beside me, and I, to my everlasting humiliation, heard myself whimper in sudden fear as I pressed closer to the body of the car.

Mr. Wong also heard that whimper and he placed his arm around me, shielding me with his massive body. "Never fear, child," he whispered. "It is not his karma that the great Chester Wong should die like a cowering cur in the mud."

And so saying, the renowned and valorous detective rose to his feet and waved his cane in the air. "Here, you, whoever you are," he yelled, "that's quite enough! You'll put someone's eye out with all that shooting."

A wicked volley of shots immediately rattled into the Ford and Mr. Wong, in a most undignified fashion, dove for the dirt. "I fear, child," he gasped, "I may be quite wrong about my karma."

"You're bleeding, sir," I said in alarm. A dark stain

was spreading over my employer's upper arm, showing wet and red against the yellow of his oilskins.

"I think it's just a flesh wound," he said, his voice shaking a little. "But I fear I may not be so lucky next time."

The shooting stopped and I raised my head as much as I dared over the door of the Ford. There was a low, flat-crowned hill about a hundred yards away, scrub pine and heavy brush covering its top. The moon was behind the hill, so that the slope facing us was in almost complete darkness.

The ambusher was there!

Slowly, a silent prayer to the lord Buddha on my lips, I reached into the back seat of the car, feeling for the Dragon Box.

I felt the hot burn of the bullet before I even heard the crash of the shot.

With a yelp of alarm I ducked behind the car again, an angry red welt raised against the pale skin of my right arm.

"Chance," Mr. Wong asked, his voice cracking with fear, "are you hit?"

"Burned," I said. "I was just creased by a bullet."

There was another lull in the shooting, and Mr. Wong whispered: "Perhaps he's gone."

I shook my head at him. "No. We're not shooting back, so by this time, he realizes we're unarmed. I think he'll come after us now."

Once again I raised my eyes over the Ford's door, and saw that my worst fear had been realized. A shadowy figure emerged from the underbrush, a rifle to its shoulder. I saw the outline of a man's hat as he walked down the hill toward us, his stride purposeful and ominous.

Now I had to reach the Dragon Box.

I stood and searched frantically in the back seat for the box, but it was gone! Because of the rough trail it had somehow dropped to the floor of the car. I ducked behind the Ford again and this time slowly opened the back door of the Ford, gently pushing Mr. Wong out of the way.

BLAM! BLAM! BLAM!

Three shots hammered into the little car and I dropped to the ground as they whistled past my head.

"It's no good, child," said my employer. "He's got us. We're done for."

"Not yet," I whispered, angry at the fear in my voice. "I must try to reach the Dragon Box."

A quick glance over the car and I realized that our attacker was getting very close, perhaps only forty or so yards away. I couldn't make out his entire shape in the gloom, but there was no mistaking the grim purpose in his stride.

Once again, I felt for the box on the floor of the car. It was nowhere to be found. It had slid to the other side, and unless I stood in full view of the gunman, it was out of reach.

This I determined to do. I would not just lie here and let myself be slaughtered. I stood up and saw the ambusher throw his rifle to his shoulder. With a loud cry of ire, I dove into the back seat of the car, my right hand scrambling around for the Dragon Box.

At any moment I expected to feel a bullet pierce into my now fully exposed body, and I felt my skin crawl, anticipating the terrible impact.

Immediately there came a flurry of shots, then the noise of pounding hooves.

I bolted upright in the back seat and made out the unmistakable shape of a huge gray horse galloping down the moon-splashed trail, urged on by a reckless rider, his chaps flapping as he urged his mount to even greater speed.

With a flutter, I realized it could only be old Big Boy, and on his back—oh, gallant young knight!—the Teton Kid.

The Kid had his Winchester to his shoulder and was cranking off round after round at our assailant. Bright orange and yellow flame flashed from his rifle muzzle and the hooves of his brave charger kicked up great gobs of mud, spattering both horse and rider.

Loudly the Teton Kid yelled, "Yippee! Yippee!" as he hammered through the mire, old Boy, the bit in his teeth, running with his neck outstretched, his mane flying in the wind.

The ambusher's shadowy figure retreated quickly up the hill, then he stopped and turned. He fired at the Kid, an easy target in the bright moonlight that left the hillside in darkness but illuminated the trail. I saw Boy shudder, stagger on a few more steps, then go down headfirst, his hindquarters cartwheeling through the air before he crashed with a terrible scream into the mud. The Teton Kid went flying out of the saddle, his rifle spinning out of his hands, and landed yards away in a crumpled heap.

A stunned silence followed, as though even the night was holding its breath. Then the sound of retreating hoofbeats echoed in the darkness as our would-be assassin made good his escape. I jumped from the car, my heart pounding with anxiety, and ran to the still, recumbent figure of the Kid.

How handsome that brave cavalier looked in the moonlight, with his fine cavalry mustache and unruly tumble of hair falling across his forehead.

"Are you hurt?" I asked, greatly fearing the answer.

"My neck's broke," the Kid whispered, looking up at me. He tried to turn to look at his horse, but couldn't. "How is ol' Big Boy?"

I glanced over at the gallant charger. There was a bullet hole in the middle of his noble forehead. Boy was lying very still, the moonlight turning his gray coat to bright silver.

"He's fine, Gary," I lied, using the young cowboy's given name for the first time. "Old Boy's going to be just fine."

"I was on my way back to the Circle O, and saw you folks being shot at," the Kid said. "Knowed it was you on account of how everybody heard that you'd rented ol' Spinster Rhodes' automobile. Figgered I'd come to the rescue." He smiled weakly. "Figgered maybe I'd get a kiss for my trouble."

"You just lie still, Gary," I said softly. "We've got to get you to a doctor."

"Too late for a doc," the Kid said. "Seen a waddie with a broke neck one time down in El Paso. He didn't last long."

Mr. Wong kneeled beside the Kid. "How are you feeling, young man?" he asked.

"Not so good," the Kid said. "I think maybe I got one boot in the pine box already."

"You saved our lives," said my employer. "You were very brave."

The Kid smiled. "Hey, Miz Lee, does that mean I get that kiss I've been dreaming about?"

"Of course," I told him, tears stinging my eyes. I bent down and put my lips to his, feeling the breath slowly go out of him.

"Sweetest dang kiss I ever had," the Kid gasped.

Then he closed his eyes and made a soft little sound in his throat and was gone.

I kneeled beside the Teton Kid's body for a few moments, then rose and turned to Mr. Wong. "Sir," I said, "I'll find this killer. I'll find him if I have to stay in Crow Creek even after Mr. Hudson is hanged."

My employer sighed and shook his head. "I fear this case is far from being solved. I believe Brad Hudson is innocent and, given the time, I know I could save him. But time is the one thing I do not have."

The grim reality of that statement was all too apparent, and with a heavy heart I realized our mission was now destined to end in failure.

Between us, we carried the Kid's body and gently as we could, for he was a tall and well-built young man, and placed him in the back of the Ford. Mr. Wong covered the dead cowboy's face with his hat, then he turned to me as I dashed tears from my eyes and said softly, "Chance, on the day we arrived in Crow Creek, we saw a funeral procession. You know as well as I do that a sad and solemn funeral is inconceivable to the Chinese mind. The lord Buddha tells us that death is merely the going from one room to another, ultimately the most beautiful room. In reality, there is no death because you are not the body. The Teton Kid's existence is always here because his soul is eternal." My employer took an immaculately white handkerchief from his pocket and dabbed my eyes. "Do you understand what I'm saying to you, child?"

I nodded dumbly, too overcome to speak.

"Good," said Mr. Wong. "Now start the car and we'll take the poor young cowboy back to town with us."

ELEVEN

There was a festive air in Crow Creek as we drove along the main street in the evening. The saloon was crowded with men, mostly out-of-town farmers with a sprinkling of miners and cowboys. Stern-faced matrons stood on the boardwalks in gossipy groups of three and four and tried their best to ignore the whiskey-lubricated clamor of their menfolk from the saloon.

A large, unshaven man in a dark suit and plug hat with the look of the habitual barroom brawler about him stopped in the middle of the street and tilted a bottle to his mouth. I braked the Ford and leaned over the door. "Excuse me, sir," I said. "Will you kindly let us pass."

"Huh?" the man asked, and I could see he was quite inebriated.

"Please, sir, will you give us the road?"

The man lurched over to the car and stood by the door. "Hic!" He looked perplexed for a moment then thumped his chest with his fist. "Hic!" He leaned into the car and I smelled cheap rye whiskey on his breath. "Whassamatter, little lady?"

"Sir, please stand out of the way and let us pass. It is a matter of extreme urgency."

The drunk waved a hand, losing his uncertain balance so he stumbled against the Ford's door. "I'm here to see the hanging," he said. "All these folks are in town for the hanging day after . . . hic! . . . tom . . . tomorrow."

"I know that, sir," I said. "Now kindly stand aside and let us pass."

The man looked into the back seat of the car and for the first time noticed the body of the Teton Kid.

"Hell, wha's he been drinkin', and can I have some?"

"Drive around him to the sheriff's office, Chance," ordered my employer impatiently. "I'll not bandy words with one who's put a thief in his mouth to steal his tongue."

"Hey, not so fast," the drunk yelled, grabbing my shoulder before I could drive away. He was a very large and powerfully built man and, since drunks don't realize their own strength, his fingers dug deeply into my flesh and it really hurt.

At my dear old school, Miss Chastity Charmaine had insisted—quite vehemently, since the world can be a dangerous and uncertain place for the genteel young lady—that the entire student body be trained in the martial arts, specifically an unarmed technique she'd seen practiced in San Francisco by the Chinese called *gōngfu*, or, as it is now known, kung fu.

Our headmistress, bless her generous and kind heart, obtained an expert instructor who originally hailed from the Japanese island of Okinawa, for this purpose. Let me introduce him only as Professor X, because this dear and learned educator came to us with a somewhat checkered background and was said to be wanted by the law in at least a dozen states for homicide and a host of other alleged crimes connected with the opium trade.

But despite his shadowy past, the professor taught us well. So, as the drunk dug his brutal fingers deeper into my shoulder and, with a vile oath, roughly demanded a kiss, I screamed *"Kiai!"* and quickly hit the inside of his elbow with the edge of my right hand, breaking his hold, then twisted his wrist around, bending his hand away from me and down so that his splayed fingers were almost pointing at his belt buckle.

The drunk squawked in pain and his feet did a fandango in the mud, and I was so upset over the death of the Teton Kid that I felt mean and furious enough to shred his tendons and break his wrist quite horribly. Of course, I didn't, because a drunk is not responsible for his actions and the young lady of quality must practice restraint at all times. I therefore contented myself with merely bending the man's wrist just a little farther, enough to make it extremely painful for at least a week—as his wild scream attested—and let him go.

As I drove away, the drunk ran to the boardwalk, squealing like a pig, his arm flopping uselessly by his side, and Mr. Wong shook his head and said: "I suppose you learned that at the finishing school I obtained for you at such ruinous expense?"

I nodded silently in reply.

"What in the world *did* they teach you at that

place?" my mentor asked loudly and in considerable exasperation.

But, as before, I lowered my eyelids and said quietly and humbly: "Generous sir, many things."

And again Mr. Wong rubbed his chin and said: "Hmmm . . ."

We pulled up outside the sheriff's office and the door opened almost immediately. Havenick came outside and walked over to the car.

"The Teton Kid drunk again?" he asked, nodding toward the back seat.

"No, Sheriff," replied Mr. Wong, "he's dead."

Havenick's jaw dropped, and my mentor quickly told him the events of the day and how the Kid rode to our rescue and saved us from the ambush of a deadly and determined gunman.

The sheriff nodded, a certain measure of pride in his smile. "The Kid didn't have sense enough to spit downwind, but I always figgered he knew how to die standin' up."

"He was a courteous and gallant knight," I said.

Havenick shrugged. "Whatever you say, Miss."

"Sheriff," said Mr. Wong, "surely this young man's death, following so close on the heels of the murder of Silas Lime, is enough to convince you that Brad Hudson is innocent and that the real killer of Victoria Grant wants me out of the way before I discover the truth."

The big lawman sighed and shook his head. "Wong, Brad was found guilty by a jury of his peers an' the circuit judge ordered him hanged come Monday morning. Now up to this moment, the judge ain't told me otherwise, so I'm gonna go right ahead an' do what he told me to do."

"You're a stubborn man," snapped the great detective. "Stubborn and pigheaded."

"Maybe so," Havenick replied, "but I'll do my duty when the time comes. An' all these folks who've come into town for the hangin', well, they know that, too."

The sheriff looked hard at Mr. Wong, his eyes narrowing. "You get a good look at the ranny who took a shot at you and killed the Kid?"

"No," my employer replied. "He was on a dark hillside. Chance has younger eyes, perhaps she can help you."

I shook my head at Havenick. "I didn't get a good look at him. I recognized Gary . . . the Kid . . . because he was riding up the trail in full moonlight. That's why . . . why . . ."

My voice petered out and the sheriff said: "Seems to me the drygulcher was Lime's partner and after he done for him, he still figgered you pilgrims was worth robbing. That's why he laid for you on the only trail back to town."

"I don't believe that, Sheriff," I said evenly. "I don't believe that for one minute. The Teton Kid is lying stiff and cold in the back of this car because the real killer of Victoria Grant wants Mr. Wong and me dead."

Havenick shrugged. "Suit yourself, little lady, but I reckon you're layin' your egg in the wrong nest."

"What will we do with Gary?" I asked the sheriff angrily. "We can't leave him lying in the back of this automobile."

"Take him over to the saloon," Havenick said. "There's a back room where we can lay him out for the undertaker. Trouble is, he'll have to lie there until after the hangin' on account of how the saloon's so busy with the folks comin' into town an' all."

"Why should that make a difference?" I asked, trying to conceal my deep dislike for this man.

"Because Heath Wilson the saloonkeeper is also the undertaker, an' until Brad's neck is stretched, he'll be busy as a bartender on payday."

We agreed to turn the Ford and drive back to the saloon while Havenick elected to walk. As he stepped up onto the boardwalk, I noticed deep scratches on the side of his muddy right boot. He could have gotten them around town—but the scuffs were white and fresh against the black leather, the kind of scratches a man gets on his boots when he crawls around underbrush and rocks in the darkness.

Willing hands helped us carry the Teton Kid into the saloon, which was crowded with noisy revelers. To a man, and to their credit, the patrons doffed their hats as the Kid was carried through the saloon and into a small back room where there was a pool table and a few chairs.

Wilson, a barrel-chested man with thinning black hair and a great walrus mustache, could not spare much time away from the bar, but he laid the Kid out gently enough on the pool table and crossed his hands over his chest.

Wilson fished in his pocket and came up with two silver dollars. He placed one over each of the Kid's eyes and said: "After the hanging I'll get the preacher and see he's buried decent."

"Is there a stonecutter in Crow Creek?" I asked.

Wilson nodded. "Swede by the name of Jan Sorenson, an' he's a good one, too."

I told Wilson to get a headstone carved, and told him what to put on it, even though Mr. Wong blanched when the cost was mentioned. But he must have realized that he owed the Teton Kid that much for saving his life, because he bit his lip and made no comment.

There was little else to do for the poor young man, so I leaned over and kissed his cold forehead and whispered, "Rest well, sweet knight," then followed Mr. Wong and Sheriff Havenick back outside.

"Just afore you arrived, I was thinkin' about going back to my house for a decent cup of coffee," the big lawman said as we stood at the door of the saloon. "Maybe you folks would like to join me an' meet my wife and son."

"Is it safe to leave your prisoner unguarded?" Mr. Wong inquired anxiously.

The town was full of drunks and a few dozen drunks can soon form a mob, a mob that could decide to push up poor Mr. Hudson's hanging by a day.

"Nah," Havenick replied, "I got a part-time deputy guarding the jail. Rode with me back in the old days an' he's a good man."

"In that case, we'd be delighted," Mr. Wong said.

But there was something I wished to check out, so I made the excuse that I needed to go back to the hotel to freshen up and that I'd make my own way to the Havenick home.

Both men accepted this as a woman thing, and the sheriff pointed out his house, a frame two-story near the creek with a small corral but no barn.

I told Havenick I'd be there in about fifteen minutes, then made my way back to the hotel. The clerk was dozing behind the desk, a newspaper in his lap, and when I palmed the bell he woke with a start.

"Oh, it's you," he said, his eyes guarded and unfriendly. "Lost your key?"

I smiled as sweetly as I could and replied: "No, I have my key. It's just that Sheriff Havenick asked me to take a look at his horse's front left tendon, since I have some experience in veterinary medicine." I fluttered my eyelashes the way I'd been taught by dear Miss Chastity Charmaine and added: "But, silly me, I forgot to ask where he keeps it."

"Why, down to the livery stable of course," the clerk said, suspicion edging his voice. "It's a big 'ol buckskin with a hammerhead, you can't miss it. See, unlike most folks in town, Havenick has no barn."

"The livery stable! Oh, why didn't I think of that?" I exclaimed, my eyelashes fluttering like summer butterflies. "You're just so clever."

"Seems obvious to me," the clerk said sourly. "Now, is there anything else I can do for you?"

I shook my head at him and smiled. "Not at the moment. I'm just popping upstairs to freshen up."

I'd just reached the bottom of the staircase when the clerk's voice stopped me. "Heard about the Teton Kid. Didn't surprise me none. He was a wild one."

"Yes," I said. "Yes, he was."

"Saved your bacon from that bushwhacker, though, didn't he?"

I nodded. "Yes, he did."

The clerk muttered something under his breath and I slowly climbed the stairs, removing my oilskins as I went. I dropped the oilskins on the second-floor landing, tucking the Dragon Box underneath, then quietly crept back downstairs again, every creak and squeak from loose boards setting my nerves on edge.

As I suspected, the clerk was no longer behind the desk. He stood at the open door of the hotel, looked quickly up and down the street, then stepped onto the boardwalk and was gone.

I followed him outside and saw his retreating figure cross the street and walk toward the alley near the bank. There was a lamp in the bank window that cast a yellow rectangle of light into the alley—apparently Ben Cranwell kept late hours—but the clerk carefully kept to the shadows. He didn't look back, so intent was he on making a report to someone he thought should have this latest piece of information.

The man obviously didn't believe my story about checking the tendon of Havenick's horse, and considered my subterfuge important enough to relay to his cohort, whomever he was. Stepping off the boardwalk into the muddy street I followed the clerk—but didn't get far.

A burly, bearded miner stepped in front of me, grinning, and yelled: "Hey, pretty lady, come an' have a drink. It's a night to have us some fun."

"No, thank you, sir," I said, anxiously jumping up to catch a glimpse of the clerk over his shoulder. "I'm in a great hurry."

"Aw come on, don't be a spoilsport," the miner said, making a grab for my waist that I easily eluded.

"Hey, you leave that little Chinee gal alone!"

A second miner, just as burly, confronted the first, his bearded jaw jutting pugnaciously.

"What's it to you?" the first miner asked, following

his question with a fist as big as a ham hock that trundled toward the second miner's jaw.

The fist landed on the second miner's chin with the sound of a sledgehammer hitting a side of beef, but the man barely flinched and cut loose with a blow of his own.

The fight was on and as the two men pounded on each other, I jumped up time and again, trying to see where the clerk had gone. A crowd quickly gathered, cheering on the battling miners, hemming me in on all sides. Being so small, all I could do was keep jumping, vainly attempting to see over the flying fists and heaving shoulders of the now bloody combatants.

But it was no use. The clerk had vanished, and with him any hope of my discovering the identity of his mysterious accomplice.

I turned and retraced my steps to the boardwalk, leaving the fight and the yelling crowd behind me.

But I had still one more destination—the livery stable.

Situated well back of the main street, the stable stood alone in darkness, a large, weathered building with a ramshackle corral and an outhouse for the convenience of patrons. A faded sign proclaiming the benefits of Anderson's Premium Chicken Feed was painted under the *V* of the roof, and an oil lamp hung on the wall to the right of the doors, throwing a circle of pale orange light that reflected in a muddy puddle below. As I drew near, an orchestra of frogs croaked a tuneless symphony to the night, and somewhere far off a dog barked.

A strutting little rooster, cut from a piece of sheet tin, stood at the peak of the roof and pointed the direction of the wind. But the bird changed its mind constantly, making a shrill little screech every time it swung around to face a different point of the compass.

I stood there for a long time, debating if I should go back for the Dragon Box, but realized it was silly to be afraid of a barn just because the darkness gave it an air of eerie mystery. Finally, pulling my uncertain courage around me like a rather threadbare cloak, I took a deep breath, then opened the stable door, the rusty hinges groaning in protest, and stepped inside.

The interior was lit by a single lamp, and a horse stomped its foot and blew through its nose in the gloom. The place smelled of horses and hay and old leather, and triangles of black shadow stood sentinel in the corners of every stall. Above my head the roof was thick with gray spiderwebs, hanging like ancient lace from every beam.

A huge rat scuttled out of the darkness and stopped, looking up at me without alarm.

"Scat!" I said, but the rodent stood its ground, its sly black eyes keenly interested in what I was doing.

I ignored the rat and glanced around the stable, trying to find Havenick's horse. Because of the crowds in town for the hanging, every stall was occupied and it took me a few moments to discover the big, hammer-headed buckskin.

The horse stood quietly enough when I came close to him and I reached out and patted his neck, whispering softly to him as I felt along his back. The buckskin had been rubbed down recently, probably with a piece of sacking, but there was still a dark sweat stain on his back from the saddle. When I looked at his legs they were spattered with dried mud.

This horse had been used earlier in the evening, and it had been ridden fast, as more gobs of mud high on its flanks and withers attested.

Was Havenick the one who'd ambushed us and killed the Teton Kid?

Our assailant had galloped away right after the Kid was thrown from his mount and there was ample time for him to get back to town and hastily rub down his lathered horse before returning home.

If it had been Havenick, he could have only one motive for killing Mr. Wong and myself—he, or someone he took orders from, feared we were getting too close to the truth.

I stood in the yellow-tinted, partial-darkness and asked myself if Havenick could be the father of Angela Hudson's baby, the vicious brute who terrified her so? And did Matt Jerrell know this, and was that the reason he'd told us to warn the sheriff to stay away?

I had plenty of questions, but no answers—just suspicions.

I was sure Mr. Wong's great mind was even now pondering these very matters and that brought me a small measure of comfort. Yet we had only one more day to prove Brad Hudson's innocence and find the real killer. But that was not enough time. Not near enough.

A floorboard creaked at the back of the stable in a corner stained by thick dark shadow.

"Who's there?" I asked, annoyed that my voice sounded thin and unsteady as my throat tightened in sudden fear.

Silence.

I stepped away from the buckskin toward the door, my heart pounding.

The floorboard creaked again, louder this time. I caught the fleeting glimpse of a shadow on the wall, moving like a ghost.

"Bitch! You have something of mine, something I want returned."

It was a hoarse whisper, coming from the threatening gloom of the shadowed corner.

"Show yourself," I said, panic rising in me. I wanted to run but found myself rooted to the spot.

"Bitch," the harsh voice came again. "You diseased little Chinese whore."

How I wished I'd brought the Dragon Box as the terrible whisper came out of the darkness again.

"You're soon going to have a good time, whore, a wonderful time. I've got something thick and hard for you . . . then I'll let you feel the sharp edge of my knife and I'll hear you squeal."

A board creaked as the man—or thing—in the corner moved.

"Oh yes, you'll squeal, all right. I'll cut that thing between your legs right out of you like I done for Doctor-high-and-mighty-Grant."

I was almost paralyzed by fear, the horrible, grating voice that I did not recognize as even human, chilling me to the bone. A shadow moved in the darkness, coming closer . . .

Could I make it to the door in time? I had to try. I turned and got ready to run for it.

Now! I ran toward the door, hearing footsteps behind me. They were close and getting closer.

"My little Chinee sweetie pie!"

The stable door crashed inward and the miner who'd accosted me in the street stood there, his bloody face split by a white grin and his arms open wide.

"They tole me you'd headed in this direction, an' after I took care of ol' Andy Sinclair I came a-lookin' for you."

Instantly the back door of the stable was thrown open, and I saw a shadowy figure dash through it and disappear into the darkness outside.

I laughed in sudden relief and ran toward the miner. I jumped into his arms, clamped my legs around his waist, and planted a passionate kiss right on his hairy, mashed lips.

"Hey," the big man yelled when he came up for breath, "this is my lucky day!"

"Not that lucky, big guy," I smiled, and slipped out of his grasp, ducking around him and out the livery stable door.

I ran, but glanced over my shoulder and saw the big miner standing in the lamplight, his arms open wide, as he yelled: "Come back, oh my little Chinee beloved!"

Then he pounded his chest, tilted back his head and howled at the moon like a great hairy wolf. As for me, I didn't stop running until I reached Sheriff Havenick's house. I stopped, caught my breath as best I could and, like a well brought up young lady, politely rapped on the door.

TWELVE

"Chance, where have you been, child?" my employer asked as Sheriff Havenick ushered me into his parlor. "Goodness, you're quite out of breath."

I decided not to mention the incident in the livery stable, saying only that I'd been watching the crowds in the street and had lost track of the time. "So I ran all the way over here," I said.

"You do dawdle so, " Mr. Wong said disapprovingly.

I was introduced to Havenick's wife, a small, thin, careworn woman in a wheelchair who gave her name as Helen.

Helen Havenick had a narrow, whining way of speaking, and her mouth was pinched in a permanent, sulky grimace as if she'd just tasted something sour. Under her gray cotton dress her breasts were slack and flat, her thighs wasted away to sticks.

"I'm sorry I can't rise to greet you, Miss Lee," she met my eyes frankly but without much interest. "I've been paralyzed from the waist down five years come the sixth of next month."

"Helen, please," Havenick pleaded. "Let's not go through it again."

"Buggy accident." Helen ignored her husband. "Burt was driving. He swerved to avoid a dog and I ended up like this."

"I'm so sorry," I said.

"So," said Helen Havenick, "am I."

"I'll get that coffee," the sheriff said, his face grim. "Just be a minute."

He walked out of the parlor toward the kitchen, and my employer asked: "I believe you have a son, Mrs. Havenick?"

The woman's reply was to cup her hand to her mouth and let out with a high-pitched: "Biiillly!"

A few moments passed then a huge, hulking giant of a boy walked into the room and stood in silence, his eyes on his mother.

"This is Billy," Helen said. "Our son."

"How are you, Billy?" asked Mr. Wong.

The boy, who looked to be about twenty, stood well over six feet with massive shoulders and a barrel chest. Under the cotton fabric of his shirt his arms were long and thickly muscled, his hands enormous, the fingers bent as though they were constantly about to pick up something and tear it apart.

"The gentleman asked you a question, Billy," Helen prodded gently.

"I am fine, sir, how are you?"

It was a coached response, delivered in the voice of a small boy and when I looked into Billy's eyes I saw they were flat and vacant, revealing little intelligence and even less interest.

Reading my expression, Helen Havenick sighed: "Yes, Miss Lee, he's retarded. Billy is nineteen years old, but he has the mind of a ten-year-old child. Don't worry, he really doesn't understand what I'm saying."

Embarrassed, I blushed and lowered my eyes. "I'm sorry. I just—"

"Don't be sorry," Helen said quickly. "Believe me, my husband bears sorrow enough for all of us. Sorrow that his only son was born mentally retarded. Sorrow that he wants to blame me for that but can't. Sorrow that a man who was once mentioned in the same breath as Earp and Hickok now has to scrape a miserable living in a town forgotten by tomorrow like Crow Creek. Sorrow that his crippled, unattractive wife inconveniently refuses to die." She smiled thinly. "Like the suffering Christ, my husband nobly carries all the sorrows of the world."

The long silence that followed this gloomy statement was thankfully broken when Havenick came back into the room bearing coffee in a blue-speckled pot and some plain white cups that he carefully set down on a small table in front of us.

"Shall I play gracious hostess and pour?" Helen asked, her face revealing nothing. "It's been such a long time I hardly remember how."

"I'll do it," Havenick said. "I doubt that you could even do that right."

"So, it always comes back to Billy, doesn't it, Burt?" Helen asked.

I sensed this was an old and worn-out topic that the woman eagerly wanted to revisit now she had a captive audience.

"Don't start, Helen," the sheriff said, pouring the coffee. "These people are our guests."

"You see," Helen said, turning to Mr. Wong as if her

husband hadn't spoken, "Burt blames me for Billy's mental state. He says I drank too much when I was pregnant and that the whiskey somehow affected Billy's brain in the womb. He's never forgiven me for that. I think maybe that's why he tipped the buggy over, hoping I'd break my neck like that poor cowboy lying in back of the saloon."

"Helen," Havenick said evenly, his face very white, "I don't blame you for a damn thing."

"And why should you?" Helen persisted. "I drank too much because you ran around with all those other women, and me with a belly out to here. Who deserves the blame for that?"

Havenick laid his cup on the table, his coffee untasted. "Helen, each day we're together is a separate little death. Why not be content with that? It's revenge enough, even for you."

I put down my cup and caught Mr. Wong's eye. The great detective, sensing my unease, rose to his feet and said: "Ahem, well, this has been delightful, Mrs. Havenick, and you dear lady are a sweet distraction. But, alas"—he consulted his gold pocket watch—"I fear it's time to leave."

Helen looked up at my employer, pushing her wheelchair around to face him. "You're still hoping to free Brad Hudson, aren't you?"

"That is my intention," replied Mr. Wong loftily.

"He'll hang," the woman said bitterly. "If my husband knows how to do one thing well, it's to hang a man. In his day, he's stretched a dozen. Funny thing is, all those dead men don't bother his conscience in the least."

"Helen, no more, please," the sheriff pleaded.

Mr. Wong pointed his great belly in the direction of the door in preparation for his exit. "Time will tell, dear lady, if Brad Hudson lives or dies," he said. "Be assured, time will tell."

He propelled his stomach forward, and his little legs gallantly caught up by the time he reached the parlor door. But then Billy's voice stopped him in his tracks.

"Pa," the boy said, "can I play treasure hunt tomorrow? Huh, can I, Pa?"

Billy had been totally oblivious to his mother's accusations, and now he was looking at his father, his eager face beaming.

"Sure, son," the sheriff smiled. "Sure you can. I went out earlier an' buried the treasure. Come sunup, I'll write you up some clues an' you can take your pony an' go find it."

Puzzled, I joined my employer at the parlor door and asked Havenick: "What kind of treasure does Billy hunt for, Sheriff?"

The big lawman shrugged. "It ain't much of a treasure, a piece of rock candy usually. I go out in the hills an' hide it, then write up some clues for Billy to follow. He loves it, an' it keeps him occupied."

"And out of your sight," Helen said viciously.

Once at the outside door, the sheriff looked from me to Mr. Wong and said apologetically: "You have to make allowances for my wife. Stuck in that wheelchair for so long . . . well, it's done something to her mind. She's not the same woman I married."

"I understand," replied my employer, but I said nothing. I was busy thinking about Havenick's sweaty and mud-spattered horse. Was that the reason for it, something as innocent as hiding a piece of rock candy for his son to find?

Deep in thought I walked back to the hotel with my employer, dodging around the drunken revelers who still filled the street.

I retrieved my oilskins and the Dragon Box from the stairs, and at the door to his room, Mr. Wong tapped an impatient finger on the box lid and said: "That was a strange and not-too-safe place to leave this precious object, Chance. I declare, whatever's gotten into you, child?"

I lowered my eyes and said I'd dawdled so much in the street that I only had time to leave the box on the stairs and hurry to Sheriff Havenick's home. I did not mention the livery stable.

"Well, that was most remiss of you," said my employer. "Chance, you may consider this a serious reprimand, very serious, indeed."

Humbly, I told my employer that I was most unworthy to be his assistant and that nothing of this nature would ever happen again. Somewhat mollified, Mr. Wong said, "Well, it had better not," then sternly warned me to be wide awake at first light in the morning.

"We have just twenty-four hours to prove Hudson's innocence, Chance," he said. "We have no time to stand in the street gawping at the antics of the local aborigines. Must I remind you yet again that an innocent man's life hangs in the balance?"

I lowered my eyes and replied in a chastened whisper: "Sir, I need no reminder, and I assure you this worthless one will be ready when needed."

My employer nodded. "Very well, then." He

opened the door of his room, stepped inside and said rather brusquely: "Good night to you, Last Chance."

As the door closed in my face, I realized my mentor's use of my full name—something he did but rarely—was an indication of his great displeasure, and I repaired to my own quarters with a heavy heart.

My father had given me my name, mostly as a sign of his disappointment in me for being born female. The poor man had six daughters and when my mother got pregnant again in her forties, father told her: "This is my last chance to have a son."

Well, he didn't.

Once in my room, I jammed the back of the chair under the door handle then quickly stripped off my clothes. Without lighting the oil lamp, I gave myself a sponge bath and brushed out my long hair, letting it fall, glossy and black, around my shoulders.

The moon had climbed to its highest point in the sky and a beam of silver light streamed into my window, turning my skin the color of cream, each breast tipped with a piece of pink coral. Eyes closed, I stood naked in the moonlight, oblivious to the sounds of revelry coming from the street below, spreading my arms wide as I bathed in pale Luna's silken radiance.

The ancient Chinese set great store by the healing powers of moonlight, and I allowed its opalescence to enter me like a lover, closing my eyes as it gently soothed away the dreadful hurt of the Teton Kid's death.

I know not how long I stood, lost in that soft, mother-of-pearl embrace, but when I next opened my eyes the moon had moved on in her course across the sky and my room was plunged into darkness.

Softly, I whispered a prayer to the compassionate Mother of Mercy, Kuan Shih Yin, she who was destined to become a Buddha yet turned away from the eternal bliss of Nirvana to save all the children of God. Kuan Yin's symbol is the white lotus blossom, and my fingertips strayed to the tattoo of that flower I bear above my right breast.

I prayed that the Teton Kid, when he was reborn, be guided by Kuan Yin and receive continued instruction toward the goal of enlightenment and perfection, so that one day that gallant young knight may himself enter Nirvana.

"Kuan Yin," I whispered fervently, "guide the Teton Kid to Amitabha's Western Paradise, the Pure Land, and from there let him be reborn under your merciful guidance."

Thus began and ended my prayer to Kuan Yin the blessed and compassionate, the burden-bearer who hears all the cries of the world.

I turned from the window and rubbed tears from my eyes with the back of my hand. Then, without lighting the lamp, I found a cheroot in my bag, thumbed a match into flame, and coaxed the tip into a cherry-red glow.

Sitting naked on my chair by the window, I watched the street, lost in thought until the cigar was smoked and sleep came tugging at my ear. I laid on the bed, closed my eyes and let the forgetfulness of slumber claim me . . .

"Not, dear lady, so much as a biscuit crumb, I beg of you!"

Mr. Wong held up a hand in horror as Ma came to

take our order as we sat in her warm and bright restaurant. The first light of dawn had still to reach out across the grasslands to the east and the town lay in darkness, the window of the restaurant casting its rectangular yellow glow on the boardwalk outside. Rain pattered against the glass panes and a rising wind was making itself known, rattling the door and sighing around the gables of the roof.

Ma's left eyebrow crawled up into her forehead as she regarded my employer with some skepticism. "Some coffee then, Mr. Wong?"

"Sufficient," declared the great detective. "One might say even more than sufficient. I have great deeds to perform this day and an innocent man's life to save. I can't be slowed down by food, even your excellent comestibles, dear lady."

"My mentor's appetite is a most delicate thing in the morning," I said, by way of explanation.

Mr. Wong nodded and smiled, as though the case for the uncertain nature of his stomach had been stated most eloquently.

"You look tired, Miss Lee," Ma said, eyeing me with concern. "Are you feeling all right?"

I nodded. "I just didn't sleep very well."

Ma smiled. "I'll fix you up something real special. How about some of them little buttermilk pancakes and a jug of real maple syrup?"

"That sounds wonderful," I replied, though, in truth, I had little appetite.

"And just coffee for you, sir?" Ma said to my employer, as though she hadn't been able to believe her ears the first time around.

"Splendid," said Mr. Wong, though his voice was tinged with uncertainty.

"Are you sure?" asked Ma, her eyebrow rising again.

"Well," said Mr. Wong, and here he sighed deeply, "if you insist. I swear, you ladies are always urging men to eat. It must be a woman thing."

"But I wasn't—"

"Just a very little something," declared my employer quickly. "Perhaps half a dozen scrambled eggs and"—he looked at Ma quizzically—"perhaps a nice chop? Do you have a nice chop, by any chance?"

"Mutton chops," said Ma. "Fresh off the range this week."

"Ah," returned Mr. Wong, "fresh off the range. How very nice. Then perhaps the odd mutton chop or two will suffice."

"Very well, Mr. Wong."

"Or even three, dear lady. If you can see your way clear."

The door opened and Ben Cranwell the banker walked inside. He looked as moth-eaten and unhealthy as ever, his back bent and his narrow face pale and drawn.

He ordered coffee, then brought his cup to our table.

"Well, Mr. Wong," he said, "how is your investigation coming?"

"Not so good, I'm afraid," replied my employer. "We're fast running out of time."

Cranwell shook his head. "Too bad. Listen, Brad Hudson is a good man, too good a man to dangle at the end of a rope tomorrow morning." He looked intently into the great detective's eyes.

"You've got to do everything you can to save Brad, everything. If there's anything I can do, any way I can help just let me know. If it's money—"

"No, Mr. Cranwell, money is unimportant, unless you can buy me some time," Mr. Wong replied, smiling grimly.

"That I cannot do," sighed the little banker. "I only wish to God I could. I'd spend every penny I have to buy you a few more days." Cranwell tilted back his head and drained his coffee. "That hit the spot," he sighed. "I've been putting in some long hours at the bank, catching up on work I should have tackled months ago." He rose to his feet. "Ah well, duty calls. Remember, Mr. Wong, anything I can do. You only have to name it."

As Cranwell left, Mr. Wong looked at his retreating back and said: "There goes a good friend to our client and a perfect gentleman."

I said nothing. The banker's greasy eyes had been on my breasts as he left and they felt like they'd been tugged one by one out of my bodice and squeezed hard.

Mr. Wong, who had perhaps noticed the little banker's greedy eyes, waggled a forefinger in the direction of my décolletage, covered his mouth with his fist, and coughed apologetically: "All this, child, is mayhap, a little . . . ah . . . revealing?" That morning I wore a Mexican peasant blouse of white poplin that left most of my shoulders bare and daringly revealed the swell of my upper bosom and the bright tattoo of the lotus, the beloved bloom of Kuan Yin.

I lowered my eyes to the table and replied: "Sir, this was my last clean garment, since you desired that I keep my luggage to a minimum."

"Well, I believe we'll be forced into our oilskins today, so your . . . ah . . . shall we say little indiscretion will not be discovered. Still, Chance, as a wise Chinese philosopher once observed, the gently-raised young lady should steadfastly keep the golden mean between revealing too little and too much."

As we sipped our coffee and waited for breakfast, I pondered my employer's observations on my mode of dress. I believe his main objection originated not altogether with my bosom, but with the tattoo above my right breast of which he vehemently disapproved.

Indeed, my breasts were quite small, though dear Miss Chastity Charmaine once told me that the ardent suitor with marriage in mind might judge their worth with a champagne glass. "And yours will fill his glass quite perfectly, Chance," she told me. "So you will pass that test with flying colors."

Unlike my headmistress, who was of the opinion that the tattoo—expertly executed and discreetly placed—inflames the desire of the ardent suitor, Mr. Wong did not care for such decoration, no matter how tasteful the subject.

Miss Charmaine herself had a rose, the very symbol of purity, tattooed above her left breast and one morning at breakfast she waxed eloquent on the subject.

I remember that she wore a beautiful dressing robe of vivid emerald green with a huge collar and puffed sleeves that set off her mane of tawny hair, and that, after discussing her rose tattoo, she told we eager young ladies that she had others, much more discreet.

And, so saying, she swung her long and shapely legs onto the table, clenched her morning cheroot in her teeth and pulled the robe aside to reveal smooth and creamy-white thighs, each one circled, very high up, with the tattoo of a single strand of barbed wire.

"Young ladies, I once had an ardent suitor, a rich and famous California rancher, who urged me, most persuasively, to get these done," said Miss Charmaine. "He said the ranches he owned totaled two hundred thousand acres, and each and every acre was circled by wire. 'I always fence off what's mine,' he said. Dear man, he was charming yet so wonderfully forceful."

In fact, when my dear headmistress put her thighs together, the tattoos joined one to the other and indeed did seem to form a barrier, fencing off that female part so avidly desired by the ardent, would-be husband and false suitor alike.

"Headmistress, after he put up his fence, did the rancher press his suit all the way to marriage?" asked one young lady—quite unnecessarily, I thought.

Miss Chastity Charmaine swung her legs off the table and modestly covered them again with her robe.

"No, he did not," she replied with that patience that made her so admirable. "Alas, he was already wed to a Boston blueblood"—here she joined her hands and raised her eyes to heaven—"a devoutly religious lady with the face of a Missouri mule who was much given to prune juice and prayer. But because of her considerable dowry and inheritances, marriage was quite out of the question."

"That was unfortunate," observed the indiscreet young lady.

"Not at all," replied Miss Charmaine smoothly. She turned the hand that held her morning glass of bourbon and flashed the ring she wore on her finger, a flawless diamond as large as a pigeon's egg.

"He didn't give me marriage, but he gave me this. *Mais, ça ne fait rien*—one is quite as acceptable as the other." My dear headmistress smiled her dazzling smile. "As for the fence he had me erect, la, are there not always daring young rustlers and is not barbed wire made to be cut?"

Dear Miss Chastity Charmaine, her words of wisdom were pearls beyond price, and the few moments I spent in sweet reminiscence helped me forget, at least for a little while, the horror of the noose that waited for poor Mr. Hudson, whose life was now measured in mere hours.

Later, despite his protestations of a frail appetite, my employer demolished his eggs and chops with gusto, while I just picked at the pancakes and syrup Ma had so thoughtfully provided. After breakfast, Mr. Wong said we should visit Brad Hudson at the jail and bring him up to date on our investigation. "Though I fear we have little enough to report," he added sadly.

The Model T was parked behind the hotel—my employer fervently wished to keep the automobile out of the sight of Spinster Rhodes since it was shot full of holes—and after a dozen cranks of the starting handle it fired up and I drove my employer to the sheriff's office.

A few streaks of lemon had appeared in the dark

sky and the first shy light of the new dawn was beginning to wash out the shadows from the alleys between the town buildings. The smell of pine and grass was in the air, mixed with the stale odors of whiskey, cigar smoke, and vomit from last night's revels that the soft morning breeze had so far done little to dissipate.

Sheriff Havenick's deputy, a thin old man with a drooping mustache wearing a black-and-white cowhide vest, nodded sourly when we arrived and led us, coughing, to our client's cell.

Hudson sprang from his bunk when we entered and ran to the bars. "Do you have good news?" he asked anxiously.

The rancher was unshaven and he had deep dark circles under his bloodshot eyes. He looked terrible and, thanks to fear and prison food, his shirt and pants hung on him like rags on a scarecrow.

"No news yet," returned Mr. Wong. "But be of good cheer, I have a whole day left and will leave no stone unturned, no avenue of investigation unexplored." Hudson's shoulders sagged. "Then it's all up with me," he groaned. "Come tomorrow morning, I'll surely hang." Hudson studied the great detective, his red eyes damp from tears. "I'm not a brave man, Mr. Wong. But I'm not a coward, either. It's just . . . just hell to die for a crime I didn't commit, a crime I couldn't commit, not in a thousand years."

My heart went out to this poor man, and I said gently as I could: "Mr. Hudson, is there anyone, anyone at all, you think could have carried out the dreadful murder of Dr. Grant?"

The rancher shook his head at me. "No. That killing

was the work of an animal, a savage beast. I don't know anyone like that, or would ever want to."

Mr. Wong laid his cane on his shoulder. "Then we must be off, Mr. Hudson. There is much work to be done. As Dr. Doyle's very fictitious sleuth says, 'The game is afoot.'"

We turned to leave, but Hudson called us back with an anguished cry. "Wait!" he yelled. "Wait, I just remembered, there is someone!"

The great detective paused in his stride and pointed his cane at the distraught rancher. "Come now, Mr. Hudson, we won't clutch at straws. There is not the time."

"No, no, listen," Hudson wailed. "There's a man called Smoke Pagan, he runs a one-loop spread that borders the northern range of the Rafter H. Talk to him. Ask him how come his wife vanished three years ago and with her his hired hand, and nobody's heard of either of them since."

The rancher joined his hands as though in prayer and pleaded: "Please, Mr. Wong, of all the people I know, Pagan is the only one who could have done this. After his wife vanished, he'd get drunk in the saloon and talk to anyone who'd listen about how much he despises women. If anybody could've murdered Victoria Grant with her high-falutin', man-hating ways, it was Smoke Pagan."

"Flimsy," said Mr. Wong thoughtfully. "Very flimsy."

Desperately, Hudson shook his head at him. "Wong, Pagan's bad, he's bad all the way through. Back in the old days he rode with the Dalton boys, an' he's fast with a gun and poison-mean with a blade.

He's a killer, like all the Pagan clan—seed, breed, and generation of them."

A few moments later we stood outside the sheriff's office in the mist-gray dawn, and my employer's face was set and grim. "Chance," he said stiffly, "we will talk to this Smoke Pagan. This much I will do and no more." He sighed, then added dubiously: "I'm afraid there will be little profit in this case, and perhaps much loss, especially when the fair Miss Rhodes beholds her shot-up automobile."

"Sir," I said softly, "this case does not end with Mr. Hudson's execution. We must find the man who has tried to kill us, not once but on several occasions. The man who is the real murderer of Dr. Grant."

The great detective nodded. "All this is true, Chance. But I believe we'll leave that up to the law when we quit this godforsaken town tomorrow and forever."

"The law? You mean Sheriff Havenick?"

"I believe he's still the law in Crow Creek," replied Mr. Wong a little pompously.

"But, sir, he may be the real killer. Or at least in cahoots with the killer."

The great detective silently walked to the car and climbed into the passenger seat, his face revealing nothing. Then he turned and looked at me most severely. "Last Chance," he said, "I believe I am better qualified to be the judge of that."

Chastened, I dropped my eyes to the ground and whispered modestly: "Sir, this one most humbly begs your pardon."

My employer nodded. "There is an old Chinese saying that the wise adult is too old a cat to take advice from a kitten. Now, start the car and let us drive on. We will confront this Smoke Pagan fellow—what a barbaric name!"

As I bent to crank the handle of the Ford, I saw Charity Hamilton walk out of the hotel and stand on the boardwalk, a carpetbag in her hand. The clerk held her horse that he had no doubt fetched from the livery stable, and was talking to her in an animated fashion. The woman, cool and aloof, ignored him, looking up and down the street as though expecting to see someone.

She turned and caught my eye and I straightened from the starting handle and waved. She did not acknowledge me, but stepped from the boardwalk and stashed her bag behind the saddle. The clerk, smiling and flustered, held Charity's stirrup and she swung easily into the leather with the careless grace of the expert horsewoman.

The beautiful paleontologist had obviously spent the night in the hotel, so, despite all her bravado, she might have been afraid to stay at the dig, even with Schramm and his vaunted British Bulldog revolver.

But who was she afraid of? Did she secretly believe that Brad Hudson did not murder Victoria Grant, and that the killer might come back for her? Or had Ghost Bear frightened her so badly that she had spent the night in town where she'd be safe from the implacable Indian and his avenging Flatheads?

As my employer called out impatiently at me to start the car, I wondered at these questions, and now, more than ever, I greatly feared for the young scientist's life. She was a woman, the natural prey of the deranged killer of Victoria Grant, and that made her achingly vulnerable.

I bent and cranked the little Model T into life, filled with new fears and a feeling of utter hopelessness.

THIRTEEN

We had no difficulty finding the Pagan ranch since after an hour's driving the road to the place branched off the main trail and was marked by a sign that read:

> PAGAN RANCH
> STAY OUT—I SHOOT
> FURST AND ASK
> KWESCHUNS LATER

"Friendly sort, isn't he?" said my employer as he studied the sign. Then he leaned back in his seat, pointed his cane up the trail and ordered: "Drive on."

Despite the promise of the dawn, the sky was gray and overcast and the distant mountains were shrouded in haze. Stunted pine and scrub brush grew alongside the muddy, rutted trail to the Pagan ranch and squabbling jays shattered the morning stillness with their clamor.

We smelled the place before we saw it, the air thick and acrid with the heavy, earthy odor of pigs. The ranch itself consisted of a small, swaybacked cabin roofed with sod, a corral, and a barn that sagged precariously to one side. There was a pigpen filled with a dozen wallowing hogs and a creaking, metal windmill stood alongside the cabin to pump water. I could see no other livestock except some scrawny chickens pecking in the yard, though I assumed there were horses in the barn. The place had a dirty, unkempt, and rundown look as though someone had made a good start on the place a long time ago, then suddenly lost interest.

Two men stood by the cabin door and watched us come.

The smaller of the two carried a rifle in his hands, and when I pulled up in the yard he pointed it at us and said with an unfriendly snarl: "Get down off that damn thing and cut the motor, you're upsettin' my hogs with all that racket. Now, get the hell over here."

It wasn't an invitation, it was an order, so I hastened to get out of the car, Mr. Wong, due to his bulk moving a little more slowly.

As we waited for my employer to join us, I studied the small man closely. This could only be Smoke Pagan.

He was perhaps an inch over five feet, and rail-thin. But his cold gray eyes were mean and he seemed to have the stored-up energy of a coiled rattlesnake, waiting at any moment to explode into action. Low on his right thigh he wore a Colt .45 with a beautiful ivory handle, and even in the holster I could see that the revolver was heavily engraved.

The lovely, expensive, and well-cared-for Colt was in stark contrast to the man's clothes. He wore baggy black pants, patched at the knees and held up by a piece of rope. His boots were scuffed and down-at-the-heels and his cotton undershirt, once white, was now gray with dirt and stained down the front from his last two dozen meals.

The man who stood to Pagan's left was Mexican, but unlike his boss he was well over six feet and his blue denim shirt and jeans were clean and neat. He looked like he'd been born wearing the two guns in crossed belts that made an ominous X on his lean hips, and his black eyes, shaded by his wide sombrero, were flat, black, and unreadable.

I instantly recognized these men for what they were: members of the old-time gunfighting and outlaw fraternity. As dear Professor Masterson was wont to say from around his cigar: "Chance, you can always read their brand, because they're snake-eyed hombres who don't wear belt guns for ballast an' their reservations in hell was made the day they was born."

Pagan, so typical of the breed, took a step toward Mr. Wong—who was making a halfhearted display of his fine broadcloth suiting and polished shoes—and pointed his rifle right at the great detective's belly.

"I know why you're here," he said, his voice silky smooth, heavy with menace. "You're that famous Chinee detective feller they're all talkin' about in town, an' you think I'm just a piece of white trash that kilt the woman who found the big animal back in the hills. Well, you're wrong, dead wrong. You can't pin that killin' on me."

Mr. Wong ended his strut and held up a dismissive hand. "My dear Mr. Pagan, detective work is a process of elimination. We merely wish to eliminate you from any possible suspicion."

"Smoke, this man does not tell the whole truth, I think," the Mexican said, smiling.

Pagan's eyes hardened, narrowing into slits. "What is the truth, Detective? You tell me pretty damn fast."

Mr. Wong hesitated, breathed deeply, then said quickly: "The truth, Mr. Pagan, is that I want you to tell me about your wife."

The gunman's face was bleak. "What is there to tell? She done left me. Took off with my hired hand."

"Why?" I asked.

Pagan laughed, an ugly snort without humor. "Hell, look around you, little lady. What did she have to stay for? This? For me? Hope and hogs never did mix. Hope and poverty didn't mix, either. When Len Quinn hired on, he had big California spurs on his boots an' a silver band on his hat an' he cut quite a dash among the ladies.

"Hope, she got to callin' Quinn her protector, an' maybe he was at first, because I was away from home a lot in them days. See, Hope fooled around with a lot of men, an' I knowed it all the time, but I thought it was just a passing fancy, something she'd grow out of eventually."

The little gunman's bleak face grew even gloomier. "Then she finally met a man who scared the hell out of her."

"This Quinn fellow?" asked Mr. Wong.

"Nah, not that strutting peacock, somebody else. See, she took to undressing in the dark, something she never did afore because she was proud of her body, especially the big rack she carried. Then, one night I lit the lamp an' saw what she was tryin' her best to hide."

Pagan shook his head. "She was covered in bruises and she had bite marks here"—his hand strayed to his shoulder—"dozens of them, real deep. I asked who done it, because I planned to call on that man an' kill him, but she wouldn't tell me. All she'd say was, 'You leave him be, Smoke. He's crazy, plumb loco, an' he'll destroy us both.'

"Well, a few days after that Hope an' the hired hand just cut out. She wore the pretty yeller dress I bought her for our wedding day when she left, an' I ain't seen hide nor hair of the two of them from that day to this."

Pagan's knuckles whitened on his rifle, "Now, Mr. Chinee Detective, that's 'bout as much talkin' as I've done in the three years since Hope left and I'm all through speechifying. So get the hell off my land an' don't come back."

"Sir, just one more question," I said, ignoring my employer's alarmed glance. "Did you know any of the men who were stepping out with your wife?"

Pagan smiled without humor. "Maybe half the male population of Crow Creek got belly to belly with her at one time or another. Matt Jerrell, that ex-Ranger at the Rafter H, Sheriff Havenick, Brad Hudson, some folks say even the little hunchbacked banker, Ben Cranwell, dealt himself a hand. Throw in saddle bums, drummers, miners, an' anybody else you care to mention an' you get some idea what kind of woman my dear wife was."

The little gunman stepped close to Mr. Wong, who, surprised, stepped back, his shoe skidding on something soft and odorous.

"What is that?" my employer asked in alarm, studying the smeared sole of his immaculate pump.

"Pig shit," Pagan said. "You'll get used to the stink after a while." He jammed a forefinger into Mr. Wong's chest. "Now, Mr. Detective, you git!"

"Señor," the Mexican smiled, "I would do as the boss says an' pretty damn quick, I think."

As my mentor and myself made a hasty retreat toward the car, Pagan, much to my surprise, stopped us with a yell. Then he walked closer and said: "You know, I hate Brad Hudson's guts, him an' all the rest of the big cattle ranchers around here who think they're too good to be seen talking to outlaw trash an' a low-down pig man like Smoke Pagan. But I'm telling you now, he didn't kill that scientist gal, either."

"Oh really," returned Mr. Wong pompously, obviously still smarting over the manure on his shoe. "Then who, pray tell, did?"

"I dunno, but I reckon it's the same man who killed young Jenny Pearson two years ago."

"Jenny Pearson? I've never heard that name before," Mr. Wong said in considerable agitation.

"Don't surprise me none," said Pagan. "There are folks around here who maybe think the girl's better left dead an' buried."

"Tell us about her, sir," I asked.

"Ain't a whole lot to tell. Jenny, she was goin' on fifteen an' real pretty, had this long golden hair that hung all the way down her back an' even at that young age she had a way with men. She was found in the hills near her paint horse, dead as a six-card poker hand. She was laying at the foot of a boulder folks around here call Squaw Rock, on account of how it looks like an Indian squaw with a papoose on her back.

"Jenny had been ravaged, if'n that's the po-lite word for it, and somebody had gone at her with a knife. Her . . ." from somewhere deep within him Pagan dredged up a distant memory of good manners. "Beggin' your pardon, ma'am . . . her tits had been cut off, and her . . . other part had been gouged and slashed to ribbons."

The little gunman shook his head. "They say, them as saw her, Jenny Pearson warn't a pretty sight no more."

"That's horrible," I whispered. "The poor child."

"Sure enough," Pagan said. "Now guess who was found standin' over Jenny's body, a bowie knife in his hand smokin' blood and more blood all over his clothes?"

"Who, Mr. Pagan?" I asked, horrified. "Who was it?"

"Well," Pagan smiled thinly, "he was man-sized even then and strong enough to tie a bow-knot in an iron horseshoe. I'm talkin' about Sheriff Havenick's son Billy."

As we drove back toward town the sky had grown darker and already a fine drizzle was slanting across the trail, promising heavier rain to come. The sun was low in the eastern sky, hardly visible behind the clouds, like an oil lamp in a fog. The burned prairie grass had begun to green from the earlier downpours, and in the distance I saw a herd of a dozen or more antelope grazing on a hillside.

"Do you think Sheriff Havenick is protecting his son?" I asked my employer as we drove. "Could Billy have murdered both Jenny Pearson and Dr. Grant, and could he be the one who ambushed us and killed the Teton Kid?"

Yet, even as I asked these questions, I thought about Billy. Could that simple boy really be capable of the vile, evil words whispered to me in the livery stable last night?

Or was Billy Havenick perhaps not quite as retarded as he pretended to be?

My employer, lost in thought, made no answer to my inquiries, and I knew that wonderful mind—defined by Scotland Yard as "the greatest criminal intellect of the twentieth century"—was grappling with the many ramifications of our interview with Pagan.

"Sir," I persisted, hoping that Mr. Wong would share his conclusions with me, "we must confront Havenick with this information at the earliest possible moment and see how he reacts. I believe the successful conclusion of this case could now be in reach."

My employer frowned, his noble brow furrowed. "You know, Chance, I've been thinking about those wonderful mutton chops I had for breakfast. I do believe I could eat them again for lunch, with perhaps a little mashed potato and just a spoonful or two of sweet garden peas."

Ah, my modest mentor. His humility was such that it would not allow him to share his brilliant deductions even with his most trusted assistant and keeper of the Dragon Box, so he must perforce hide his dazzling light behind the façade of a simple lunch menu.

Truly, as a wise Chinese philosopher once said,

those who aspire to greatness must first humble themselves.

We drove the rest of the way to town in a silence broken only by the hiss of the rain and the hum of the automobile as I pushed the machine to its limit in our race against time to free poor Mr. Hudson. Mr. Wong made no comment on our breakneck speed, but every now and then he licked his lips and whispered, "Mmmm," and I realized this was a symptom of his nervous energy as he grappled with the facts of the case.

Mud spattering high in the air from all four tires, we roared into town and I headed straight for the sheriff's office.

My employer, looking behind him, said in alarm: "Chance, we just passed Ma's!"

But I knew he was making a little joke, since time was now very much our enemy and we had no time for lunching.

I braked outside the sheriff's office and the door opened almost immediately. Havenick's tall, grim-faced old deputy stepped on to the boardwalk and shook his head at me, waving his arms. "If'n you're lookin' for the sheriff, he ain't here."

"Then where is he?" I asked, irritated by the man's absence.

The deputy shrugged. "He left more'n an hour ago. If he ain't down by the cottonwoods along the creek, then maybe he's along to Ma's to eat."

"Ah," said my employer, "an excellent meeting place. Chance, turn around and let us repair to Ma's at all possible speed."

I was unreasonably annoyed at Havenick for not

being where I expected him to be, and was about to turn the car around when I spotted the huge, shambling figure of his son standing on the porch of his home looking intently at us.

Quickly, I straightened up the wheel and headed for Billy.

"Chance," Mr. Wong wailed, "we're going the wrong way, child."

"Sir, Billy's on the porch," I said. "Now is an excellent opportunity to talk to him."

"I doubt that we'll get any sense out of that boy," my employer sighed. "But proceed if you must."

I pulled up alongside the porch and waved. "Hi, Billy."

The boy looked surly and made no reply. He came down off the porch and stood beside the car, and I was uncomfortably aware of how huge he was and how he loomed over me. The rain was coming down steadily and Billy's lank brown hair was plastered over his head and he smelled of dampness and yesterday's sweat.

"Would you like to come in the car and sit down out of the rain?" I asked, offering him the uncertain shelter of the Ford's canvas top.

Billy shook his head at me. "I don't like cars. I like horses."

"Can we talk to you, Billy?" I asked. "It's something very, very important."

Immediately suspicion clouded the boy's surly features. "What about?"

"It's about Jenny Pearson, Billy," offered Mr. Wong. "Do you remember Jenny?"

Billy nodded. "Jenny was pretty. But she wouldn't

talk to me. She said I was stupid." The boy's face was suddenly disconsolate. "She said I was ugly and smelled bad."

"Billy," I said softly. "I'm sure she didn't mean all those things. She was only a child and sometimes children can be thoughtless."

The boy shook his head. "She said bad things, nasty things."

"You were found with her body, I mean after poor Jenny was murdered, weren't you, Billy?" I asked, giving him no rest. "Did you want to hurt Jenny for all the nasty things she said to you? Did you hurt her, Billy? Maybe you didn't mean to hurt her, but it just happened."

I saw the boy's face harden. "My pa says I don't ever need to talk about that to anybody. It was a bad thing an' he says I got to forget it ever happened."

"Why were you there with Jenny?" I asked, gently as I could. "Were you out riding and just happened to meet up with her?"

"Treasure hunt!" Billy said, his sullen face suddenly brightening.

"Ah, your pa sent you on a treasure hunt and it led you right to Jenny," I said. "Is that how it happened, Billy?"

"Somebody killed Jenny. It was a bad man killed her with a knife."

The boy studied me for a few moments, then he yelled: "You're a bad lady. Pa told me to stay away from you. I don't want to talk about Jenny no more!"

He turned and ran, disappearing behind the house. A few moments later I saw him run along the creek bank then vanish into the stand of huge cottonwoods, scattering the crows roosting in their branches.

As I watched Billy, something else down by the cottonwoods caught my attention, something that froze the blood in my veins and made me gasp in sheer fright.

"Chance, what is it now, child?" asked Mr. Wong, his face showing his annoyance.

"Look, sir, down by the creek, that tree that stands alone to the right."

My employer glanced in that direction without much interest. "I see the tree, what of it?"

"Look on the lower branch, do you see what's hanging there?"

This time Mr. Wong peered at the cottonwood more intently. "Ah yes," he said. "A noose."

"That's where the sheriff plans to hang poor Mr. Hudson," I exclaimed in horror. "From a cottonwood tree."

My employer shrugged. "Chance, there isn't a gallows in town, so if Brad Hudson must hang, the tree makes perfect sense."

"Then he must not hang!" I exclaimed. "Oh, sir, you must save him, you must!"

"I'm doing my best, child," returned Mr. Wong. "There just isn't time, I'm afraid, even for me."

"Sir, I believe that Sheriff Havenick murdered young Jenny Pearson and Victoria Grant," I persisted. "That must be the immediate direction of your inquiry."

My brilliant mentor nodded. "That may indeed be the case, but I believe the sheriff to be a desperate and dangerous gunman and we are no match for such a man. We must, therefore, enlist help."

"But who is willing to help us?" I asked, overcome yet again by that increasingly frequent feeling of utter hopelessness.

"Ben Cranwell the banker," Mr. Wong said. "He's offered his help, now we must accept it."

I had no wish to have the little man undress me again with his eyes, but I saw the logic in what my employer was saying. Cranwell was rich, powerful, and influential. It would take such a man to bring Sheriff Burt Havenick to justice.

FOURTEEN

When I stopped the car outside the bank, I studied the alley closely. This is where I'd seen the hotel clerk vanish when we'd first arrived in town and I was sure he'd been heading in this direction before I lost him last night.

The bank was the first building, standing on the right of the alley. Beyond there was only a vacant lot, overgrown by grass and brush. Opposite there was a large warehouse with two doors to the street that had painted on their fronts, B. SULLIVAN, EGG AND CHEESE IMPORTER. EST. 1888.

To the right of the warehouse a couple of disused shacks huddled disconsolately together and beyond that a small barn and corral where a tall, American horse hung his head over the top rail, seemingly enjoying the coolness of the rain and freedom from flies.

Where could the clerk have been going to in such a hurry? The warehouse looked like it hadn't been used in years, and the shacks were windowless, their doors hanging askew in the frames. I could only guess that the clerk somehow left messages here, messages for someone that he knew would pick them up regularly—like the sheriff who would visit this alley to check on the bank in the course of his rounds.

"Come, Chance, don't dawdle," said my employer as he turned and saw me study the alley, frowning in concentration. "There is no time for gawping and woolgathering."

The banker welcomed us to his office pleasantly enough, and in the full light of day he looked even grayer and sicker than he had at breakfast. His feverish eyes were sunk deep in his head and his shoulders were hunched, as though a heavy weight was bearing down on him.

Outside the rain was coming down in torrents and thunder rumbled in the distance. Both Mr. Wong and I were wearing our oilskins and I was thankful that Cranwell could not further explore the nuances of my bared bosom and shoulders.

"And what can I do for you nice people?" he asked. His voice was remarkably strong, but his smile seemed forced and without warmth.

Quickly Mr. Wong described our talk with Smoke Pagan and our discovery that Billy Havenick had found poor little Jenny Pearson's body while on a treasure hunt.

At my employer's urging, I finished the story, telling the banker about our conversation with Billy and how we suspected that Havenick was the murderer of both Jenny and Dr. Grant. Instinctively, I held back the terrifying episode in the livery stable, believing it would have introduced a jarring note that could undermine our whole story. I wasn't sure the whispered voice in the barn, though disguised, was that of

Sheriff Havenick's—though it could have belonged to an accomplice.

After I'd stopped speaking, Ben Cranwell sat back in his chair and studied us over steepled fingers.

A few slow moments passed, then he said: "There is no real, hard evidence to back up what you two are saying."

I made to protest, but the little banker held up a hand. "Hear me out. I don't want to see Brad Hudson hang anymore than you do, but it's a damnably dangerous thing to interfere with the workings of the law. Remember, Brad was found guilty by a jury and sentenced by a legally appointed circuit judge."

My shoulders slumped. "Then you won't help us."

"Not won't—can't," Cranwell replied.

Again he steepled his fingers, studying my gloomy face. At last the banker sighed deeply, leaned forward in his chair and said: "Okay, okay. Look, there are still men in this town who were part of the Crow Creek vigilante committee back in the old days. I'm talking about good, solid men like Heath Wilson the saloon-keeper, Doc Lawson, and maybe half a dozen others. You bring me something tangible, some hard evidence that I can place before them, and I'll call a meeting of the committee tonight and put a stop to this hanging."

Cranwell waved a hand toward the town. "I know these men. Along with the sheriff they kept the riffraff out of this town—two-gun men and bunco artists, the dance hall loungers, and the saddle bums. The vigilante committee made Crow Creek a decent place to live, a place where a man could bring his wife and raise a family without fear. Those men will do what has to be done, as long as they have the law to back them up, and the law requires hard evidence."

The banker shook his head at me. "Don't ask me to go beyond that, young lady. Believe me, as it is, I could be wildly overestimating my influence in this community."

There was little more to be said, so Mr. Wong rose to his feet and I followed.

"Rest assured, Mr. Cranwell," said the great detective, "I will do everything in my power to uncover the evidence you need. I will bring to you, sir, the evidence of Sheriff Havenick's guilt."

"Mr. Wong, I have no need to remind you that time is of the very essence in this matter," replied the banker. "The bank closes at noon today, but I'll be doing bookwork at my home for the rest of the day. My humble abode is a little ways out of town to the east, but anyone will tell you where it is."

"You have my gratitude, sir," quoth Mr. Wong, extending his hand.

Cranwell smiled as he warmly shook hands with my employer. "As for gratitude, sir, you'll have plenty of opportunity to show that later."

But he was looking right at me as he said that, the tip of his yellow tongue curling along his top lip, and I felt my skin crawl.

Once outside we quickly sought refuge from the rain under the inadequate shelter of the car's canvas roof and Mr. Wong instructed me to drive, with all possible haste, to Ma's Kitchen.

"We may well see Sheriff Havenick there," he said,

"and have an opportunity to confront him with the facts we've recently uncovered."

"Beware, sir," I said, as I turned the Ford in the narrow alley. "He's a dangerous man and such information could make him desperate. If he believes himself to be cornered, he could resort to gunplay."

Mr. Wong shrugged. "The private detective's life is fraught with danger, Chance. I accepted the risks a long time ago and I will not shrink from them now. As the great Confucius says, 'To see what is right, and not do it, is want of courage.'"

My employer puffed out his chest and nodded his sleek head this way and that in an elegant and animated display. "It has never been said, nay, not even hinted at, that Chester Wong is lacking courage."

My employer would not allow me to park in front of the restaurant, lest the spinster Rhodes discover her shot-up car, so we drove behind the building and I braked to a halt.

The rain was fairly hammering down and the gray clouds forked vivid lightning, accompanied by tremendous crashes of thunder. The air smelled of electricity and danger and I felt a terrible unease as if something dreadful was about to happen.

"Indeed, this is a miserable day to be about such a task as ours," said Mr. Wong gloomily, glancing up at the lowering sky as we made our way to the front door of Ma's Kitchen and walked inside.

The little restaurant was warm, bright, and welcoming and I gratefully removed my clinging oilskins and sou'ester hat, ignoring my employer's annoyed "tut-tut-tut" as he disapprovingly regarded my suddenly revealed cleavage.

"My, my, don't you look pretty," said Ma when she came to the table for our order. "You look like a little china doll." The lady put her hand to her mouth. "Oh, I meant no offense."

"None taken," I said and smiled. "A compliment is always acceptable."

Mr. Wong and I had immediately ascertained that the sheriff was not here, and now I made bold as to inquire if he had perhaps lunched earlier.

Ma shook her white curls. "I haven't seen hide nor hair of him," she said. "I suspect he's too busy getting ready for the hanging tomorrow. He's an efficient one, our sheriff, a hard, unforgiving man when all is said and done, but he knows what he's about."

"Ah well," said my mentor, and I thought I detected a note of relief in his voice, "perhaps he'll be in later. Now, dear lady, since I am extremely pushed for time, if you will please take my order." The mutton chops had been very much preying on Mr. Wong's mind and he now anxiously inquired if there were any left, having made ravenous inroads into Ma's stock earlier that morning.

"I'll see," said Ma, turning toward the kitchen, leaving my employer in a highly agitated and nervous state.

"Good news," beamed Ma on her return, "I have four left. Would you care for one, Mr. Wong?"

"Nay, dear lady, not one, but all four," declared my delighted employer. "I can't bear the thought of them going to waste."

"Potatoes?" asked Ma.

"Mashed," said my employer.

"They're boiled," declared Ma.

"Excellent," said Mr. Wong. "And peas."

"Only carrots," said Ma.

"Excellent," said my employer.

"I also have some nice boiled onions," observed Ma.

"Bring 'em on," said my mentor, clapping his hands in delight.

"And you, young lady?" asked Ma, pencil poised over her order pad. "I have some nice chicken and dumplings."

After a while, the vegetarian stops declaring an aversion to meat, since a raised eyebrow at the very least, outright hostility at the worst, usually greets such a declaration. I therefore made the excuse of a less-than-healthy appetite—at that moment the honest truth since I was on the one hand worried about Mr. Hudson and on the other fearful of Sheriff Havenick—and asked for some boiled potatoes, onions, and coffee.

"You young ladies," declared Ma in pretended exasperation, "always thinking about those slim figures."

As the old lady toddled away to fill our orders, my employer sniffed and declared haughtily: "Truly, Chance, if the path to enlightenment lies in abstinence, your place in Nirvana is most definitely assured."

But I, thinking of my love for Burmah cheroots, pretty clothes, and gallant young men, modestly lowered my eyes and whispered: "Sir, this unworthy one is far from breaking the cycle of death and rebirth, though I pray nightly to the divine Kuan Yin that this might one day be the case."

"Moderation is the key!" exclaimed Mr. Wong, as though he'd just thought of it, adding a vehement exclamation point to his statement. "Remember, child, the wise old ones of China say everything that exceeds the bounds of moderation has an unstable foundation. Now," he added, slapping his great stomach, "where is that confounded woman with my mutton chops?"

We had only begun to eat when the door to the restaurant was thrown wide and Sheriff Burt Havenick, looking grim and tall and terrible, stormed inside, a crash of thunder and a sudden gust of cold rain announcing his entrance.

The lawman strode quickly to our table, sweeping his slicker back from his holstered gun, and I felt a sudden, white-hot jolt of fear. The Dragon Box was within reach on the next chair, lying atop my oilskins, and I pulled the chair toward me, close to hand.

Mr. Wong froze, a forkful of dripping mutton suspended between his plate and open mouth, and for a single moment it seemed time stood still.

"What the hell did you do to my boy?" the sheriff roared, shattering the tense silence like a rock thrown through a plate glass window.

He looked mean and angry clean through. The man was set on a hair trigger and I believed the slightest wrong move or ill-chosen word could send him reaching for his gun.

"Whatever do you mean, Sheriff?" my employer said carefully, laying his fork gently on his plate. "We did nothing to your son."

"You were grilling him about Jenny Pearson,"

Havenick gritted between clenched teeth. The big lawman's killing rage was threatening to buck out of control and his despairing eyes told me he was doing his utmost to rein it in. "Now he's really upset and says you're going to hang him."

"Billy was found standing over poor Jenny's bloody body with a knife in his hand," I said as evenly as I could. "He said he was on a treasure hunt, a hunt you set up for him, Sheriff. Did you send him on that hunt, knowing he'd find the girl's body and be blamed for her murder?"

The stark accusation now lay between us, an immovable rock I'd thrown in Havenick's path that he could not tiptoe around. I'd left him with just two choices—deny it, or draw his gun.

In the few moments of stunned silence that followed my statement, I eased the clasp open on the Dragon Box, knowing I'd be at least a second too slow if it came to gunplay—and by that time my employer and I could well be dead.

Unexpectedly, it was Ma who stepped in and defused the situation.

"Here," she said, "this won't do. I'll have no fighting in my restaurant." She walked right up to Havenick, showing not the slightest fear. "Burt, this is an eating place, not a Texas barroom."

"Huh?" the sheriff asked, like a man who'd just wakened from a sound sleep.

"Sit down and have some coffee," Ma said. "I'll have no gunplay here, mind."

Havenick's shoulders slumped. "I'm not gonna draw down on nobody, Ma," he said. "Them days is long gone."

"Yes they are," said Ma, "and good riddance, I say."

The sheriff looked at Mr. Wong and then me, his face stricken. "I didn't send Billy on a treasure hunt the day he found Jenny. Maybe he made one up for himself. He loves to ride in the hills." Havenick sat down in a chair opposite me. "My boy didn't kill Jenny Pearson. I guess you was told what happened to the girl. I mean, how she died. When Billy was found standing next to her body, there wasn't a spot of blood on his clothes. You can't kill a person that way she was killed without getting yourself covered in blood. That's how the folks here in Crow Creek saw it. They knew Billy, an' they knew that boy couldn't hurt anybody."

"Smoke Pagan says there was blood on Billy's clothes," I said softly.

"Smoke Pagan is a liar and a piece of trash."

"Sheriff," I said, knowing I was playing a dangerous game, "you could have murdered Jenny Pearson and left her body for your son to find. That way, he'd get the blame and you'd be in the clear."

My hand slid inside the Dragon Box.

Dear Professor Bat Masterson once told me you have to win a gunfight in the first half-second. "Slower than that and you'd better light a shuck for the pearly gates, little lady," he said, "'cause you're gonna be dead as hell in a parson's parlor."

Havenick looked stunned. He sat there without moving, his pale, gunfighter's eyes fastened on mine.

Did I have half a second? The sheriff's eyes would telegraph his move, but he would be very sudden.

I'd never seen this man draw and shoot, but many times I'd watched Professor Buckskin Frank Leslie pull a Colt as fast as a striking cobra, and, from all I'd heard, Havenick would be even faster.

But the big lawman made no move toward his gun. He just shook his head and said: "You don't know me, do you? You don't know me at all."

"Sheriff, I think I know you all too well," I said.

Mr. Wong gulped loudly as he swallowed a huge mouthful of mutton chop. "Getting cold," he said, by way of explanation.

Havenick ignored the great detective, talking directly to me. "They say I've killed eight men, an' maybe I have. Maybe even a couple more. But I never hurt a woman in my life, an' all the men I killed, I done for them standin' straight up, lookin' right into their eyes."

The lawman's leathery face was tight and drawn. "I never tried to blame anyone else for my killings, I took them all on myself. An' the last person on the face of the earth I'd try to blame is my own son."

"Nevertheless, the fact remains that Billy followed your map to Jenny's body," I said, uncertainty gnawing at me. I'd been so sure of this man's guilt, now his obvious sincerity was troubling me.

"I told you, I never drew that map," he said. "When Jenny Pearson was killed, I was up in the mountains sheep huntin'. I didn't even know about it until I got back, then me an' Ben Cranwell got up a couple of posses and we scoured the hills around here for days. We didn't find nothin'."

"Ah yes, well, that's all settled then," said Mr. Wong. "I can see quite clearly that our suspicions were misplaced, Sheriff."

"Sheriff," I said, choosing to ignore my irritated

employer, "what do you know about the disappear-
ance of Smoke Pagan's wife?"

The lawman shook his head at me. "Nothin'. She
took off with that hired hand of Smoke's, flashy kind
of ranny by the name of Len Quinn. They ain't been
heard of since."

"You were . . . stepping out with her?" I asked.

"Now and again. Me and maybe a dozen other
rannies."

"Sheriff," I said, "Matt Jerrell out at the Rafter H
gave us a message to give to you. He said to tell you
to stay away from Angela Hudson." I flashed him my
sweetest smile. "Now, why do you suppose he'd ever
dream of saying such an unfriendly thing?"

Havenick took a deep breath and let it out with a
shuddering sigh. "You've met my wife. Me an'
Helen, we haven't been man and wife for a long
spell, if you know what I mean. She goes her way,
an' I go mine."

"Difficult for a woman in a wheelchair to go anywhere," I said.

"Helen doesn't need that chair. She can walk if she
wants to. The chair, well it's just her way of crucifying
me a little more every single day of her life. She
blames me for Billy, you already know that, an' she
blames me for the kind of life I've given her, rotting
away in this backwater town. Helen was beautiful
once. I realize that's hard to believe when you look at
her now, but there was a time when she was the
purtiest gal in San Antone, Texas, bar none."

The man's wide shoulders slumped and his chin
sank onto his chest. "After we arrived in Crow Creek,
Helen's beauty left her day by day. It was kinda like

watching one of them night-blooming cactus flowers slowly fade and wither in the sun."

Havenick looked up, his anguished eyes searching mine. "Am I to blame for that? Was it really all my fault? Or was it this town and all it stands for—the end of the line, a few ramshackle buildings standing beside a railroad track that leads to nowhere?"

I ignored these questions because I had no answers for them anymore than the sheriff did, and said: "Tell me about Angela."

"What's to tell? She's young, she's fresh, she's alive. She"—Havenick's face was suddenly alight—"she . . . pleases me. I love being around her."

"Did you ever beat her?" I asked.

"Beat her! What kind of question is that? I'd never harm a hair of her head and I'd kill any man who did."

Mr. Wong had been silent, but I knew that great mind was ceaselessly at work even as he ate. Now he finished his mutton chops and beckoned over Ma, who was keeping a discreet but watchful vigil over our table.

"How were the chops?" she asked, her voice thin and strained as she took my employer's plate. Ma was speaking to Mr. Wong, but she never took her eyes off Sheriff Havenick.

"Excellent," quoth my employer. He raised one perfectly plucked and trimmed eyebrow. "Pie?"

"Apple," replied Ma.

"With raisins?"

"Of course."

"And, dare I hope, a touch of cinnamon and clove?"

"Indeed, Mr. Wong."

"Then," said my employer happily, "since we three are perfect friends again, apple pie all round."

"I don't want pie," Havenick said sourly.

"Nor do I," I added, for I had little appetite left.

"Ah well," said Mr. Wong gloomily, "pie for one. But make it a large slice, if you please, Ma."

Havenick rose to his feet. "I'm shovin' off, but I've got a word of advice for you two. Stay away from Billy, an' stay away from me until after the hangin' tomorrow. Then I'm gonna put you on the noon train back East an' I don't ever want to see your faces again in Crow Creek."

"Sheriff!" I said. The big man had started away, now he turned back. "I should tell you that I've spoken to Ben Cranwell and he's putting the old vigilante committee back together again to stop the hanging of poor Mr. Hudson."

Of course, I wasn't telling the whole truth—that we didn't have a single shred of evidence that would encourage the committee to act. But I wanted to see the sheriff's reaction. Fear, I hoped, or maybe even guilt.

His face betrayed none of those things.

"You tell Ben Cranwell that if the vigilantes try to stop the hangin' tomorrow, there will be dead men on the street," he said, without emotion. "Ben's a good friend of mine, but you tell him that."

As Mr. Wong closed his eyes and delightedly forked his first piece of pie, Havenick walked to the door then stopped. He turned toward me and his face was puzzled.

"You know," he said, "I didn't give Billy a treasure

map, but maybe someone else did, an' you can believe that or not, it don't make no difference to me. But I'll tell you something about my son, he has this little quirk—he throws nothing away. He's even got the first piece of rock candy he ever found on a treasure hunt. See, Billy, he collects things, colored rocks, feathers, old Indian arrowheads, worn-out horseshoes, you name it. He's got everything he ever found or was given to him, and he never parts with any of it."

The sheriff hesitated for a moment as though deep in thought, then said: "If there was a treasure map that led to Jenny Pearson's body, then Billy's bound to have it somewheres."

I only half believed Havenick, but I did want to see that treasure map! "Hold up, Sheriff," I said. "You may have an excellent point there."

Mr. Wong was busy with his apple pie, but I lightly touched the back of his wrist and said: "Meditative sir, I infer by your silence on the matter that you believe the treasure map, if it exists, could have a great bearing on this case."

My employer nodded, chewing thoughtfully. "Your analysis of the current state of my mind is most accurate, Chance. Indeed, I, Chester Wong, must personally inspect this map."

"Then there's no time like the present," Havenick said, as a crash of thunder rattled the restaurant window. "Let's go."

I rose, quickly donned my oilskins and hat and snapped shut the Dragon Box, stowing it under my coat where it would be protected from the rain.

My employer got to his feet, but still held his plate under his chins, forking huge chunks of pie into his mouth at a great rate of speed. When he'd eaten the last crumb, dabbing it up with his forefinger, he put on his oilskins and declared himself "keen as mustard and ready for action." "Though I must confess, all this hurried eating is sure to give me indigestion," he added unhappily, laying coins on the table to pay for our meal.

FIFTEEN

We left the Model T behind Ma's restaurant and walked with Sheriff Havenick toward his home. The sky was iron-gray, enormous clouds banked one on top of the other like menacing giant boulders ready to tumble down onto Crow Creek and flatten it to the ground. The mountains to the west were hidden in a thick haze and the clouds hung so low even the grasslands were invisible but for a half mile or so nearest town. The rain fell heavily, cheered on by the relentless thunder, and lightning lit up the clouds like the flash of distant cannons.

The sheriff made no conversation as we walked, nor did I or Mr. Wong, each of us busy with our own thoughts.

Oh, how that magnificent brain of my employer's must have been considering, analyzing, rejecting the nonrelevant, pondering the pertinent, as we struggled through the mud and the downpour to the sheriff's home.

"You know, Chance," he said at last, breaking his silence. "I think Ma has a too heavy hand with the cinnamon, though I must confess, her piecrust ranks with the very best I've eaten, perhaps even comparable to that of the Chez Petit Garçon in Paris."

"Sir," I said, "I know you tease, and have indeed been pondering weightier matters."

"Well," returned my mentor, "that is true. The mutton chops do deserve some consideration."

And he lapsed once again into a profound and ruminative silence.

How Mr. Wong loved to conceal his true brilliance under the concealing cloak of the mundane!

My employer, despite his dazzling brilliance, was at heart a humble man. Does not the lord Buddha tell us that humility is the path to immortality, vanity the path to endless births and deaths? Assuredly, Mr. Wong was well on his way to breaking the reincarnation cycle, his noble soul knocking on the very gates of Nirvana.

When we finally reached the sheriff's house, Billy wasn't at home. But Helen Havenick met us in the hallway. "Where are you going?" she asked her husband suspiciously.

"Billy's room," replied the sheriff. "We're looking for something."

Helen moved her wheelchair, arms pumping angrily, across the hallway. "You're not going in there, Burt." The woman's face was pale, but her washed-out blue eyes were ablaze with fury.

"Out of my way, Helen," Havenick said.

"For God's sake, Billy's got nothing else. At least leave him his privacy!"

Mr. Wong forced his great belly past both me and the sheriff and lightly laid his hand on the woman's thin shoulder. "Dear lady, I have no wish to invade

Billy's privacy, but the matter is of the utmost importance. You see, the boy may have a treasure map that could lead us to the real killer of Victoria Grant."

"Billy has nothing!" Helen exclaimed. "There is no map. He throws them all away."

"Helen," Havenick said quietly. "You know that's not the truth."

Suddenly the woman began to sob. "Billy didn't kill Jenny Pearson. Billy couldn't kill anybody."

I moved next to Helen, put my arm around her shoulders and looked into her tear-splashed eyes. "Mrs. Havenick, we don't think for one moment that he did. But we have to find that map. Someone directed Billy to Jenny's body, someone who hoped he'd be blamed for a terrible, savage murder. We've got to discover who that someone was."

Helen Havenick sat in silence for a few moments, then, without a word, rolled back her wheelchair, leaving the hallway open.

"Go," she said. "It doesn't matter. None of it matters anymore."

Mr. Wong and I followed the sheriff as he quickly walked to a door at the end of the hallway and opened it wide.

Billy's room was much as I'd expected.

The boy's bed was pushed against one wall and a rag rug covered the rough wooden floor. There was a dresser piled high with bits and pieces that looked like junk to me, but apparently were regarded by Billy as great treasures—ancient, rusty horseshoes picked up from the trails around town, quartz crystals, dozens of stone and metal arrowheads, colored rocks, spent cartridge cases, a collection of gaunt, dejected hawk feathers, a battered, stringless fiddle, lengths of dried and cracked leather, mostly from old mule harnesses, yellowed newspaper clippings . . . just about everything the lonely, disturbed boy had found or acquired in his sad, empty life.

But I saw no maps.

"He probably keeps the maps in a dresser drawer," Havenick said, anticipating my question. "They've got to be around here somewhere."

The sheriff opened one drawer after another, noisily banging them shut as his frustration grew.

"Damn it," he said, straightening up, "I know they've got to be here."

Helen Havenick appeared in the doorway. "I told you he didn't keep those stupid maps," she said. "Why would he? They'd be a constant reminder of how his father wants him out of his home and out of his sight."

"That's not true, Helen," the sheriff said. "Billy loves his treasure hunts and I enjoy making them up for him. He'd never throw the maps away." He waved a hand around the spartan bedroom. "He's kept everything else he ever found."

"This is most disconcerting," said Mr. Wong. "My logic tells me that without the map, our chances of solving this case and freeing Brad Hudson are slight in the extreme."

"Then he must hang tomorrow," Helen said, her mouth twisted into a cruel, triumphant smile. "At least he'll escape Crow Creek, unlike the rest of us who just remain here and rot, like the town itself."

Despairingly, I looked around the room. As always, my employer was right, without the map our investigation was stalled and poor Mr. Hudson surely doomed.

I now had serious doubts that Sheriff Havenick was the guilty party, and even if he was, we had no hard evidence to tie him to the murders. And without that evidence Ben Cranwell and the vigilantes would not act.

I studied the room, trying to determine if there was a place we'd overlooked, a nook or cranny big enough to hide a stack of paper maps. There was no such place.

My eyes wandered to the window, the rain running down its glass panes like tears, and my glance was arrested by something on the sill. I walked over and picked it up, rubbing it between my fingers. It was mud, and not yet dry.

"What do you have there?" Sheriff Havenick asked.

"Mud," I replied. "It's all over the sill."

The big lawmen walked over to the window. "That's strange," he muttered.

"What's strange?" I asked.

"This window. Billy painted his room last year, an' he painted right over the window and the frame, since he never opened it. He was always afraid that someone would come in and steal his treasures. But look, the paint's cracked all the way up the frame. This window has been jimmied open and quite recently."

"That would explain the mud on the sill," I said. "Someone forced the window open and climbed into the room."

In a stately manner, Mr. Wong strolled over to the window and examined it closely. After a few moments he straightened up and said haughtily: "This tells me nothing." He waved a dismissive hand. "The boy may have climbed through the window himself and left mud on the sill."

"But he'd have no reason to do that," Havenick said.

The great detective shrugged. "Boys are wild, unpredictable creatures. Just being a boy is reason enough."

"Sir, could it not also mean," I prompted gently, "that someone knew Billy still had the map and wanted it back?"

Mr. Wong frowned as his powerful intellect analyzed my question, then he replied: "It's possible, I suppose. But most unlikely." He turned to Havenick. "Sheriff, it would have to be someone who knew Billy very well. How many people in town are aware of the fact that he holds on to his treasure maps?"

The sheriff thought for a while then shook his head. "I don't know. Not many. Maybe none."

"Precisely," nodded my employer. "Once again, we are dealing with trivia and not the true facts of the case."

Indeed, I admitted to myself that the great detective was correct. The mud on the sill told us that someone could have entered this room quite recently, but who? It might have been a person looking for the treasure maps, but quite equally could have been Billy himself, that moody and strange boy.

Alas, it seemed our investigation was no further forward and I felt most dejected, especially when my thoughts turned to the poor Teton Kid lying in the back room of the saloon, stiff and ice-cold with silver dollars on his eyes. Was his death a futile thing, all in vain?

Would we ever find the man responsible for his murder, for surely it was murder? I could not bring myself to answer that question.

"We will not burden you any further, ma'am," said Mr. Wong, bowing to Helen Havenick. "Good day to you, dear lady."

"Wait!" I exclaimed.

"What now, child?" sighed my employer in considerable exasperation.

I dug in the pocket of my riding skirt and pulled out the mud-encrusted silver arrowhead.

"I want to see if Billy has an arrowhead in his collection like this one," I said.

"Let me see that," Havenick said, extending his hand.

I placed the arrowhead in his palm and the big man looked at it, then laughed. "You're not from the West, are you?" he asked.

"I believe you already know that, Sheriff," I said stiffly, annoyed by the man's wide grin.

Havenick shook his head at me. "Little lady, this isn't an arrowhead." He rubbed mud away from the surface of the object with his thumb. "It's the tip from a belt. See"—he placed the arrowhead, or whatever you want to call it, over the silver tip of his own belt at the end of the short, narrow length of leather that passed through the buckle—"it's identical to my own."

"More trivia," sighed my employer, waving his cane around and jogging from one foot to another in a highly agitated manner.

But the sheriff's fancy belt had jogged my memory and I took the silver tip from him and again compared it to the one on his own belt.

The tip was scroll engraved, a style much favored by dear Professor Masterson who had his personal six-gun covered all over in similar fashion. The engraving on the belt tip was just as finely executed as that on the professor's Colt, and I could see at a glance that it had been carried out by an expert.

"Sheriff, when Mr. Wong and myself first met you on Friday morning, you told us your belt buckle was a gift from Brad Hudson, did you not?" I asked.

Havenick nodded. "Yeah, it was a Christmas present." He hesitated, then added: "An expensive Christmas present, made by a holster an' gun belt company in El Paso, Texas. Me, I gave Brad a pair of woolen gloves. Value-wise, they didn't hardly match up, though."

"You said someone else received a belt buckle from Mr. Hudson. Who was it?"

The big lawman smiled. "The only other man he wanted to keep on his side—his banker, Ben Cranwell."

A little alarm bell was going off in my head as I pressed on: "Sheriff, I found this belt tip at the dinosaur dig where Victoria Grant was murdered. How do you suppose it got there?"

Havenick thought for a moment, then replied: "Ben often rode out there to take a look at the big skeleton. He may have lost it. Or maybe somebody else has one just like ours."

"I don't think so, Sheriff," I said. "This tip matches yours exactly and the work is very fine. Mr. Hudson placed a special order for just two buckles, both of them very expensive, so it's unlikely the company made more of them."

Havenick's face was suddenly grim. "Little lady, are you tryin' to implicate Ben Cranwell in this? He's a friend of mine, an' a good man."

"No, not at all," I said, backing down hurriedly. "As you say, Mr. Cranwell probably lost it."

"If'n it's really his in the first place," the sheriff said. He reached under his slicker and brought out a watch, thumbing open the case. "It's almost noon, I have to get to Ma's an' rustle up some grub for my prisoner. This will be the last meal Brad will ever eat."

"Ah," said Mr. Wong, his interest piqued. "Did he ask for anything special?"

"Nah, I don't take requests. He'll get his beans, beef, an' coffee like always."

"Oh," said my employer, his face revealing a vague disappointment.

"Well, Chance," said my mentor as we trudged through the rain back toward the hotel, "it seems the map and the silver arrowhead were but other dead ends in a case that now suddenly appears to be full of them."

"I'm not so sure about that," I said.

"Whatever do you mean, child?" asked my employer testily. "There is no map and you heard the sheriff, the arrowhead is a belt tip. If it did belong to Ben Cranwell, a most respectable and concerned citizen, he could have lost it when he went out to visit the dig."

"Patient sir," I said, "we must investigate every lead, no matter how small, if we are to save poor Mr.

Hudson's life. Desperate times call for desperate measures, and Mr. Cranwell has now become a suspect."

"But he's not a suspect," wailed my employer, the rain battering off his sou'ester. "The belt tip proves nothing."

"Sir, it was found at the murder scene. Surely that's suspicious enough in itself?"

"Trivia, Chance. It means nothing."

"Nevertheless, I plan to investigate Mr. Cranwell," I said stubbornly. "If it was he who climbed into Billy's bedroom and stole the maps, he did it during working hours, that is, before noon. The bank is now closed, but the maps may still be there."

Mr. Wong stopped dead in his tracks. We were on the boardwalk, almost at the hotel, and there were only a handful of other people in the street, the rain having driven everyone else indoors.

A cart hauling a load of wood squelched past, drawn by four mud-splashed mules, a hunched and miserable driver at the reins. My employer waited until the wagon was gone then said: "Chance, what is your plan? Surely you aren't thinking of—"

"—breaking into the bank? Yes, I am."

I heard a sharp intake of breath from Mr. Wong. "Last Chance Lee, I forbid it!" he exclaimed.

"Stern sir," I said, "poor Mr. Hudson's life is now measured in hours, and very soon he will partake of his last meal. If we do not act now, it will be too late."

"But," said the great detective in horror, "you're asking me to rob a bank! I could get twenty years in Sing Sing for that."

"We're not robbing the bank, sir," I explained, pushing my ill-fitting sou'ester up from over my eyes with my wrist, since the sleeves of my oilskins hung inches over my hands. "We're merely investigating it."

My employer stood for a few moments pondering this new development that had taken him quite by surprise. I could see his great mind working as he considered the pros and cons of my proposal, his round moon of a face shadowed with doubt.

"I don't know, Chance, this is a highly irregular course of action you're contemplating," he said finally. "To break into a respectable banker's place of business just because he may have lost part of his belt at an archeological site he visited many times is . . . well . . . radical. Almost anarchistic."

"Sir, it is not only an archeological site—it is a murder scene."

Again Mr. Wong lapsed into deep thought.

"The chances of Mr. Cranwell being guilty of the terrible murder of Victoria Grant are, perhaps, a million to one," he observed after a few moments silence.

"Sir, if you were to ask poor Mr. Hudson, now sitting in the shadow of the noose, I'm sure he'd ask you to grasp at any chance, no matter how slight."

"But . . . but . . . how will you gain access to the bank? You have no key. Unless . . ."

"Yes, perceptive sir, I believe I can pick the lock."

Mr. Wong sighed. "Something else they taught you at that damnable finishing school I obtained for you at such great expense, I suppose?"

I modestly lowered my eyes to the ground and replied most humbly: "Sir, your noble generosity provided this unworthy one with a truly excellent education."

"Hmmm . . ." said my mentor, rubbing his chin.

In truth, picking locks was not part of Miss Chastity Charmaine's curriculum, and she at no time formally touched on the subject.

But a dear friend of mine, a fellow alumni named Miss Emily Ferguson, was the daughter of the celebrated New York safecracker Mr. Thomas "Fingers" Ferguson. That gentleman passed on his knowledge of all things pertaining to the profession to his only child, she being, in his own words, "the apple of his eye."

Miss Emily, a girl of a most generous and open nature, passed that intelligence on to me, and was quick with her praise when I proved to be a keen and adept pupil.

At breakfast one morning, when Emily and I were taken to task by another student for our growing expertise with locked doors, Miss Chastity Charmaine did say that, on reflection, the safecracking profession was quite ancient and honorable, though one that required a long apprenticeship and much skill.

"Above all, it is clean work," she said. "I know Emily's dear—and generous—father went about his nocturnal business dressed like a fine gentleman, and that is much to his credit."

Alas, Mr. Ferguson was at that time enduring a long stretch in federal prison, but he had left his daughter a considerable inheritance and later many ardent and handsome suitors vied for her hand in marriage.

Oh, benevolent Miss Emily, little did you know as we sat side by side at our dear old school that the exceptional skills you taught me might one day help save the life of a man who languished in even more depressing circumstances than your own beloved papa!

As we stood in the downpour, the thunder crashing above our heads and the scent of pine and grass in the air, Mr. Wong thought long and hard about our course of action.

Finally he sighed deeply and said: "What must be done, must be done. The Irish have a saying, 'In for a penny, in for a pound,' and, since the die is cast, I can only go where fate leads me." He raised his arms in an attitude of surrender and added dolefully: "Lead me where you will, Chance."

"That, sir, will be no farther than the bank," I said.

SIXTEEN

When we arrived outside the bank, it was indeed closed as I'd expected, the shades drawn and no lights showing inside. The alley was deserted but for a thin and rain-soaked dog that snuffled hungrily, poor thing, around an empty peach can that someone had carelessly tossed aside. Although it was just a few minutes after the noon hour, the dark sky had cast a gloom over Crow Creek and there were deep shadows in the doorways of the warehouse opposite the bank. Down by the corral the big American horse that had stood there earlier was gone, giving the place a lonely and forlorn look.

To my utter joy and relief, the lock on the bank door, though large, was a simple mortise with a spring bolt and very easy to open. I took a pin from my hair and thanked Ben Cranwell for trusting Sheriff Havenick's infamous gun to keep his establishment secure instead of a good, sturdy pin-tumbler lock that could have proved a much tougher nut to crack.

"Sir," I said to Mr. Wong, who was anxiously looking up and down the alley, "when I kneel down to pick the lock, please stand close to me and shield me from view."

"Pick the lock!" wailed my employer in anguish. "Oh God, how low the great Chester Wong has sunk."

"Now sir, if you please." I kneeled down and readied my pin. "Stand close."

My employer did as I asked, his mighty bulk between me and any prying eyes that might enter the alley.

I was somewhat out of practice, so I made several failed attempts to open the lock and had perforce to stop, push up the sleeves of my oilskins and straighten the pin before making yet another attempt.

"Have you opened it yet, Chance?" whispered my employer apprehensively.

"Sir," I replied, "not yet. But I think I'm on the right track."

"Hurry then, and for heaven's sake don't dawdle."

This stern statement was followed by a sharp intake of breath, and I knew at once that someone had entered the alley.

"Good day to you, sir," I heard Mr. Wong say.

At first I did not hear the muffled reply, but as the unwelcome intruder came closer a man's voice sounded clearly as he inquired: "In town for the hangin' are ye?"

"Oh yes, yes, indeed," replied my mentor, and he moved so close to me that his great hips crushed my body against the door and my face was jammed hard against the lock. Worse, the cheap sou'ester had been forced down over my eyes and I couldn't see a thing.

"Brung my wife and young 'uns," the man said. "A good hangin' is something to see."

"Indeed," replied Mr. Wong, pressing me even harder against the door so that I could hardly breathe.

·

"Hope the weather clears, though," the man said, obviously wanting to talk. "Brung us a picnic an' my wife always says you can't eat fried chicken an' watch a hangin' in the rain."

"No, indeed, sir," said Mr. Wong, as I tried to catch my breath, my inner voice clamoring, *Go away, go away.*

"I guess you know the bank is closed an' won't re-open until after the hangin'?" the man said.

"Ah yes, I'm well aware of that," replied my employer. "I . . . um . . . just like standing out of doors and watching the rain. It's what you might call a hobby of mine."

That, I thought, was a most inadequate speech. I felt like screaming, "Get rid of him!" but I couldn't find the breath. I was now so crushed against the door the brass plate around the lock was gouging deep into my cheekbone and Mr. Wong's huge posterior was slowly suffocating me.

"Rain's good to see, if'n you're a farmer like me," the man said. "Been at farming, man and boy, for this past thirty years."

"An excellent profession, farming," said Mr. Wong. "Wheat and some dairy, I presume?"

"Just so," the man said. "It's a rewarding profession, but hard work by times."

Go away! I thought desperately. *Oh, please, please, Mr. Farmer, just go away!*

"Salt of the earth, farmers," observed my employer loftily. "Always said that, always will."

"Well, thankee, that's nice of ye to say so," said the farmer. "Not everyone thinks that way, especially around these parts. See, what we have in this neck of the woods are mostly cattlemen, an arrogant breed that don't cotton much to farmers."

My chest was so compressed by Mr. Wong's enormous hips I was now in very real danger of passing out for lack of oxygen. My head was swimming and my breath, when I could breathe, came in short little gasps.

That's when the terrifying thought came to me that I could die this way. I could go down in the annals of criminal history as the unworthy assistant who was suffocated by the large and soft derriere of the world's greatest detective.

Dimly, as though from the end of a long tunnel, I heard the man's voice say: "Well, good day to ye, sir. Perhaps I'll see ye at the hangin' tomorrow."

"Depend on it, sir," replied Mr. Wong. "I will be there."

A few moments passed then—oh blessed relief!—my employer took a step away from me, glanced over his shoulder and said: "Come now, Chance, pick the lock quickly. For pity's sake, no more dawdling, child."

I took a few deep breaths of welcome air and my head began to clear.

"Bear with me, sir," I gasped. "The door will be open very soon."

This time, fearing that I might once again be crushed by my employer's huge bulk should someone else enter the alley, I worked with a will and very quickly managed to tumble the spring bolt so that the lock clicked open.

I reached up to the brass door handle and pulled on

it, wriggling free of Mr. Wong as the door swung in my direction.

"Sir, I believe we may now enter," I said, rising to my feet.

"Oh dear," returned my employer with feeling. "This is most irregular and, I fear, very much against the law."

I opened the door wider and slipped inside, Mr. Wong opening it wider still to allow the passage of his mighty physique.

Once we were both safely inside, I quietly closed the door and looked around me.

Despite the fact that the hands of the railroad clock on the wall pointed to just fifteen minutes past noon, the gloominess of the day had plunged most of the bank into darkness. But now and then a flash of lightning illuminated the room and the metal grilles at the teller stations cast shadows on the far wall, like stark, black prison bars.

It was a melancholy scene, the loud tick-tock of the clock adding a somber counterpoint, and my body trembled with a shudder of nameless dread.

In the threatening darkness I could not but recall the voice at the livery stable, and half-expected to hear that raspy whisper come out of a dark corner, full of malice and vile obscenity.

"What now?" Mr. Wong asked softly.

"Now we visit the office of Mr. Ben Cranwell," I replied.

My employer gulped loudly and, his voice unsteady, said: "Chance, this isn't right. This is burglary of the very worst kind."

"No, sir," I replied humbly. "I believe this is called investigation."

I opened the partition at the counter and quietly laid it flat, then beckoned for Mr. Wong to follow. The great detective reluctantly pointed his belly at the gap in the counter and propelled himself forward.

CLAAANG!

A brass cuspidor went tumbling across the wood floor, accidentally kicked by my employer's toe, since he had great difficulty seeing his feet due to his quite exceptional portliness.

"Shhh, sir." I put my finger to my lips. "We must be very quiet."

"Damn it, Chance," whispered Mr. Wong in great agitation. "I wasn't meant to skulk around in the dark like a common criminal."

"Let us proceed," I said, ignoring the great detective's outburst. "Softly now."

The door to Cranwell's office wasn't locked and we made our way inside, Mr. Wong's head swiveling this way and that as though he expected the little banker to appear at any moment and demand to know what we were doing there.

I walked over to Cranwell's desk. If the maps were in the bank, they'd be here.

A sudden flash of lightning bathed the office in stark white light, and behind the little banker's chair the picture that hung on the wall seemed to come to life as the thunder crashed.

I hadn't really noticed the picture on our last visit—a painting of a stern and exceptionally hairy Civil War officer in a Union uniform—but now his blazing eyes

bored into me, apparently outraged by this unwarranted intrusion.

Walking closer to the painting, I studied the brass
plate on the bottom of the frame. It read: BRIG. GEN.
EBENEZER DEAKINS. 101ST. MASS. INF.

This soldier must have been one of Ben Cranwell's
close relatives, and he looked to be a harsh and un-
bending man.

"Come, Chance," my employer whispered.
"There's no time to dawdle. Let's look for the maps
and be gone, for I fear we're in the utmost peril of
being discovered."

With the general looking down on me in disapproval, I quickly searched the drawers of Cranwell's
desk. There were no maps. If it was Cranwell who had
climbed into Billy's room, he had taken the maps with
him, and may have by this time destroyed them.

But in the top drawer, amid a jumble of papers, I
discovered something that shook me to the core and
made the hairs on the back of my neck rise.

There were three bottles, each full of a silvery liquid, and I immediately recognized them for what they
were. On our first visit to the banker's office, I had
caught a glimpse of Cranwell shoving a bottle into his
drawer and at the time thought it might be whiskey
and that he was a secret drinker.

But these bottles did not contain liquor—they were
filled with something much more sinister, and suddenly many things began to fall into place.

In that instant, as the lightning flashed outside and
the thunder rumbled angrily, I realized there could
well be a deranged monster on the loose—and that he
was without doubt homicidal and very dangerous.

I had seen the silvery liquid the bottles contained once before—on the lecture podium of my dear old school's resident physician, the beloved Dr. Hans.

Dr. Hans—we young ladies were never allowed to know his last name—was an old and valued friend of our headmistress, Miss Chastity Charmaine. Indeed, the doctor had previously been medical consultant to her earlier establishment, an institution for genteel young ladies located on the San Francisco waterfront.

Dr. Hans was very learned on those disorders peculiar to the weaker sex, and he was an expert on the social diseases that were then rampant along the West Coast, brought to our shores by sailors who had sampled the delightful, if tainted, fruit of distant and exotic lands.

Miss Charmaine, ever solicitous of our welfare, warned we young ladies that the ardent and suitable suitor, could, by close inspection, be deemed disease free and therefore allowed to press his suit.

"This examination, which only takes a few moments and in no way destroys the amorous mood, can be conducted before any penetration is permitted," she told us one morning at breakfast. "It is known in the hooking profession as 'a short-arm inspection' and should never be overlooked by the genteel young lady, even in the heat of passion."

Miss Charmaine, bless her kind heart, then motioned toward Dr. Hans with her bourbon glass. "The good doctor here will give a lecture on the social diseases later this morning, and will describe in detail what signs and symptoms you must look for in the course of any precoital inspection."

Dear Dr. Hans was a wonderful man who had received his MD from the University of Heidelberg, but at the time he joined our school he was somewhat under a cloud, since he was very much wanted by the law.

Alas, it seemed that the great physician had been caught in the bed of one of his patients, and, as he so quaintly put it, "was in the very throes of the short strokes," when the bedroom door was thrown open and the lady's husband entered, a huge brute of a longshoreman wielding a large and murderous club.

The doctor, who was never very far from his trusty Derringer, eluded the first blow of the club, then shot the man neatly between the eyes. Dr. Hans then thought it prudent to flee San Francisco, the law barking at his heels, and for a while dropped the practice of medicine, turning instead to the gambling profession.

When he heard that Miss Charmaine had established yet another institution for young ladies, this time in Boston, he applied for the post as physician-in-residence and was welcomed most warmly.

Our dear headmistress did let it be known that the doctor had once been caught "in the act" so to speak, and was, as a result, a wanted man.

"And for what?" she asked. "Does not a veterinarian, when he has cured a horse of what ails it, try the animal out to make sure it's sound? All dear Dr. Hans did was to trot a young filly around the corral a few times to reassure himself that she was once again fit to be under saddle. If only her brute of a husband had known our house physician was doing him a great favor. But he didn't, and, alas, he reaped the bitter consequences of his ignorance."

And it was dear Dr. Hans, during one of his lectures, who first brought the silvery liquid in the bottle to my attention, and now I instantly knew it for what it was.

"What is in those bottles you're studying so closely?" asked Mr. Wong, walking to my side.

"Sir," I said, "did not Sheriff Havenick mention that there was a doctor in Crow Creek?"

My employer thought for a moment, then nodded. "Yes, Dawson, Dobson . . . something like that."

"Lawson," I said, snapping my fingers.

"What of it?"

"Sir, we must go talk to him without a moment's delay. There is no time to be lost."

"But why, Chance?" asked Mr. Wong, and I could see that he was on the point of getting himself worked up into a highly agitated state.

"Sir, I believe there could be a very dangerous murderer on the loose like a wolf among sheep. He is a man so deranged that he could have completely lost his grip on reality and that he will kill again and again if he is not stopped."

"You mean Mr. Cranwell? Or is there someone else?"

I shook my head at the perplexed Mr. Wong. "Sir, I will answer that question only after we've spoken to Dr. Lawson."

Hurriedly I left Cranwell's office and rushed to the front door of the bank, my employer following at his best rate of speed.

I opened the door and stuck my head outside, studying the rain-swept alley. I felt Mr. Wong beside me and he too put his head through the open door above mine.

"All clear?" he asked, anxiously looking up and down the narrow little street.

"Yes," I said. "Now, let's leave quickly."

As fast as we could, we exited the bank and I pulled the door closed.

"Aren't you going to lock it?" asked my employer.

"Sir, there is no time. But I believe Mr. Cranwell's assets are safe."

"This," said Mr. Wong, "is highly irregular."

"But necessary, sir," I said as I walked toward the main street. "I fear the clock is running out on us and that the killer of Victoria Grant, Silas Lime, and the poor Teton Kid will add another death to his grim total very soon."

SEVENTEEN

A passing miner, soaked through with rain and annoyed at being stopped by our question, pointed the way to the doctor's office, a low, white-painted house near the railroad tracks with a corral and small barn in back, no doubt for Lawson's horse and buggy.

We crossed the mired street, my oversized oilskins trailing in the mud, and walked toward the physician's house, apparently a combination home and consulting office.

If anything the rain was getting heavier, and it fairly bounced off my shoulders and hat as I struggled, head bent against the rising wind, alongside the tracks.

At last, after considerable effort, Mr. Wong and I stood on the doctor's porch. Above our heads, suspended from a beam with chains, a sign read, THOS. J. LAWSON MD, and reassured, I rapped on the door.

There was no answer.

I rapped again, this time harder.

Still no answer.

"Here, let me try for heaven's sake," said Mr. Wong testily. He raised his dragon-headed cane and banged hard on the door several times.

"Hold your horses, hold your horses," came a cracked and tremulous voice from somewhere inside. "I can hear you."

The door opened wide and a small, white-haired old man stood there in a vest and slippers, the neck of his collarless shirt open. He carried a newspaper in his hand and peered at us over the top of rimless half glasses.

"What can I do for you?" he asked, after giving Mr. Wong and myself a quick inspection.

"We'd like to talk to you, Doctor," I said, after I'd made the necessary introductions.

"So, Last Chance Lee, is it?" the physician asked. "Pregnant, are ye?" He nodded at my employer. "Is this great hulking lout the father?"

"My dear sir," spluttered Mr. Wong, outraged, "how dare you even suggest such a thing. This young lady is my ward."

"Eh?" asked the old man, cupping a hand to his right ear.

"Sir," I said quickly, "we wish to talk to you."

"Eh?"

"We wish to talk to you!" I yelled.

"No need to shout, I can hear you," the old doctor said. He studied us both for a few moments, then added reluctantly. "Come inside, both of ye."

Dr. Lawson led us past his parlor, where there was a cheery fire burning, and into a cold and gloomy room at the rear of his home.

"This is my surgery," he said. "We can talk here."

A padded leather couch, apparently for his patients, took up the middle of the floor. There were a few chairs scattered around the room and the walls were bare but for the doctor's diploma, from a fairly good Eastern university.

In one corner stood a grinning skeleton on a stand, a battered Stetson hat on its yellow skull. Following my eyes, Dr. Lawson smiled grimly and said: "That there is Sad Sammy Sinclair. He was hung for a horse thief here in Crow Creek in the summer of 'eighty-nine, and I claimed his body." He walked over to the skeleton, grabbed an arm and made the dry bones rattle. "Needed this for my practice, you see." He lifted the hat off the dreadful thing's head. "This was his. Claimed that, too." Dr. Lawson looked me up and down, his shrewd old eyes finally coming to rest on my belly, hidden under my oilskins. "So," he said, "you think you're pregnant, do ye?"

"I'm not pregnant," I said.

"Eh?"

"I'm not pregnant!"

"Well, why did you come here?" He glanced at Mr. Wong. "Is it him? He looks well enough to me. At least he's eating regular."

"Sir, I am not sick. I am never sick," said my employer pompously, and he went into a little display, shuffling his feet and bobbing his sleek head to show how perfectly fit he was.

"Eh?"

"I'm not sick!" roared my employer, adding in an annoyed whisper, "You deaf old coot."

"You have the croup?" asked Dr. Lawson.

"No, I—"

"Please, Doctor, I must talk to you," I interrupted.

"Talk away," the old man said. "But my consulting

fee is two dollars." He gave Mr. Wong a distrustful look and added: "In advance."

With a long-suffering sigh my employer dug into his pocket and came up with two silver dollars, placing them in the doctor's open palm. The old man bit each one, then salted them away in his vest pocket.

"Now," he said, "what can I do fer ye?"

I reached into the pockets of my oilskins and produced the three silver bottles, lining them up in a row at the bottom of the couch.

"Have you ever seen these before?"

"Eh?"

The doctor's face was stricken and I saw a glint of something that could be concern, or even fear, in his washed-out blue eyes.

"Have you ever seen these before?"

The old man threw up his hands. "Wait," he said. "Hold on there just a durned minute."

He rushed out of the room, then returned after a few moments, an ear trumpet in his hands. He put the trumpet against his right ear and said: "Now, young lady, what did you say?"

"Have you ever—"

Dr. Lawson winced and jerked the trumpet from his ear. "Not so loud! I can hear pretty good with this goldurned thing."

"Doctor," I said in a more normal tone, speaking directly into the bell of the trumpet, "have you ever seen these before?"

"Why are you asking me these questions?" the old man asked suspiciously. He turned to Mr. Wong. "You're that private detective feller Angela Hudson hired, aren't you?"

"Indeed," said my employer.

"Eh?"

"*Yes I am!*" yelled Mr. Wong.

"Well, I saw that paleontologist gal's body, and mister, if Brad Hudson was her murderer, he deserves to hang."

There was a note of uncertainty in the old man's voice, as though he was holding something back, something he didn't want to confront, even in his own mind.

"That's why we're here, Doctor," I said into the trumpet. "We believe Mr. Hudson is innocent and that the man who owns these bottles could be the guilty party."

"Where did you get these?" the old man asked, picking up one of the bottles and examining it closely.

"From Ben Cranwell's office."

The old man did not ask how we got the bottles, but merely nodded. Then, speaking almost to himself, he said: "They're all full, and that means he hasn't been using them. I reckon he knows it's already too late, that he's too far gone."

"Tell us about Ben Cranwell," I urged.

The doctor shook his head at me. "Young lady, I never discuss a patient with anyone. Besides being a private matter, it's unethical and could get me struck off the physician's list."

"Sir," I said, "an innocent man's life is at stake here. Brad Hudson has a date with the hangman's noose at dawn tomorrow down by the cottonwoods along the creek. We just don't have time to discuss ethics."

"Ben Cranwell is a fine man, well respected in this town," Lawson said, straightening up and dropping his folksy old country doctor act. "He supplied the money to build the schoolhouse and he's putting up all the cash for a church we're planning to build next spring. Without Ben Cranwell and his bank, Crow Creek wouldn't exist. Young lady, I won't say a single word against him."

"Doctor Lawson," I said evenly, "you just said Ben Cranwell was too far gone. What did you mean by that? Sir, you must tell us all you know about his medical condition."

"Damn you!" the old man snapped. "Damn you for being here! You'll destroy everything." The physician angrily yanked the trumpet from his ear, walked over to a small cupboard affixed to one wall and opened it. He reached inside and took out a bottle of bourbon and a couple of glasses.

"Nowadays I keep this handy for my more nervous patients," he said, breathing deeply as he fought to keep his anger in check. "But back in the old days I used it as an anesthetic on Sunday mornings when I was digging bullets out of perforated cowboys." He held up the bottle. "Anyone?" Both Mr. Wong and I shook our heads, and the old man said: "Well, I'm sure you don't mind if I do."

Dr. Lawson poured three fingers of whiskey into a glass and gulped it down in a single draught. He shuddered as the hot fire of the bourbon hit his belly, then palmed the cork back into the bottle and found a chair and carried it close to me and sat down.

The old man buried his face in his hands for a few long moments, and when he finally looked up it seemed like he'd aged a dozen years. The lines on his face had deepened and he was very pale.

"What do you want to know?" he sighed.

"Everything," I replied. "We must know everything."

"You're asking me to betray a trust. You're asking me to destroy a man, a fine man."

"Doctor," I said, anger edging my voice. "If Brad Hudson hangs, I'll bring a United States marshal to Crow Creek and live to see you charged as an accomplice to the cold-blooded murder of an innocent rancher. You'll be as guilty as any drunken lout who ever formed part of a lynch mob. You'll have murdered Mr. Hudson, not with a rope, but with your silence."

"Are you threatening me?" Lawson asked, the hatred in his eyes a living, growing thing.

"Yes, Doctor," I said. "I'm doing just that."

The old man studied my face for a few long moments, trying to determine the strength of my resolve. I believe what he saw scared him, because he let out a strangled sound that was half groan, half sigh and asked: "Young lady, in your opinion, is Brad Hudson a madman?"

The doctor's question took me by surprise. I shook my head at him, then said into the trumpet: "No. I believe the rancher as sane as you and I."

The old man nodded. "Victoria Grant was murdered by a madman. I did the autopsy on her body and she'd been raped and torn apart, as though by a vicious wild animal." His faded eyes looked up at me. "The question now is: Who in Crow Creek is mad? Who could be completely insane?"

I nodded: "I believe I know the answer to that question. But I want to hear it from you."

"I believe there is someone whose brain is so rotted he's no longer capable of rational thought. He could be mad. He could be stark, raving mad yet so sly, he can hide it from others and put up a front that seems perfectly sane."

The old doctor picked up one of the bottles. "This man—no names, mind—has stopped using the medication I prescribed for him. This medication is topical, that is, you rub it over your skin. But this individual is no longer using it, as the full bottles indicate. He must know he is beyond a cure and I believe he is now teetering on the brink of disaster."

"Chance, ask him what's in the bottles," Mr. Wong ordered, adding loftily: "I refuse to yell at the old coot."

"Sir," I replied, "I can answer your question. The bottles contain mercury, the most modern and effective treatment for syphilis."

"Syphilis!" exclaimed the great detective. "Are you telling me that Ben Cranwell is suffering from that terrible disease?"

"Yes, sir," I replied. "I learned a great deal about the dread ailment at my dear old school."

"For heaven's sake!" exploded Mr. Wong, his round face flushed. "What did they teach you at that place?" He held up a hand. "I know, don't tell me, many things, right?"

"Sir," I said softly, modestly lowering my eyes, "my education was most complete."

"Hmm," said my employer, rubbing his chin thoughtfully.

"This man I was telling you about," interrupted Dr. Lawson, who now seemed eager to talk. "He began to suffer from complete mental breakdown about two years ago. I diagnosed his condition as paretic neurosyphilis, also known as the general paralysis of the insane. The mercury treatment was all I had to offer, all medical science has to offer. Typically the insanity begins gradually as behavioral changes in people in their early forties, as this man was a couple of years ago, and it gets worse from there."

The old doctor thought for a couple of moments then added: "The physical symptoms are an odd, moth-eaten appearance accompanied by hunching of the shoulders as the disease begins to break down the body's bone structure."

So that's why Cranwell looks like a hunchback, I thought.

"Doctor," I said, in my eagerness my mouth was very close to the trumpet, "Jenny Pearson was murdered two years ago, about the time your patient's mental breakdown first began."

"Yes . . . yes, I am aware of that," the old man said quietly.

"And you did the autopsy on her body?"

"Yes, I did. She was a beautiful young girl and she'd been raped, torn apart."

A surge of anger rising in me, I pulled the ear trumpet from Dr. Lawson's hand and threw it against the wall. The trumpet was made of thin porcelain and it shattered into a thousand pieces, showering Mr. Wong with fragments.

"Doctor, you're no more deaf than I am," I said hotly. "You knew why we were here, and you just didn't want to answer our questions. You pretended to be deaf, hoping we'd give up and go away."

"But how . . . how . . . ?"

I walked over to where Mr. Wong was standing and picked up a roll of dollar bills. "When I got close to the trumpet, I saw these shoved inside. My guess is someone paid you for treatment and you stuffed the bills inside the trumpet for safekeeping, then forgot about them. The trumpet was blocked, so it didn't take a genius to realize that it wasn't doing you any good." My hands on my hips, I stepped close to the old man. "Doc, you may be absentminded, but you're not deaf."

The old physician hung his head. "I knew you might come here." He nodded toward my employer. "I reckoned if the fat man there was half the detective he's rumored to be, he'd eventually figure things out and maybe come looking for me."

"Sir," said Mr. Wong in considerable pique, "I am portly to be sure, the ideal state for a man, but fat I am not."

"Doctor," I said, letting my employer stew for a while, "you must have made a connection between the deaths of Jenny Pearson and Victoria Grant."

"Yes, I did."

"And who did you suspect?"

"I knew Ben—I mean, I realized this man I was telling you about was mentally unbalanced, maybe dangerously so, but even then I didn't allow myself to suspect him. I refused to entertain the possibility that he was capable of such horrible crimes. He and I were on the vigilante committee back in the old days and when I rode with him he was considered a brave and honorable citizen. I just couldn't bring myself to even think that this man was a rapist and a killer."

"Young Billy Havenick was found bending over Jenny's body. Would you have spoken up if he'd been accused of her murder?"

The old doctor looked up at me, his eyes hard. "Maybe. But there are many Billy Havenicks in this world, and few like this man."

I let that cold statement pass, and asked: "If this man you're talking about murdered both young woman, why on earth would he do such a thing? Would it be for mere sexual gratification?"

"Chance!" Mr. Wong protested, shocked. "That is not the language a young lady should use."

"Sir, I most humbly apologize," I returned. "But we must get to the heart of the matter."

"The madness of paretic neurosyphilis manifests itself in different ways," Dr. Lawson said, his face bleak. "The disease turned Ivan the Terrible of Russia from a benign, Renaissance monarch into a neurotic, suspicious, and homicidal monster who murdered his own son, believing he was plotting against him. In this man's case—"

"Ben Cranwell's case, let's cut right to the chase, Doctor," I snapped.

The old man sighed. "Ben Cranwell caught his terrifying disease from a female. It's possible he now harbors an irrational hatred for all women, blaming them for his condition. Starting two years ago with Jenny Pearson, that hatred could have driven him to rape and kill. Notice I say 'could have.' I'm not saying Ben is guilty. But if he is, he considers what's he's doing a reckoning. It's his revenge on all women, and the more feminine and pretty they are, the more he's likely to target them."

"Doctor," I said, "why didn't you tell all this to Sheriff Havenick? Why did you not mention it at Brad Hudson's trial?"

The old man shook his head at me. "Until I saw those full bottles of mercury, I didn't realize Ben was quite so far gone." He looked into my eyes. "Young lady, you have to believe me, up until you knocked on my door and brought these bottles, I just couldn't allow myself to think that a fine man like Ben Cranwell could be a killer."

"Doctor, you've been a healer and played God for so long, you've lost your own grasp on reality," I said, anger edging my voice. "It could be that in the eyes of heaven, poor, simple Billy Havenick has more right to exist than a dozen Ben Cranwells."

"Let this go," Lawson pleaded. "Just walk away from it and get back on the train for New York or wherever you came from. You people don't understand the West. You don't understand towns like Crow Creek. A community like this, it lives or dies by a man like Ben Cranwell. Before he came here, this town was dying. It's his bank, his money that keeps us all going. He's our lifeblood, and there isn't a man within a hundred miles who doesn't owe him one way or another." The old man's tired, disturbed eyes sought mine, silently pleading. "Please, please think about it. What was a silly young girl with not a thought in her head but clothes and boys, and an uppity female scientist to this community? Nothing, nothing at all. Ben Cranwell may be mad, but let him be, I tell you. Let this town be."

I made no reply to the old man but walked to the surgery door and opened it.

"What will you do now?" the doctor asked anxiously as I made to leave, Mr. Wong trailing after me.

"Find Sheriff Havenick and ask him to arrest Ben Cranwell for the murder of Jenny Pearson, Victoria Grant, and Silas Lime, and for complicity in the death of the Teton Kid."

Lawson laughed, a harsh cackle. "Silas Lime was a hopeless opium addict. He was no great loss."

"And I suppose Ben Cranwell gave him money to support his addiction?" I asked.

The old man nodded. "He was beholdin' to Ben, as all the folks are around these parts."

"Thank you, Doctor," I said. "You've been most helpful."

Angrily the physician jumped to his feet, his slight old body quivering with rage. "Damn you!" he yelled. "Damn you both for coming here. Destroy Ben Cranwell and you destroy this town. You destroy me! Don't you see that?"

"Doctor," I said, "like Silas Lime, you and Crow Creek will be no great loss."

EIGHTEEN

My employer and I left the doctor's house and trudged through the mud toward the sheriff's office. The great detective was lost in thought, no doubt pondering the ramifications of Ben Cranwell's apparent guilt in this matter and I did not think it wise to interrupt his reverie.

The rain was hammering down out of low clouds, and in the distance by the cottonwoods the creek was threatening to overflow its banks. Foaming white crests showed on the surging water as it carried debris from its high source in the far mountains, great skeletal tree branches and the slender trunks of felled pines tumbling like matchsticks in the powerful torrent. Even from where we walked in the street, I could hear the roar of the swollen creek as the mustard-colored water raced along. The flood was still confined within the high cutbanks, but it was perilously close to running over into town if there was no break in the downpour.

No one was abroad in the street except Mr. Wong and me, a fact shrewdly noted by the great investigator when he at last broke his silence.

"Everyone is probably at lunch," he said wistfully. "Where we should be, Chance."

"Alas, sir," I replied, "I fear we have no time to eat, not while this case hangs in the balance."

A shadow of disappointment crossed my employer's face. "I suppose you're right, but I'm in danger of wasting away," he observed gloomily. "It seems I've been slowly starving to death since I first set foot in this jerkwater town."

We reached the sheriff's office and, after shooing a sleeping dog from the front of the door, walked inside.

Havenick had his feet up on his desk, a dime novel in his hands, but he set it down and rose quickly when we entered. "So, it's the great private eyes," he said. "Come to see Hudson for the last time? If'n you are, you'll have to wait your turn. Right now he's with the preacher makin' plans for the sweet by an' by."

"Sheriff," I said quickly, "as much as we'd like to talk to poor Mr. Hudson, we're here on a matter of even greater urgency. I'm happy to say that Mr. Wong—as a result of his diligent detection—has much to report."

My employer nodded, smiled, and waved a dismissive hand, as though I'd clearly stated his value as a criminologist and his dedication to duty. "You inform the sheriff of our conclusions, Chance," he said loftily. "That is the task of an assistant."

Havenick walked to the stove and lifted the coffeepot, motioning with it in our direction as his eyebrows rose in a question.

"Please," I said, but Mr. Wong said he did not care for coffee.

The sheriff put a steaming tin cup in my hand and I sipped the bitter black brew gratefully. I badly wanted a cheroot, but I'd left them in my room. Besides, Mr. Wong would have been shocked if I'd smoked in his presence and might have confiscated the whole box.

"Is this about the missing maps?" Havenick asked, perching himself on the corner of his desk.

"Yes," I replied, "but there is much more."

"Then shoot the breeze. Let's hear it."

Quickly I outlined the events of the morning, sparing no details about our entering the bank and not finding the maps but discovering the full bottles of mercury. I told the stunned lawman about our visit with Dr. Lawson and how the old physician, very reluctantly, stated that Ben Cranwell could be insane and dangerously homicidal.

"The doctor says it's possible that Mr. Cranwell could be responsible for the deaths of Jenny Pearson and Victoria Grant, to say nothing of Silas Lime and the Teton Kid," I finished.

Sheriff Havenick sat and stared at me in disbelief, his long jaw dropped on to his chest. "You . . . you . . . " he struggled, and found himself unable to finish.

After a few moments of stunned silence he tried again. "You . . . broke . . . into . . . the . . . bank?"

"Yes, we did," I said. "I picked the lock and then this farmer came and I almost got suffocated and Mr. Wong was talking to him and my face was jammed against the door and the farmer said—"

"I mean . . . you robbed the bank?" Havenick's face was a study in shocked disbelief.

"No, Sheriff," I smiled sweetly. "We entered the bank, but we didn't rob it."

"But that's still burglary. I could get you twenty years for that."

"My sentiments exactly, Sheriff," intoned Mr. Wong pompously. "But the young will not listen to wiser, older heads who advise caution. Certainly they receive advice, but few profit from it."

"Sheriff," I said, "how we discovered those full bottles of mercury is, at this moment, neither here nor there. If you want to charge us with bank robbery, do it after Brad Hudson walks out of here a free man."

Havenick rose to his feet, his eyes hard. "Oh yes, we will speak of this later, depend on it. We will talk at great length, believe me."

The big lawman studied Mr. Wong and myself in silence, then seemed to make up his mind about something. "What you're telling me about Ben Cranwell doesn't mean a thing. So he's got the clap real bad an' it's snapped a link in his trace chain, that still don't prove he killed them women."

"No it doesn't, Sheriff," I said, "but we did find part of his belt at the murder scene. And that's why we have to go to his home and look for the maps that were stolen from Billy's room. If Cranwell gave Billy a map that led to Jenny Pearson, poor thing, then he knew exactly where the girl's body was located."

"Billy says the only maps he had were ones drawn up by me," Havenick said. "That puts a big hole in your theory."

I pushed my sou'wester hat up from my eyes. "Billy is scared. He doesn't know what he's saying. I believe Cranwell has that map and if we can find it, it's evidence enough to tie him to Jenny's murder. I know it doesn't link him to the murder of Victoria Grant, but both killings were so similar I think it should sow enough doubt in your mind to at least postpone Mr. Hudson's hanging."

Havenick sipped his coffee, his face troubled.

"Little lady, your talk is full of ifs an' buts n' maybes an' it's a mite short on facts."

"Sheriff—" I began.

But the lawman cut me short. "Let me be," he snapped. "I'm studyin' on this some."

A few moments passed, the silence punctuated by the rattle of the rain on the roof and the distant rumble of thunder.

Finally Havenick laid his cup on his desk, grabbed his yellow slicker from a nail behind the door, and took down a Winchester rifle from the gun rack. "Let's go talk to Ben Cranwell," he said. "And take a look-a-here at them maps if he has them."

Once outside, Havenick glanced up at the dark sky and remarked that the little banker's place was a ten-minute horse ride outside of town. "It's too far to walk in this weather," he said. "Where's that damn Model T auto-mobile of yours?"

I told him it was behind Ma's restaurant and we trudged miserably through the mud and rain to the car. Havenick and Mr. Wong immediately climbed inside under the welcome shelter of the canvas top, then after the few moments it took for the men to settle themselves, my employer leaned out the door and said imperiously: "Chance, you may start her up when ready. Don't dawdle now."

I cranked the handle, the cold rain battering off my oilskins finding its way down the back of my neck and between my breasts, but the car steadfastly refused to start.

After a dozen futile attempts, Havenick stuck his head out the door and suggested helpfully that I try cranking just a half-turn at a time.

"An excellent recommendation, Sheriff," said Mr. Wong, who had his head out the other side. "Try that at once, Chance. And no dawdling now."

I did as the sheriff said, and after maybe two dozen half-turns on the handle, the Ford gave an asthmatic cough and spluttered into life.

"Works every time," Havenick told Mr. Wong. "But, of course," he added, nodding his head wisely, "you have to put your back into it."

"Did your hear that, child?" asked my employer as, soaking wet and exhausted I climbed behind the wheel. "That's something to store away in your mind for the future. Put your back into it, Chance. That's the secret."

"I will try to remember that, sir," I said, driving toward the corner of the restaurant. I suddenly yanked the wheel to the right, much more than needed to get around the corner and back into the street, so that Mr. Wong's great bulk fell heavily against Havenick, crushing the sheriff so hard against the car door that he let out a gasping bellow of pain.

"So sorry, Sheriff," I said sweetly, "I was so busy remembering your advice that, silly me, I quite forgot how to drive."

Ben Cranwell's house was a large, rambling structure set close to the trail from town. It was painted white, with a picket fence outside, and was shaded by a huge and ancient oak tree. There was a small barn at the back of the property and a neatly planked corral.

Sheriff Havenick peered through the mud-splashed windshield as we drew close. "I don't see his buggy," he said. "And that big American horse of his has took a sudden notion to stand in the rain, but I don't see him neither."

"Is that the horse I saw in the corral near the bank?" I asked.

"Yeah," Havenick replied. "Ben keeps it there when he's in town."

I braked the car outside Cranwell's house and we walked up to the front door.

"I don't think he's to home," Havenick said, trying to peer through the panel of plain frosted glass set into the top half of the door.

He rapped on the door several times, muted booms that echoed hollowly inside the house. We waited, but heard no sound of feet coming to answer our knock.

"Like I said," Havenick sighed, "he ain't to home."

"Sheriff, we must get those maps," I reminded him urgently.

The big lawman tried the door, which was locked, then shook his head at me. "Lady, if he ain't to home, he ain't to home. We'll have to come back later. Besides, Ben may have taken the maps with him, that is, if he even has them."

"This is most inconvenient," said Mr. Wong, "most inconvenient indeed. There's no telling when he'll be back."

I stood there, somewhere between anger and

amazement, stunned by the fact that two grown men—one the world's greatest detective, the other a tough, gunfighting cow-town sheriff—could believe themselves stalled by a locked door, most of it glass.

There was no time for the niceties of lock-picking, but thank goodness for my wonderful old school and my dear Okinawan kung fu instructor!

As the two men turned to leave, I stepped quickly up to the door. I pivoted on my left leg, let out a mighty, *"Kiai!"* and side snap-kicked the door with my right, using the whole bottom of my foot as a battering ram. This kick is devastating and is normally used against human opponents, being delivered to the groin, knee, rib cage, solar plexus, or throat. But it does, from experience, take out even the stoutest door quite nicely.

In fact, probably due to my being more than a little vexed, my kick splintered the door completely away from the frame taking a three-foot length of timber with it. At the same time there was a loud *CRASH!* as the glass shattered into a thousand pieces followed by *BANG!* as what was left of the door slammed hard against the wall.

The pulverized portal was now hanging wide open and askew on just one of its hinges as I bowed politely, my eyes modestly cast to the ground, and said most humbly: "Sirs, I believe we may now enter."

Sheriff Havenick looked at me in horror. "What . . . did . . . you . . . do?" he gasped.

"This," I said politely, extending my right hand toward the doorway. "I opened the door."

"Chance," said Mr. Wong, his face betraying even more horror than that of the sheriff's, "this is hoodlum behavior. I declare, it's . . . it's . . . breaking and entering."

"This, sir," I said, "is investigation."

I walked inside, leaving my employer and his stunned companion to follow me or not.

Cranwell's parlor lay to the right of a long hallway. As far as I could see when I popped my head inside, it was unremarkable, looking like any other middle-class parlor at that time and place. It was, however, quite masculine, lacking the woman's touch. There were no flowers in pretty vases and the bare legs of the piano were without the embroidered bloomers women sew for modesty's sake. A gun rack holding half a dozen rifles and shotguns occupied most of one wall, where a woman would have hung a picture, and the scuffed wood floor was badly in need of varnish and wax.

Of the missing maps, there was no sign.

"I don't like this," Havenick said as he stood beside me. "What do we do if Ben Cranwell comes home?"

"You might try shooting him, Sheriff," I said.

With Havenick and Mr. Wong—who was wringing his hands in anguish and seemed most agitated—following in my footsteps, I searched the entire downstairs of the house and found nothing. "Now we go up," I said, as self-assuredly as I could, but I felt my confidence waning as the fruitless search continued.

"Little lady," declared the sheriff sternly, "you'd better pray we find them maps an' they tell us something. If'n we don't, you're facing charges of bank robbery an' breaking and entering. An' believe me, the judge is gonna toss you in the juzgado an' throw away the key."

With those melancholy words ringing in my ears, I climbed the staircase and stopped on the landing while the men caught up with me.

"Bedroom's up here, I guess," Havenick said. "Now I feel like we're really invading Ben Cranwell's privacy."

"So do I," declared Mr. Wong in a great state of agitation, and he did a little strut and wrung his hands even more to show how distressed he was.

"Sirs, we are invading Cranwell's privacy," I said. "But I believe our cause is a worthy one."

"It had better be," Havenick said ominously. "If it ain't, we're in a heap of trouble."

There were two bedrooms upstairs, neither of which looked as if it had been used for a long while—but no sign of the maps in either.

"This, I'm afraid," declared Mr. Wong piteously, "has been a fool's errand."

In the second and smaller of the two rooms, a large oak armoire stood against the wall just to the left of the door. I stepped over to it and opened the door wide. It was empty but for a ragged frock coat that had seen much wear hanging from the rail on a hanger.

Bending, I opened the drawer at the bottom of the armoire and slid it open. It contained a large wooden box and several leather belts, each coiled neatly, and an empty .45-caliber cartridge box. The drawer smelled of gun oil, and when I opened the box I saw that its green velvet interior had been designed to hold two short-barreled Colts. Both guns were gone.

I quickly unrolled the belts. One was identical to

the belt Havenick was wearing—but the arrowhead-shaped silver tip was gone.

I reached into my skirt pocket and found the tip, and it matched the shape of the belt exactly.

"Hey, let me see that," the sheriff said.

He took the belt and studied it closely. "It's an exact match for mine," he said. "This is the other belt Brad Hudson had made up, the one he gave to Ben Cranwell."

I nodded. "And Cranwell was wearing it when he raped and killed Victoria Grant. Somehow, in the struggle, the silver tip was torn loose and he didn't notice it was gone until it was too late. By then it had been buried by the mud falling into the dinosaur dig."

Havenick shook his head. "I'm starting to get buffaloed by all this. It just don't make any sense. Ben Cranwell isn't a killer. I'd stake my life on that."

"You may have to, Sheriff," I said. I glanced around the room. "And I'll tell you something else, this room doesn't make any sense. There's something very strange going on here."

We were in the bedroom at the back of the house, its windows overlooking the barn and corral. The room was small, too small. Judging by the parlor downstairs, which shared the common wall at the gable end of the house, I calculated that this room should have been at least four feet longer.

I walked quickly to the wall, where there was a bed and a small dresser, and tapped on it. I didn't hear the solid thunk of solid wood, but a hollow sound.

"Sheriff," I said, "I believe this is a false wall and that a hidden chamber lies beyond."

Havenick thumped on the wall with his fist. "Sure does sound hollow."

"And look!" I pointed to some tiny clumps of mud that lay on the floor where it met the wall. "How could mud from a person's feet get that close to the wall? Unless—"

"Unless this wall opens somehow," Havenick said quickly.

"Let me see, make way there," declared Mr. Wong importantly, thrusting his great belly between the sheriff and me. "Is this another one of your"—he sighed—"clues, Chance?"

"Sir," I replied, "we believe there is a secret chamber behind this wall."

"I," said my employer, "will be the judge of that."

He rapped on the wall with his cane, being rewarded with a hollow boom, boom, boom, like someone beating on a bass drum.

"There is," declared Mr. Wong loftily, "a hidden concavity behind this wall that we will investigate at once." He turned and addressed Sheriff Havenick. "Quick, officer, draw your revolver. We must be prepared for any danger that lies within."

The sheriff pulled his Colt, a slick, practiced movement that reminded me of dear professors Masterson and Leslie, and asked: "How do we get in there? An' suppose it's just a place where Ben Cranwell hides his money?"

"That's what we're here to find out, Sheriff," I said, pushing on the wall at various places. There was no give anywhere and I stood back, completely frustrated.

The house was uncomfortably hot and close, and I

quickly removed my heavy oilskins. Unfortunately as I struggled out of the coat, the neckline of my peasant blouse slipped, showing rather more breast and lotus blossom tattoo than I cared to reveal, at least all at once.

"Oh dear," declared Mr. Wong when he saw my sudden state of undress.

And Sheriff Havenick smiled, appreciatively I thought, put a fist to his mouth and coughed politely behind it.

I quickly hiked up my blouse as my employer said sternly: "Chance, in future we must be more careful, especially in mixed company."

But my thoughts at that moment were not on my décolletage, because when I was removing the oilskins I happened to glance at the wall behind the bed, a four-poster with a large oak headboard.

It seemed to me there was a seam in the wall, as though the planks didn't fit well at that point—or could the quarter-inch gap be an indication of a hidden doorway?

"Sheriff," I said, "help me pull this bed away from the wall."

The big lawman did as I asked, and when the bed was clear I studied the seam, noting that it ran all the way from ceiling to floor.

Now we were closer to the wall at that point, I noticed a smell, a cloying, sickly-sweet odor that clutched at my stomach.

Havenick must have smelled it too, because he raised his gun to waist height, the palm of his left hand on the hammer and said: "Push on that wall, an' if it opens stand clear right quick. I don't know what's behind there, but if'n it's something I don't like even a leetle bit I'm gonna cut loose an' burn some powder."

I pushed on the wall, and to my surprise it gave way easily. A whole panel of wood moved, one half sliding into the hidden room as the other half swung out into the bedroom. The panel was hinged in the middle, top and bottom, and the hinges themselves were well oiled and soundless. The smell, like something long dead, hit me like a fist.

"Move away," Havenick said, his gun ready. "I'm not boogered by ha'nts an' sich, but if something horrible walks out of there I want a clean shot at it."

But nothing moved within the chamber, nothing but the slow, curling drift of the vile smell. Havenick pushed me aside, his bandanna covering his mouth and nose, and stepped inside. I followed, peering over his shoulder.

The hidden room had no windows and was in complete darkness. The gray early-afternoon light slanting through the doorway did little to illuminate the interior, but there was a small oil lamp on a table by the bed and the sheriff came back into the room, gasping for breath, picked up the lamp, and thumbed a match into flame.

"I don't know what's in there," he said, addressing Mr. Wong and myself as he lit the lamp. "But if you two want my advice, I reckon you should stay out here."

"Don't worry about us, Sheriff," I said. "The maps could be in there and three pairs of eyes are better than one."

Havenick shrugged. "Suit yourself, but you're playin' leapfrog with a unicorn."

Mr. Wong and I followed the sheriff into the chamber, the orange light from the lamp casting an eerie glow on the walls and ceiling.

And what we beheld was a chamber of horrors.

NINETEEN

As Havenick lifted the lamp above his head, the better to light up the room, I saw on the wall opposite a series of hooks, and hanging from these what appeared to be a dozen small brown leather sacks, graded in color from almost black to tan to yellow.

As I looked closer, with a dawning horror, I realized what the sacks were. On each, withered and tiny, was a nipple!

These were female breasts, each cut from a living victim.

Mr. Wong reached that conclusion at the same time I did, because I heard him gasp: "The horror! Oh the horror!"

The sheriff, slower to recognize what they were asked in a whisper: "What are those things?"

I told him, and Havenick trembled so much, the lamp shook in his hand.

"But how . . . I mean . . . when?" he asked.

"These are trophies," replied my employer. "Some are old. The darker ones, dried by time, could go back ten years or more. Those two there"—he pointed to two of the yellowish specimens—"are not so old. I believe this one, he indicated the smaller of the two, once may have graced the fair young body of Jenny Pearson, and this other and larger, the paleontologist Dr. Victoria Grant."

Those poor, tortured women, how horribly they died at the hands of a vengeful lunatic! Involuntarily, my own shaking hand strayed to my own breasts, almost to reassure itself that they were still there.

"How many . . ." Havenick's voice faltered and he tried again. "How many women do you think, Wong?"

The smell in the small, enclosed room was almost unbearable and the great detective grimaced as he studied each severed breast closely.

"They are all different," he said finally, "all of them from different women. I'd say the oldest dates back ten years and what you see here represents twelve murders. No, make that thirteen." He picked up what I'd taken to be a deerskin pouch filled with tobacco lying next to a pipe on a small table in the chamber. "Here is another. Yes, I would say thirteen women. Cranwell would come in here, smoke his pipe and enjoy his collection, reliving his triumphs, savoring the sweet reminiscence of his kills."

Mr. Wong deduced from the color and texture of each breast that the oldest dated to around the time Cranwell first arrived in Crow Creek.

Horrified, I wondered how many women, prostitutes, drifters, runaway teenagers, hopeless alcoholics, and other poor souls had trusted the little banker and didn't realize until the moment of their terrible deaths that their kind benefactor was an unspeakable monster?

"Where are . . ." I didn't quite know how to say this, so I just blurted it out ". . . the rest of their bodies?"

The sheriff waved a hand. "Buried around here most likely," he said. "This is an isolated house, a lot could go on here that nobody would see."

I shook my head in bafflement. "How could that many women just disappear from Crow Creek without questions being asked? It doesn't make any sense."

"They didn't disappear from town, at least not all of them," Havenick said. "When the soiled doves were still on the line, they came and went and no one bothered to keep track of them. Now that I think about it, Ben Cranwell was one of their best customers. But when the hookers was run out of town by the wives of the vigilante committee, Ben took to going on trips an' now and again he'd bring back his own woman. Sometimes she was pretty, sometimes she wasn't, but pretty or not, she'd stay with him for a spell, then she'd be gone. An' then Ben would mope around an' tell folks that his woman had grown tired of Crow Creek an' jest up an' done left him."

Havenick smiled. "That's when the womenfolk around here would cluck their tongues an' say Ben had no luck with the ladies, an' that was a cryin' shame because he was a fine catch for anybody."

The sheriff looked around the chamber and shuddered. "Little did they know."

The wall to the left of the hidden doorway was in darkness, and Mr. Wong suddenly jumped away from it with a surprised yelp, swiping at the sleeve of his immaculate gray suit.

"Damn!" he exclaimed. "Wet paint!"

"Let me see that," Havenick said. He walked over to the wall and raised the lamp—and I saw myself!

Or, at least, it was supposed to be me.

A crude drawing had been daubed on the wall with red paint, the slant of my eyes exaggerated and my straight black hair much shorter than I wear it. I was depicted as lying on my back with my legs wide open to reveal . . . well, that which should remain a sweet secret except to the ardent and well-qualified suitor.

Above my head were the words:

DIE CHINESE WHORE

And it looked like a knife blade had been plunged into my nether regions again and again in a frenzy of lust and uncontrollable hate.

Angela Hudson had fared no better. There was a similar drawing of her, and the words:

DISEASED WHORE FILTH

As in the drawing of me, a sharp knife had been plunged into her repeatedly.

"Jesus," Havenick gasped as he studied the crude graffiti. "Who would ever have guessed Ben Cranwell had a mind that could come up with something like this."

"Ben Cranwell no longer has a mind, Sheriff," I

said. "His brain is a vile, rotten cesspit and he is no longer capable of rational thought."

"We got to find him," the lawman said. "I reckon he's going to make his way back here, an' we can hole up an' lay for him."

I did not think Cranwell's return was likely, and as I moved toward the door of the chamber, something rustled under my foot. I looked down and saw a small, square piece of paper that seemed to be covered in writing of some kind.

It had to be one of Billy's treasure maps.

"Sheriff," I said urgently, "direct the light of the lamp toward the floor."

Havenick did as I asked, and we saw that the entire floor was covered in papers.

"Those are the maps," the sheriff said, and he kneeled and one by one picked them up.

I'd had quite enough of the horrible trophy chamber, and I asked Havenick to bring the maps with him into the bedroom.

There were at least a hundred of them, dating back years to when Billy was just a boy. The sheriff spread them out on the bed, and we quickly leafed through them. Several were smudged with red paint, which suggested Cranwell had first drawn his vile caricatures on the wall and then in a rage scattered the maps over the floor.

After a few moments, during which there was no sound but for the rain battering against the bedroom windows, Havenick straightened up from the bed, brandishing a map in his hand. "These maps are all in my handwriting," he said. "All but this one." The sheriff handed it to me. "What do you make of it?" he asked.

I studied the map closely. It wasn't really a map in the strict sense of the word, more a set of handwritten clues with roughly drawn physical features of the landscape that Billy could search for and identify.

It was the last clue that caught my attention, just a line of writing, all in capitals, with no drawing:

> NOW SEEK THE PLACE WHERE THE INDIAN
> MAID TOOK ROOT, THE TREASURE YOU SEEK
> LIES BENEATH HER FOOT

It could only be a reference to Squaw Rock—the spot where poor little Jenny Pearson was murdered.

Mr. Wong stepped beside me and haughtily looked down his nose at the map. "This tells us nothing, Chance. How do we know Ben Cranwell even wrote it?"

"Wait," I exclaimed, "I believe we can verify that."

I reached into the pocket of my riding skirt where I'd stashed Cranwell's directions to the Hudson ranch. Opening up the crumpled piece of paper, I quickly compared the writing. Cranwell's directions had also been scrawled in block capitals—and they matched the writing on the map exactly.

"Sir," I said to Mr. Wong, "I believe both these notes were written by the same hand."

"Chance, Chester Wong will be the judge of that," my employer said, reminding me by his stern demeanor, if not his words, that I was but a humble assistant and my opinions were of little account in the matter of criminal detection.

With agonizing slowness Mr. Wong took a small tortoiseshell case from his vest pocket, opened it, withdrew a tiny pair of pince-nez glasses, breathed on the lenses, pulled out his pocket handkerchief with an elegant flourish, polished the spectacles at great length, settled them on his nose, adjusted the glasses to a more comfortable position, sighed deeply, extended his hand, and said: "Now, the map and the Cranwell directions, if you please."

After a few moments contemplative study, the great detective nodded to himself, handed the map and the directions back to me and declared with much solemnity: "Both these documents, in my professional opinion, were written by the same hand. And my opinion will stand up in any court of law, I do assure you."

"Brilliant!" exclaimed Sheriff Havenick, genuinely impressed. "Not for nothing, Wong, are you called the world's finest detective."

"Indeed," said my mentor, and he removed his oil-skins and hat and went into a wonderful display, nodding his handsome and glossy head as he swung his mighty belly this way and that and lifted his knees high as he strutted around the room so that we could see and admire his small, well-formed feet.

After this gorgeous exhibition, Mr. Wong addressed Sheriff Havenick in a most friendly manner: "Sir, now that I have uncovered vital evidence in this case, including this ghastly charnel house, I want your assurance that you will mount a posse, hunt down Ben Cranwell, and apprehend him for the murders of Jenny Pearson, Victoria Grant, Silas Lime and, yes, the Teton Kid, and many others as yet unidentified. And, of course, that you will release Brad Hudson at the earliest possible opportunity."

"You can depend on it," Havenick said. "Brad Hudson will be a free man by the time the sun sets on this day."

"Bravo!" declared my employer. "Then my work here is done."

"Sir," I said, my eyes humbly lowered to the floor, "this unworthy one believes our work is far from done but, on the contrary, is just beginning."

"What did you say?" inquired my employer in a most irritated tone. "Speak up now, child, what is the meaning of this unwarranted outburst?"

"First of all, sir," I replied, my eyes still fixed on the floor, "I think Ben Cranwell will not come back here and that even as we speak he is on his way to the Hudson ranch to commit another murder. There is no time to return to Crow Creek and form a posse, we must act now and hunt him down ourselves." I looked up at Mr. Wong. "Oh, sir, I beg of you, we do not have much time."

"Why do you think Cranwell is headed for the Hudson ranch?" Havenick asked quickly. "I reckon he's lit a shuck out of the county an' it will take a posse, maybe two or three, to hunt him down."

"Precisely, Sheriff," said Mr. Wong, and he looked at me in considerable annoyance, shook his head and added: "Tut-tut-tut."

"Sheriff, you're not dealing with a rational man here," I said, anger rising in me. "Cranwell wants Angela Hudson, and he wants me, too, for that matter. Look at the drawings in his secret chamber. Look what he did with his knife. His evil intent is written all over the wall!"

"Chance, I hardly think—" began my employer, but Havenick cut him short.

"Wait," he said, "she may have a point. Maybe, jest maybe, killing Angela is what he has in mind, or what's left of his mind."

Now I stated a thought that had been troubling me deeply for some time.

"Sirs," I said, "there is more. I don't think Ben Cranwell is acting alone. There is someone else, someone behind the scenes manipulating him and using his madness as you would a puppet. Cranwell is evil, but he's being controlled by an even greater evil, and the use of evil is creating even more evil."

"Who is this man?" Havenick asked.

"I don't know," I replied. "But, please, I'll tell you the rest of what I believe in the car. We must get to the Hudson ranch as quickly as possible."

"I agree with her, Wong," Havenick said. "I think maybe we should head out there pronto an' take a look-see."

My employer shrugged, his face expressionless. "Whatever. But it's a wild goose chase. I can assure you that Ben Cranwell is long gone. Right now, knowing that Chester Wong is closing in on him, he's running for his life."

Once more in my oilskins, I pushed the sleeves up off my hands and cranked the handle of the Ford. To my joy it started at once, and I climbed in behind the wheel.

The rain was lashing down, driven by thunderclouds that rolled toward us off the mountains like a vast and endless sea. I pushed the little Ford hard, mud spattering over the windshield in great wet globs as we splashed through the countless deep puddles that had turned the trail into a quagmire.

As I drove closer to the Hudson place, the flat prairie gave way to gently rolling hills, most of them crested by sparse stands of timber. Nothing moved. This was a rain-swept, silent land and the eye, trying to penetrate the distances, saw only gray piled on gray, the gray-shrouded hills merging with the darker gray of the sky.

Havenick moved his Winchester out of the way of his knees and leaned over, speaking almost into my ear above the roar of the struggling engine. "Okay, little lady, spill. What makes you think Ben Cranwell isn't just a crazy man acting alone?"

"Sheriff," I said, turning my head slightly as I spoke over my shoulder, "Silas Lime was paid to murder Mr. Wong and I, but, as it turned out, he was a mediocre swordsman and an even poorer assassin. At that time Ben Cranwell had no reason to think we were closing in on him. He even offered to help us and he knew we considered him an ally. He had no reason to hire a man to kill us. Besides, the way his mind is right now, he would have preferred to murder us himself."

"That's possible," Havenick said thoughtfully, though I heard Mr. Wong snort his vehement disagreement.

"There's another thing," I said. "Lime was killed by a sword thrust from behind. He turned his back on someone he thought he could trust. He would never have trusted Cranwell that much. Lime was a gambler and he'd spent a lifetime reading people. He was smart enough to know the man was crazy and a killer. You don't give a man like that an opening."

We drove in silence for a few moments, then I said: "When my employer and I were ambushed on the way back to town from our visit to the Hudson ranch, the killer used a rifle and fired from a distance. Again, Sheriff, that just wasn't Ben Cranwell's style. If it had been him who was trying to kill us that night, he would have done it up close and personal, preferably with a knife."

Reluctantly, because I knew how Mr. Wong would react, I then told Havenick about my terrifying experience in the barn, skirting around the fact that I was checking out his own buckskin horse. "I now believe that vile man in the shadows was Ben Cranwell," I said. "He could have used a gun that night and killed me easily, but he didn't." I shuddered. "He wanted me alive to . . . to . . . rape me and then torture me with his blade. A monster like that doesn't use a rifle from ambush."

"Last Chance Lee!" exclaimed Mr. Wong, his use of my full name betraying his annoyance. "Why didn't you inform me of this? I would have taken steps to protect you. In fact," he added with great finality, "I would have sent you away from Crow Creek on the very next train."

"Sir," I said, turning my head to look at him, "I didn't wish to burden you with more troubles, since this case was already taxing even your great powers of deduction to the limit."

"This is true," Mr. Wong agreed, somewhat mollified. "But don't ever let a thing like this happen again without informing me. You also neglected to carry the Dragon Box that night, an unforgivable lapse of judgment." My employer was silent for a few moments, then added sternly: "Chance, you may consider this a severe reprimand."

I hung my head, though I still kept my eyes on the treacherous trail vanishing into the misty grayness ahead of us. "Sir," I said, "this unworthy one apologizes most humbly."

"Just don't let it happen again, that's all. Now, if you please, pay attention to the road."

But Sheriff Havenick wasn't about to let the matter rest.

"Chance," he said, rain from his wide-brimmed Stetson trickling down the back of my neck, "you believe the man who's using Ben Cranwell drygulched Silas Lime an' laid for you with a Winchester? Do I savvy that much?"

I nodded. "That's what I think."

"But who would stand to gain from all that? I mean, where's the motive?"

I shook my head at him. "That, I don't know, Sheriff. And I must admit, it's puzzling me greatly."

"And that's why this is all balderdash," said Mr. Wong. "I have thought on this, and my conclusion is that Ben Cranwell acted alone while the balance of his mind was disturbed. The felon is now on the run and must be apprehended at the earliest possible opportunity."

The great detective turned to look at me, then Havenick, his utter contempt for my guesswork plain.

"Chester Wong has now made his position clear.

He has accurately stated the facts of the matter and there can be no more argument. Now, Chance, drive on and keep alert for I see we are nearing the Hudson ranch where I am sure you will find Angela Hudson alive and well."

TWENTY

The Hudson ranch showed no signs of life as we drove toward the main house, and I feared we were too late. Behind me, I heard Sheriff Havenick crank a round into the breech of his Winchester.

As we drew closer, I saw that the front door hung wide on its hinges, an open invitation to the rain that slanted around the ranch house like a ragged gray curtain blowing in the wind. The creek rushing under the bridge was swollen and as I drove over the wooden slats the tires of the Model T hissed in ankle-deep water.

I braked to a halt outside the house and Havenick immediately jumped out of the car, his rifle at the ready.

Mr. Wong and I joined him, standing at his shoulder in the downpour as thunder crashed overhead and lightning split the sky, the smell of ozone heavy in the air.

"Wait," Havenick whispered, extending a hand to stop me as I tried to go around him to enter the house. "What the hell is that?"

I listened for a few moments, but heard nothing. "What do you hear?" I asked the sheriff.

"Shhh . . . there it is again."

This time I heard it, a muffled boom, boom, boom, coming from somewhere in the house.

"What the hell!" Havenick said.

"It sounds like a drum," I said. "Like somebody slowly beating on a bass drum."

Boom, boom, boom . . .

"This is most peculiar," declared Mr. Wong. "Who would be pounding on a drum at the Rafter H?"

"Maybe it's Injuns," Havenick replied, smiling without humor.

"I suggest," I said, "we go investigate."

We walked carefully toward the open door of the ranch house, the sheriff in the lead, his knuckles white on his Winchester.

Above our heads the sun was obscured by the towering masses of thunderheads, and, although the day was cool, I was perspiring under my oilskins.

Boom, boom, boom . . .

Havenick stopped. "Dammit," he said to no one in particular, "that there drum is spookin' the hell out of me."

"Lead on, Sheriff," I whispered. "This is no time to dawdle."

Without another word, Havenick walked through the open door of the house. To our left, the door to the parlor was closed, and the sheriff tried the handle. It turned in his hand and he whispered to me: "Watch out!"

Havenick threw the door wide open, charged inside, dived to his right, rolled, and came up on one knee, his Winchester ready for action.

The room, which was neat and clean and filled with fresh wildflowers, was empty.

Boom, boom, boom . . .

"It's coming from the kitchen," I whispered as Havenick regained his feet.

Mr. Wong's mighty bulk was blocking the narrow hallway and the sheriff had to squeeze past him, holding his rifle over his head.

Once free of the great detective, Havenick stepped to the door and tried the handle. The door opened a couple of inches, then stopped.

"It's jammed. There's something behind it," he said.

BOOM . . . BOOM . . . BOOM . . .

The sheriff turned and motioned toward the door with a nod of his head. "Wong, get your weight against this door and see if we can get it open."

My employer did as he was asked and he and Havenick put their shoulders to the door and pushed. It opened slowly, inch by inch, then a bloody hand, small and delicately formed, flopped into sight, thudding limply to rest on the floor.

Havenick jumped back. "Jesus Christ! Who is that?"

Boom-boom-boom . . . The drum grew louder, the pace of its beats faster.

"Is it Angela?" Mr. Wong asked, his face horror-stricken.

"No," I said, "that's a man's hand. It's Mr. Chang, the cook."

"Let's get this door open, Wong," Havenick said urgently.

This time the two men pushed and the door swung

open wide, sliding the dead body of the cook across the polished wood floor of the kitchen. Chang had been shot twice, once in the chest, the other between his eyes. He was on his back, staring at the ceiling, a look of terror frozen on his dead face.

· *BOOM-BOOM-BOOM-DA-DA-BOOM . . .*

The drumbeat was coming from the other side of the kitchen, behind a heavy butcher-block work table that had been overturned in a desperate struggle.

Sheriff Havenick leveled his rifle in the direction of the table and, his voice soft and deadly, said: "You, behind the table. Come out with your hands in the air or I'll drill you fer sure."

"Damn you," a man's voice from behind the table said weakly. "Havenick, you was always a low-down, ornery skunk and you ain't improved none with age. Hell, you'd even shoot a dead man."

"That's Matt Jerrell, the Rafter H foreman," I said.

"I know who it is," Havenick said. He lowered his rifle. "An' he ain't improved much with age, either."

Matt was lying behind the table, blood covering the front of his shirt. His gun was still in his hand and he leveled it at the sheriff. "Havenick, right about now I ain't in the mood to trust anybody. One move that don't look right to me an' I'll let some daylight into you."

"Please, Mr. Jerrell," I said. "We're here to help." I looked quickly around the kitchen. "Where's Angela?"

"Took," Matt said.

A huge cooking pot lay at the foreman's feet, and he tapped it with his toe, producing a hollow boom.

"Figgered if'n I hit this often enough and loud enough, somebody would hear me," he smiled weakly.

"Who took Angela, Matt?" I asked as Havenick kneeled beside him and opened the wounded man's shirt. Matt had lowered his gun now he knew we presented no danger. "Was it Ben Cranwell?"

"Yeah," Matt replied, "except his name ain't Cranwell. It took me a spell to figger it out, but when he came here lookin' for Angela, I recollected who he was."

Havenick was studying the wound in the foreman's chest, shaking his head.

"Cranwell's real name is Chick Modell, and I first saw him around San Antone back when I was a Ranger. He was a gambler then, an' poison-fast with a gun. He'd already killed a couple of men in Texas an' a couple more up in the Territory. Next I heard he was runnin' with the Wild Bunch and had took to train robbery. I heard he'd killed another man, a sheriff, in Denver, an' then about ten years ago he just dropped out of sight."

"And that's about when he came to Crow Creek," I said.

"Yeah," Matt said, coughing, blood staining his lips. "I guess he started his bank with stolen money and set himself up as a respectable, law-abiding citizen."

"Jerrell," Sheriff Havenick said, his face grim, "we got to get you to a doctor. You're all shot to pieces."

The foreman shook his head. "No time for that. You've got to go after Angela."

"We can't leave you here, Matt," I said.

"Yeah you can," replied the foreman. "I ain't going anyplace. I'll still be here after you stop Modell, or Cranwell, or whatever you want to call him."

Havenick rose to his feet. "Jerrell's right. We got to go after Angela or we could end up with another murder on our hands."

Matt nodded. "Now you're showin' a lick of sense, Havenick, an' that's a mite unusual for you."

The sheriff ignored this and said to Matt: "How good is he? Modell, I mean. How does he rank?"

The young foreman looked up at Havenick, his face bleak. "Better than me. He killed poor ol' Chang and then drilled me afore I'd even cleared leather. He's better than you, Sheriff. He's fast as a striking rattler and he generally don't miss what he's aimin' at."

Havenick nodded. "Thanks for the warning. I'll be careful."

"How much of a start does he have on us, Matt?" I asked.

"I dunno, an hour maybe. I'd look at my watch, but one of Modell's bullets hit the dang thing an' most of its works are in my chest. Listen"—the foreman struggled onto one elbow—"he don't think anyone will follow him, an' with the creeks in the hills swollen by the rain, he'll keep to the main trail. Did you drive that there auto-mobile of yours?"

I nodded.

"Then maybe you can catch him. Go, just don't let anything happen to Angela."

"You love her, don't you?" I said.

"Yeah," Matt said. "Now get after her."

We made Matt Jerrell as comfortable as we could, then climbed back into the Model T, which again started with a single crank of the handle, as though providence was now on our side.

"I think, Chance, that given the unpredictable nature

of Ben Cranwell, let us now refer to him by his real name, Chick Modell. And given his skill with arms, it is time to open the Dragon Box," Mr. Wong said as we splashed across the bridge and headed for the trail. "If ever we needed your particular talents, it is now."

"Sir," I said humbly, "whatever small skill I have is at your disposal."

I pulled over to the side of the trail and retrieved the box from under my oilskins, laying it on my lap.

The Dragon Box had been a graduation gift from dear Miss Chastity Charmaine, imported from San Francisco's Chinatown at great expense to contain yet another gift—a Colt Single Action revolver given to me by sweet Professor Bat Masterson.

The Colt was ordinary enough to look at as it lay in the box's interior of scarlet satin, blued with rubber handles and a four-inch barrel. But the action had been fine-tuned by Professor Masterson himself so that it was slick and smooth as silk, the trigger bound back to the guard by silver wire. There were places for five cartridges, each one hand loaded by the professor, and each bullet made from a melted-down silver dollar.

"Chance," Professor Masterson told me on graduation day, "every one of them bullets will fire true an' as straight as a gut with a pup pullin' on it. You do your part and they'll do theirs."

I took the Colt from the Dragon Box, half cocked the hammer and began to feed the rounds into the cylinder, and Sheriff Havenick cried out in alarm. "Hey, be careful with that thing! You could hurt yourself."

But my employer immediately came to my defense.

"I assure you, Sheriff," he said, "that Chance is quite the expert with the revolver."

"How come the trigger's bound back that-a-way?" Havenick asked suspiciously. "If'n you ask me, that piece ain't safe."

I finished loading the Colt, thumbed the gate shut and placed the gun on my lap under my oilskins.

"It's safe, Sheriff," I said. "At least most of the time."

As I eased the Ford back onto the road then accelerated to its best speed, mud flying high into the air from our spinning wheels, my thoughts went back to my dear old school and the day Professor Masterson discovered my hidden talent with the revolver.

Indeed, the first person to recognize it was a fond and special friend of mine, a fellow student named Prudence Chapman. Prudence was a very genteel and well-born young lady from McCulloch County, Texas, a member of the extensive Miller/Clements/Hardin clan, being cousin to both Killin' Jim Miller—something of a black sheep that one!—and the great adventurer of the family, the handsome and dashing John Wesley.

Our revolver and archery range was a disused gravel pit set at some considerable distance from our dear old school's ivy-covered walls, and it was there, during a practice session, that I confessed to a transgression that, in the past when committed by other students, had made even mild-mannered Professor Masterson go extremely red in the face and curse like a trooper.

"Prudence," I said miserably, "I'm a gun fanner. It's the only way I can hit the target. If I hold the Colt out at arm's length and sight along the barrel as we've been taught, I just can't hit anything."

Dear Prudence, that sweet girl, was shocked. "But both Professor Masterson and Professor Leslie, especially Buckskin Frank, call gun fanning a tinhorn's grandstand play that's wildly inaccurate, and they've threatened to crucify anyone who tries it."

"I know," I said unhappily, "but it's the only way I know how to shoot."

My friend shook her head sadly. "Oh, Chance," she said, "you'll be in so much trouble if you even suggest fanning your gun."

"But Professor Masterson did say that the genteel and well-brought-up young lady could clear an alley by thumb-slipping the hammer," I pointed out.

"I know, but that's not quite the same thing as fanning, is it?" declared Prudence. She stood in silence for a moment or two, then looked over her shoulder. Satisfied, she turned to me and said: "There's no one around right now. Let me see you fan a gun."

She handed me her own practice revolver—a first-class shot, Prudence kept what she called her Sunday-going-to-prayer-meeting-Colt—in a locker at the foot of her bed.

"It's loaded," she said, "so let 'er rip."

Professor Masterson had set up man-sized silhouette targets at ten paces, and I brought the Colt to waist level, fanning the hammer with my left palm. In those days we only loaded five cartridges, the hammer resting on an empty chamber as a safety measure. So, in the time it takes to blink an eye, I fired three times, stepped out of the smoke, and fired twice more, all five of my bullets finding their mark in the belly area of the target.

Our ears ringing, Prudence and I looked at each other for a few moments, then that fine girl jumped into the air, her arms high above her head, and yelled: "Huzzah! That was as slick as owl snot an' as fast as a settin' hen on a June bug!"

"You see what I mean?" I asked as I punched the empty shells out of the gun. "I can't shoot any other way."

"Then you got to fess up," Prudence said. She wore a long white dress, embroidered around the neck, and a pink bow that held back her beautiful black hair from her face. "I think when Professor Masterson sees shooting like that, he maybe will forgive the fanning."

"I sure hope so," I said miserably. "Though he seems to be dead set against it."

As it happened, I didn't have long to wait before my confrontation with both my dear professors. Miss Chastity Charmaine, always solicitous of the welfare of the young ladies, had the two professors in residence—a most unusual occurrence—and called a practice shoot the next Sunday, right after church.

When Professors Masterson and Leslie were together at the school, they tippy-toed around each other, for both were well aware of the other's formidable reputation.

When the two men met, at mealtimes mostly, they greeted one another with the most elaborate courtesy and a great display of fine manners and good breeding in which elegant little bows and meticulously worded inquiries after family and loved ones played a major part.

On the Sunday in question, the student body had been split into two, fifteen young ladies being with each professor at widely separated parts of the range.

I was with Professor Masterson, and I had no secrets from him since that sharp educator missed very little that was happening around the school.

"Chance," he said sternly, his mild blue eyes suddenly hard, "I hear tell you have been fanning a gun. That is a grandstand play and is for the tinhorn and the wannabe and not for the young lady of quality."

I lowered my eyes to the ground and most humbly begged the professor's pardon, stammering in my own defense that fanning was the only way I knew to shoot.

Professor Masterson immediately called for a demonstration, warning me that it would end in disaster and would reflect badly on him, especially before the critical eye of Professor Leslie. But, as I had previously shown Prudence, I drew my gun from the holster and fanned five balls unerringly into the target in about the time it takes to snap your fingers, each one finding its mark. After the smoke had cleared, Professor Masterson stepped close to me—a shocked, puzzled expression on his round face—and said: "Chance, that was slick, an' I never seen the like in all my born days. Hell, you're a natural-born gun fanner, the first one I ever knowed."

The professor immediately called over to Professor Leslie, asking if he could spare a minute, at his convenience, to join him.

"Why certainly, Professor Masterson," Professor

Leslie replied, walking over to our little group. "This is indeed a rare pleasure."

Quickly Professor Masterson outlined what he'd just witnessed, and then asked me to give Professor Leslie—who suddenly looked very stern indeed, but so handsome with his roguish blue eyes and dashing cavalry mustache—yet another demonstration.

This I did, drawing the Colt and bringing it up to waist level, fanning the hammer as soon as I lined the gun up with the target.

"She's a natural," gasped Professor Leslie as soon as the demonstration was over and the target was once again perforated. "I don't think I seen John Wesley handle a Colt's gun better. Hell, I don't think I seen anybody handle a Colt's gun better. I just seen it for my own self, but I don't believe it. It's something I didn't think was possible."

Dear Miss Chastity Charmaine—wearing an after-church dressing gown of vivid scarlet silk that revealed a great deal of firm breast and shapely thigh, her mass of tawny hair tumbling over her shoulders—had strolled over from school to check on the progress of our lessons.

Our dear headmistress placed great emphasis on the martial arts, confessing that she found much of our curriculum, especially mathematics, physics, and chemistry, tedious in the extreme. As a measure of her interest, she brought along her entire entourage, both her pretty French ladies maids, her piano player, and her personal bodyguard in the huge and grinning form of the famed prizefighter, Willie "the Trenton Tar Baby" Johnson.

Now, as I finished my demonstration, Miss Char-

maine laid her morning glass of bourbon at her feet,
placed her cheroot between her dazzling white teeth,
and applauded: "Wonderful! Oh, *c'etait fantastique!*"

Professor Masterson bowed to our dear headmistress and said: "Indeed, madam."

He was thoughtful for a few moments, then addressed Professor Leslie in these terms: "The Chinese
are said to have invented gunpowder and cannon
hundreds of years ago. Could it be, Professor Leslie,
that their long association with firearms has made
them natural-born gun fanners?"

Professor Leslie had listened intently to this question, his head tilted to one side. Now he considered
Professor Masterson's entire statement at some
length. Finally he nodded in agreement, as though the
explanation for Chinese genius with revolvers had
been most accurately stated.

"I believe you have hit the nail on the head, Professor Masterson, and are spreading the gospel," he declared. "For I believe the Chinese race is indeed
ancient and that they are an inscrutable people much
given to secret skills of all kinds."

"Then we have solved the mystery at last," declared Professor Masterson, giving his fellow educator a graceful little bow.

Professor Leslie elegantly returned this courtesy,
then, before taking his leave, said to me: "You have
great talent, young lady. Gunfighting skills are rare as
a tear at a Boot Hill buryin', and are not given to everyone. Use them well, and then only judiciously."

That night, in honor of my prowess, Miss Charmaine broke out the champagne and there was

Mumm's all round and a full box of Burmah cheroots to be shared by both student body and faculty.

"A word with you, Last Chance," said Professor Masterson at one point in the evening, drawing me into a quiet corner away from the festivities. "You are a natural-born gun handler, with more skill than anyone I've ever seen in my life, an' I've seen the best. I want you to promise me that you'll use your gun on the side of the law and will not ride the owlhoot trail and be drawn into the company of outlaws, footpads, and all manner of low persons, including dancehall loungers, brothel keepers, thieves, tinkers, and razor grinders."

Modestly lowering my eyes, I blushed and replied softly: "Sir, my esteemed and famous guardian, the great detective Mr. Chester Wong, has offered me a post as his assistant in the field of criminal detection. My future, I believe, lies in that direction."

"Then all is well," responded Professor Masterson, sipping on his champagne. "I know you will make me proud of you."

Now, as I drove the Model T in pursuit of a demented and deadly gunman, I quietly prayed to Lady Kuan Yin that my skills be up to the task that lay ahead and that I would indeed make dear Professor Masterson proud.

Yet fear clutched at my stomach and I could not but think that we were in hot pursuit of a vicious predator who knew not mercy or remorse—so like the fanged and clawed horror that had been uncovered on the hillside, its white and silent bones gleaming wet in the endless rain.

TWENTY-ONE

"Pull over, Chance," Havenick ordered. "I gotta get out an' take a look-see."

I did as the sheriff asked and he jumped out of the car, his Winchester at the ready.

"Hoofprints, an' not too old," he yelled against the noise of the rain. Havenick was down on one knee, studying tracks along the side of the trail where the ground was higher and less muddy. He rose and scrambled back into the car. "Those prints are fresh because they haven't yet been filled up by the rain. Two horses an' riders an' just a few minutes ahead."

The sheriff rested the butt of his rifle on his thigh. "If there's shootin', and I'm pretty sure there will be, leave it up to me, little lady. I don't want you sprayin' lead all over God's creation with that there tricked-out six-gun. Somebody could get hurt, an' that somebody could be me."

"Sheriff," I said, "I'm quite a competent marksperson, you know."

"Yeah, well, competent don't cut it. Ben Cranwell or Chick Modell or whatever you want to call him is a ranny best left alone by amateurs. You saw how he done for Matt Jerrell, an' he's no tenderfoot."

"As you wish, Sheriff."

"Now, drive on, but go slow an' keep a sharp look-out."

The terrain as it opened before me was a succession of shallow hills, some of them crested by rocky outcrops, stands of aspen growing on their lower slopes. Far to the west the mountains were shrouded in cloud, but the wind brought me the scent of pine and the sharp, clean promise of the coming winter snows.

Like a wild animal, Havenick sniffed the air. "We're mighty close. I can smell Angela's mare."

TING! TING! TING!

Three rounds tore through the bodywork of the car, followed by the roar of the rifle, and the sheriff yelled: "Get out!"

I skidded to a halt and opened the door of the car, tumbling into the mud, Sheriff Havenick and Mr. Wong following close behind me.

"Oh, the car," wailed my employer miserably as he flattened himself against the rear door. "Chance, if we keep getting shot up like this, there will be nothing left of Miss Rhodes' automobile except four wheels and a frame."

"Keep down!" Havenick yelled, pushing Mr. Wong lower behind the Ford's body. "Worry about the damned car later."

"Easy for you to say," said Mr. Wong petulantly. "You don't have to pay for the damages."

BLAM!

The windshield shattered into a thousand pieces, and Havenick smiled at me and said: "Maybe that's Modell's way of thankin' you for breakin' down his door."

Without waiting for a reply, the sheriff rose to his feet and cranked off three fast rounds in the direction of the hidden gunman, then ducked behind the car again.

"He's up on a ridge with plenty of good cover, rocks an' scrub pine an' sich," he said grimly. "Gonna be hard to winkle him out of there." He raised his head as high as he dared, cupped his hand to his mouth and yelled: "Angela!"

There was no answer from the ridge.

"Angela, are you all right?" the sheriff tried again.

"Up here! I'm—"

Angela Hudson's voice was suddenly cut off, followed by a sharp cry of pain.

"Damn you, Modell, you low-down skunk!"

Havenick rose to his feet and fired at the gunman, cranked a round into the chamber, and fired again.

BLAM!

Modell's rifle roared from the hill and the sheriff took the bullet full in the chest. He staggered backward, still working his rifle. He fired, fired again, then collapsed in a heap, a sudden gush of bright scarlet blood filling his mouth, tumbling down the front of his slicker.

I heard a drumbeat of pounding hooves. A horse was running toward the car. Instantly I leaped to my feet, my Colt waist-high and ready.

BLAM! BLAM!

Modell was standing upright and he fired twice at Angela Hudson as she galloped toward us. The girl was flattened along her horse's neck, her blond hair flying in the wind.

Modell was on his feet, working his rifle, but was

well out of range of my revolver. I threw the Colt onto the seat of the car and picked up Havenick's rifle, cranked a round into the chamber, and fired at the gunman. My bullet chipped fragments of rock from a boulder at his feet, and I fired a second time, kicking up a fountain of mud between his legs and the man dived behind the rocks.

Angela reached the car and pulled her horse to a skidding halt, the animal's back legs kicking up great gobs of mud as it screamed and went down on its haunches.

Angela kicked free of the stirrups and half jumped, half fell out of the saddle. I fired the Winchester at Modell's position as she ran toward us and dived down behind the Ford.

"Be careful, Angela," I said urgently. "You've got a baby inside you."

The girl shook her head. "I'm all right and the baby's all right."

She had a welt on her right cheek, bright red against her pale skin, and when she saw me looking at it, her fingers strayed to the spot.

"He thought he'd knocked me cold," she said, "and I let him think that. When Burt Havenick stood up and started shooting, I took my chance and ran for it." She looked over at the sheriff's lanky, blood-splashed body. "Is he . . . is he . . . ?"

I nodded. "He's dead, Angela. A man like Burt Havenick, well, he just couldn't go any other way."

"So many deaths," Angela whispered. "So many people."

"As my Chinese ancestors say, death would be a terrifying thing indeed," whispered Mr. Wong, "if there were not alongside it resplendent immortality. Even as we speak, Angela, the good sheriff is being re-born into a higher state."

"I hope you're right," Angela said. "Oh, how I pray you are right."

"I know I'm right," declared my employer. "Chester Wong is never wrong."

A horse was thundering toward us. As I had antic-ipated, Chick Modell, insane and impatient as he was, would not for long be content to snipe at a distance.

I looked over the car and saw him coming in our direction at a full gallop, showing considerable prowess in horsemanship and skill at arms as he worked the lever of his Winchester and fired again and again from the shoulder.

I pressed the butt of poor Sheriff Havenick's rifle to my shoulder, sighted carefully on Modell's chest, and squeezed the trigger.

Click.

The gun was empty.

Throwing down the rifle in disgust, I reached for my Colt. Modell was now only fifty yards away and closing fast, so close I could see his crazed bloodshot eyes and the mud splashed on his banker's frock coat.

Breathing deeply, aware of Angela's frightened lit-tle squeal of fear, I let the gunman get closer. Then I opened up on him, fanning off five quick shots, the Colt bucking and kicking in my hand like a wild stal-lion.

Scared as I was, the strange, unbidden thought came to me that I'd just fired five silver dollars—my entire salary for a week.

I'm the first to admit that I'm not a great shot with

a long gun, but happily I did great execution with the
Colt. Modell screamed in agony as one of my bullets
smashed into his left hand where it held the forestock
of the rifle, blasting away a couple of fingers. The
Winchester spun from his grasp, arcing high into the
air before thudding into the mud. Another bullet
grazed the right side of his neck and instantly blood
splashed over his shirt collar. A third slammed into
his big American horse and the wounded creature,
poor thing, staggered forward, Modell keeping it on
its feet by sheer brute strength and his own deranged
will.

I had no idea where the two other rounds went, but
now I had an empty rifle and Colt and was at the
madman's mercy.

But his crazed charge was over.

Modell yanked the head of his wounded horse
around, screaming vile obscenities at me, and galloped back the way he had come. I saw him ride over
the ridge and disappear into the gray curtain of the
falling rain.

Quickly I reloaded Sheriff Havenick's rifle and my
Colt from the dead lawman's full cartridge belt and
passed his six-gun to Angela. "Keep that close," I said.
"You may need it."

"How is Matt?" she asked urgently, her face
stricken.

"He's in bad shape," I said.

"Will he live?"

"For you, Angela, I believe he will."

"I must go to him now."

Angela rose to her feet and moved toward her

trembling horse, but I put out my hand and grabbed her arm.

The girl showed her annoyance by pulling away from my grip, but I stood right in front of her. "Angela, before you leave, there's something you must know."

"What is that?" Angela asked, her blue eyes flashing.

"The man you knew as Ben Cranwell has a disease, a terrible disease, and he may have passed it on to you and the child within you."

Angela looked at me in puzzlement. "What do you mean?"

"Cranwell, his real name is Chick Modell, is the father of your baby, isn't he?"

"No, no he's not. This is Matt's baby. We're in love," she added defiantly, "and we plan to marry."

Now it was my turn to be puzzled. "But . . . but you told me to let Cranwell be, that you needed him."

"Yes, I needed him all right, needed his money to keep the ranch going." Angela shook her head at me. "I never let Cranwell make love to me, and he never asked me to. He said I was one of the most feminine women he'd ever met, and that he just wanted to . . . to slap me around."

The poor girl took a shuddering breath. "In return for money for the ranch, I'd go to him and he'd beat me. Sometimes he'd beat me real bad. You saw the bruises on my face and shoulders, but there are others . . . hidden. He'd go at me with a leather belt, sometimes for an hour at a time. He'd bite . . . bite—"

Angela broke down into sobs and I put my arms around her, holding her close.

"Your father never knew this?" I whispered.

"No," she said. "Cranwell warned me that if I ever mentioned a word to Dad, he'd foreclose on the ranch and we'd lose everything. I . . . I couldn't let that happen."

"But your father . . . Matt . . . didn't they see the bruises? Didn't they wonder?"

The girl shook her head. "Usually Cranwell was careful to avoid my face. It was only that last time that he got careless. Then he acted like a madman, like he didn't care if anyone knew or not."

"But you made love to Matt. I—"

"Only in the dark. I pretended I was too shy to take my clothes off in front of him. We always made love in darkness, like it was something criminal or evil, something to be ashamed of. And I was ashamed of letting Cranwell use me the way he did."'

I touched Angela's cheek. "Now you can make love in the light, as God intended."

The girl pulled away from me and ran to her horse. "I must go to Matt."

As I watched Angela gallop away, Mr. Wong came to my side.

"Oh calamity," he groaned, framing each cheek with an open palm. "When Miss Rhodes sees her car she'll have a fit, then she'll faint, then she'll charge me a fortune in damages. Chance," he said grimly, "this enterprise is costing us dearly and my bank balance may never recover."

"Sir," I said, "we must consider such things later. Right now, do you think what's left of the car can climb mountains?"

"I have no idea. Why do you ask?"

"Because we must in all haste pursue Chick Modell and bring him to justice."

"But that is a job for . . ." his voice trailed away.

I nodded. "You are right, sir, there is no longer a sheriff."

"Alas, then there is only us," said Mr. Wong gloomily, his fingers straying to the sore on his ear where he'd been shot during the terrifying ambuscade of the night before.

"Sir," I said, "once again your powerful intellect has gone right to the heart of the matter. There is only us."

"Then," said my employer in a tone of voice suggesting a man going to his own funeral, "let us proceed."

Modell's trail over the hills, even in the rain, was not hard to follow. Blood from his mangled hand and wounded horse spotted the grass, and I could even tell where he'd stopped to bandage the stumps of his fingers with a piece torn from his shirt.

The little Model T, a triumph of modern engineering, performed perfectly over this difficult terrain, and I silently pledged that I would endorse Mr. Henry Ford's fine product at the earliest possible opportunity.

Mr. Wong and I rode side by side without talking, listening for any sounds that might come to us over the roar of the engine. Now that the windshield was gone, rain battered into our faces and soon I began to feel the cold, shivering in my clammy oilskins.

Gradually it dawned on me that the trail of the man called Chick Modell had been curving in a gradual arc and was now headed almost due west, toward the distant mountains crowned with cottony gray clouds.

A wounded man fleeing for his life on a faltering horse would avoid the uncertainty of the mountains and instead ride south toward the anonymity of Helena or Virginia City where a new mount could be purchased. There was only one place in a western direction that could interest Modell: the dinosaur dig and, alone and vulnerable, the museum representative Jeremiah Schramm . . . and the beautiful Dr. Charity Hamilton.

I pushed the Model T harder, the rear wheels skidding and fishtailing on the wet grass, and headed back to the trail where I could set a better pace.

I told Mr. Wong of my terrible fears and added: "Now we are in a race against time. It could be that Modell believes if he can't have one woman, he can have another."

"And that would be Dr. Hamilton, I presume?"

"Indeed, sir, and I believe she is in deadly danger."

"I never liked that Schramm fellow," observed my employer. "There is a shifty, dishonest look about him."

Could Schramm be the unknown puppet master? I thought in alarm. *Could he be the one who used the mad Ben Cranwell for his own schemes, perhaps to take credit for the discovery of a new dinosaur species and the worldwide fame it would bring him?*

The thought filled me with horror, and I told Mr. Wong to hold on as I opened up the Ford's throttle. The churning wheels immediately threw mud into our faces as we roared along the muddy trail, scattering a startled herd of antelope that had come down out of the hills to graze.

"Onward, Chance!" yelled my employer as he waved his cane over his head like a saber. "There is an innocent life to be saved!"

And right at that moment the front wheels of the car plunged into a deep hole with a sickening *CRUNCH!* and the motor quit.

TWENTY-TWO

"What has happened?" cried Mr. Wong in alarm. I jumped out of the Model T and inspected the damage.

Disaster!

The heavy rains had washed out a large, horseshoe-shaped section of the trail, and I, thinking it was just another puddle, had driven right into it. The depression was several feet deep, and the gallant little Ford was nose first in muddy water that rose all the way up to the top of the hood. Worse, the right wheel was bent inward at a strange angle and it was obvious to me that the car would need major repairs before it could be driven again.

"Oh calamity!" wailed Mr. Wong. "When Miss Rhodes sees her car, she'll faint once because of the bullet holes, faint twice because of the wheels, and then present me with a horrible bill."

"Sir," I said urgently, stripping off my oilskins, "the dinosaur dig lies a short distance ahead, 'round the bend of yon hill. I will run there and you must follow at your best speed."

My employer was aghast. "But . . . but that's miles!"

I shoved my Colt in the pocket of my riding skirt.

"Please, sir, there's not a moment to be lost if we are to save Dr. Hamilton."

The rain was coming down so hard I was already soaked to the skin, my hair falling lank to my shoulders and the wet peasant blouse clinging to my breasts.

Bidding the somewhat dejected Mr. Wong to follow, I ran in the direction of the dig, praying that I'd be in time.

I spared but one backward glance for my employer, and saw him following me, picking his fastidious way through mud and mire. But I thought the posture of his stocky, oilskin-clad figure revealed both determination and resolution—at least, that's what I fervently hoped.

The bend in the trail came in sight and I ran on, splashing through puddle after puddle as the rain continued without let up. Above me, the clouds were iron-gray touched with black and in the distance thunder roared and growled like a wounded animal.

I staggered on, my head bent against the driving rain, the heavy Colt in my pocket weighing me down like a lead weight.

My breath was coming harder now, in short little gasps, and my chest felt like it was on fire. Yet I ran without slacking my pace, my hand on the Colt lest it fall out of my pocket and be lost in the mud.

I pounded around the bend, the lofty hill to my left crowned with pine and aspen, and saw the dinosaur hill about a mile ahead. I could make out the tents on its slope, but saw no sign of life.

Was I too late?

That fearful thought made me quicken my pace,

and a startled jackrabbit bounded away from me into the long grass as I ran past him.

Fit as I was, the run was taking its toll on me, and I stumbled and fell flat on my face, covering my entire front in mud. I rose quickly and felt for the Colt. It was gone. I kneeled down and frantically scrabbled around in the oozing mire. My fingers touched something hard. Thank God, it was the revolver. But the barrel and cylinder of the gun were thick with slimy mud and I dare not trust it in that condition.

Time was running out but the needs of the Colt had to take priority.

Sitting down on a patch of wet grass, I yanked my blouse over my head, shivering as the cold rain beat on my naked back and breasts, and began to clean the revolver with the soft cotton garment.

Chance, there is no time for this! my mind screamed. Yet it had to be done.

Working quickly, it took but a few minutes and the Colt was as clean as I could make it. The cylinder spun freely and the barrel seemed to be clear of mud and I inspected each cartridge and wiped it off thoroughly before reloading.

I pushed the gun back into my pocket, hoping for the best, and pulled on the muddy wet blouse. A quick glance back along the trail told me that Mr. Wong was not in sight, so I rose to my feet and began to run again.

Drawing closer to the hill, I saw no movement. But the dinosaur dig lay toward the crest, hidden from sight by a stand of aspen, and Modell and the others could be there.

I slowed my pace to a jog, not wanting to arrive out

of breath, and finally walked into the cover of the aspen. Gun in hand, I quietly made my way though the trees—and beheld a sight that froze my blood.

Chick Modell stood at the edge of the dinosaur pit, his damaged left hand hanging limp by his side. But his right fist was on the holstered butt of his Colt as he watched Jeremiah Schramm, who was bent over in the pit, digging with a small shovel, throwing dirt onto the parapet. Charity Hamilton, her face pale, stood close to Modell and she looked scared and tense.

It was now or never.

I walked out of the cover of the aspen toward the pit, and Modell turned and saw me. He made no move to draw his Colt. Was the gunman that confident in his ability to draw and shoot before I could even react? It seemed that way, and the realization chilled me.

"Well, well," Modell whispered as I drew closer—the same, vile whisper I'd heard in the barn—"the little Chinese whore come to join the party, and it looks like she's just in time, too."

I glanced into the pit where Schramm was digging. The man looked frightened, his long hair plastered over his face by the rain.

Behind him, the skeleton of the dinosaur lay glistening wet, its fangs bared as though ready to strike. The great curved hooks on its crouched legs gleamed like scimitars, terrible, slashing weapons that could slash and rip and disembowel.

But Schramm had uncovered two other bodies, one still wearing the remains of big-roweled California spurs on the rotted leather boots that covered the

skeletal feet, the other with long blond hair still clinging to the skull and scraps of a yellow dress blowing
on the slatted rib cage like hideous ribbons.

"Yeah, look at them," Chick Modell said, his eyes
wild, insane. "Miss High-and-Mighty had no time for
me, but she run off with a saddle tramp cowboy. They
were gonna be *sooo* happy together. Well, look at
them. How happy are they now?"

"That's . . . that's Mrs. Pagan," I said tightly, horror
clutching at my throat.

"Yeah," Modell smiled. "I killed 'em both. The
woman took a long time to die an' I had a lot of fun
with her while she was doing it. The cheap, little diseased whore."

The gunman spat into the pit, a twisted, evil look
on his face.

How different he looked now, hunched, shabby, a
bloody bandage wrapped around his ruined hand,
from the dapper little banker Ben Cranwell.

Charity Hamilton was watching me with wary
eyes, tense, expecting something to happen.

"When Dr. Grant was digging out the dinosaur, she
found the bodies," I said. "It scared her, and you
killed her to keep her quiet."

Modell smiled, a smile touched with pride and triumph. "She was a screamer that one. Screamed the
whole time I was doing . . . things . . . to her with my
knife." The crazed gunman's voice took on a vile
singsong note. "In an out . . . in and out . . . that's the
way the knife goes." He threw back his head and
laughed, an insane, demonic cackle.

"You later hid the knife in Brad Hudson's barn," I

said. "You knew it would be found and point to his guilt."

Modell shrugged, still giggling, wiping his watering eyes with the back of his bandaged hand. "Better him than me."

"What you didn't know was that you lost the silver tip of your belt when you were burying poor Mrs. Pagan. I found it and eventually it led me to you."

"Yeah, I knew you had that belt tip and I'd have gotten it from you in the barn if that drunken idiot of a miner hadn't interrupted our little get-together." He spat into the pit again. "You ruined a perfectly good belt for me, you little whore."

How did he know about the belt tip? my mind clamored. Only two people had seen me take it from the pit—Schramm and Dr. Hamilton.

I realized now that Schramm had been the puppet master, but right now I shook my head at Modell in disgust. "And you murdered poor little Jenny Pearson, didn't you?"

"Another whore," Modell snarled. "A snooty bitch that wouldn't give me the time of day. But I showed her, didn't I? Now she's spreading her legs in hell."

I'd heard enough.

"Chick Modell, alias Ben Cranwell, I'm arresting you for the murder of Dr. Victoria Grant and many others," I said with more confidence than I felt. "Throw down your gun and put your hands in the air."

"Go to hell!" Modell yelled, and he went for his holstered Colt.

But in that instant two things happened very quickly.

With a loud cry, Schramm jumped from the pit, the shovel above his head as he charged the little gunman.

Modell drew and fired. I'd never seen anyone present a Colt with such blinding speed and in that split second I knew why he'd been held in such high esteem by the Wild Bunch. He was faster, much faster, than either of my dear professors and more accurate, because his shot took Schramm between the eyes and the man screeched and tumbled back into the pit.

Like a striking rattler, Modell whirled very fast in my direction, his gun up and ready.

I fanned the hammer of my revolver, and, despite its bath in the mud, the finely honed action was as smooth as silk.

BLAM! BLAM! BLAM!

The three rounds sounded like a single shot, the Colt bucking wildly in my hand. Modell screamed and threw up his arms, his body jerking convulsively as he was hit and hit again. He staggered back toward the pit, his Colt hammering useless shots into the air, lost his footing, and tumbled over the edge.

I ran to the parapet and looked down at the fallen gunman.

His eyes were wide open, staring at me in disbelief, the front of his shirt stained bright scarlet with blood.

"You couldn't have beaten me," he gasped. "You just couldn't have. No one can beat Chick Modell with a gun."

"Poor sick, demented creature," I said softly. "You were close, quite close."

"You hit me," Modell choked, blood rushing into his mouth. "Damn you, bitch, you hit me twice."

I did not reply, because the gunman was looking over my shoulder and up at the gray sky, his eyes filled with unspeakable horror.

I do not know what Modell saw in that moment, the last instant of his life. Perhaps it was the imminent destruction of his monstrous soul.

Vile, horrible creature that he was, I nevertheless whispered a prayer to Lady Kuan Yin the compassionate that Chick Modell be born to another life where he could perhaps atone for his terrible sins in this one.

BLAM!

The angry whine of a bullet zipped past my head, and I crouched and turned quickly toward the sound of the gunshot. Charity Hamilton was standing there, Schramm's British Bulldog revolver extended straight out in both hands.

Stunned by this unexpected turn of events, I was rooted to the spot. Charity fired again, the bullet tugging at the sleeve of my blouse.

This time I moved, bringing up my Colt, the palm of my hand hovering over the hammer.

The paleontologist tried to get off another shot, but she was having trouble with the gun and it looked to me as though the cylinder was jammed with dirt.

"Throw the hogleg down, lady!" I yelled. "Or by God, I'll drop you right where you stand." (Oh thank you, dear professors Masterson and Leslie for teaching me the proper language of the genteel lady gunfighter!)

"Don't shoot!" Charity screamed, letting go of her gun like it was suddenly red-hot.

"You . . . you tried to kill me," I said.

"And I would have, if the lousy gun hadn't jammed," Charity returned bitterly.

"But why? I saved your life?"

"You stupid bitch, you don't understand a thing, do you?"

"What don't I understand, Dr. Hamilton? Tell me."

The woman, even soaked by the rain, was a stunning beauty, her dress plastered against the curves of her tall, lithe body like a second skin.

"She was going to have it all, the fame, the fortune," she said. "I couldn't let that happen."

"I don't understand," I said. "Are you talking about Dr. Grant?"

"Who else? Of course I'm talking about Victoria Grant. The dinosaur"—she waved a hand toward the pit—"was her discovery. The credit for a great new find in paleontology would be all hers, and there would be nothing left for me. No crumbs from the great lady's table, nothing."

Charity took a step toward me, but I raised the muzzle of the Colt and she stopped.

"Do you know what it's like to be a woman in a man's profession?" she asked. "A woman can never break through to the top, never. But a discovery like this one, well, it brings the respect of one's peers, even the grudging respect of the male scientists. It's a ticket to the very heights of paleontology and all that entails—money, respect, lecture tours, New York, London, Paris, Rome . . . I couldn't let all that slip through my fingers, now could I?"

"Doctor Hamilton," I said evenly, "in your own way you're just as crazy as Chick Modell was."

"Chick's brain was rotted with his filthy disease, but he was useful to me," Charity said without emotion.

"You had Modell murder Dr. Grant most horribly," I said. "That is unforgivable."

Charity shrugged. "I'm not looking for forgiveness. Victoria found the skeletons of the Pagan woman and her lover when she was digging around in the pit, just before Schramm came back from scouting the hills. What she saw scared her real bad, and when I came in from my own ride, she told me to leave at once and bring the sheriff. I realized now was my chance to get rid of her and I told Ben Cranwell, as he was then known in town, that she was here alone. He did my work for me."

"But how did you know Cranwell was a killer?" I asked.

"I knew. Trust me, I knew."

That last statement was puzzling, but I did not pursue it because I had yet another and more urgent question.

"You planned to get rid of poor Mr. Schramm, didn't you?"

The woman nodded, smiling. She showed no fear and that disturbed me.

"He could have given me away. In fact," she smiled, "he was covering up the two bodies and digging his own grave when you arrived. Still, his efforts won't be wasted. Soon you and that lunatic Modell will share it with him."

Again this was a disquieting statement. Surely this

woman was so crazy she'd lost all touch with reality, especially the .45-caliber reality in blue steel I was holding steady as a rock in my right hand.

"Once you started killing, you realized you had to kill again and again," I said.

Charity nodded. "If that's what it took, I was prepared to do it. In this godforsaken wilderness people disappear all the time. No one would suspect me."

"Yet you were afraid the great detective Mr. Chester Wong would uncover your terrible scheme as he tried to prove Brad Hudson's innocence. That's when you hired Silas Lime to murder us. But when I saw you in Crow Creek yesterday morning, you'd been there to kill him because he'd failed you."

"Lime was an incompetent fool, and he knew too much. I had to get rid of him. A quick sword thrust in the back as he looked for his gin bottle. It was almost too easy."

"And it was you who fired on my employer and myself as we were returning from the Pagan ranch."

"Yes, and I would have killed you both if that stupid cowboy hadn't interfered."

"He's dead. You killed his horse and he was thrown and he broke his neck."

Charity shrugged. "That was his bad luck. He should have minded his own business."

"You're under arrest," I said, anger rising in me. "I'm taking you back to town and into jail where you belong."

"You fool," Charity smiled, her lovely face perfectly calm. "Do you think, after all I've gone through, that I'd let a silly little whore like you arrest me?"

"Lady, you've no choice," I said.

"Oh yes she has," whispered a voice at my shoulder. I felt a cold steel muzzle press against my neck and the unmistakable triple click of the hammer being pulled back on a Colt revolver.

TWENTY-THREE

I slowly turned my head and beheld the scowling, wrinkled face of Dr. Thomas J. Lawson, MD.

"Don't try any sudden moves and drop that gun," the old man said.

I did as he told me, my Colt thudding onto the grass at my feet.

"Now turn around and face me, real slow."

Again I did as I was told, and Lawson called out over my shoulder. "Charity, get that gun."

The woman stepped behind me and picked up the Colt. "Tom," she said, her voice puzzled, "I can't use this. It's got no trigger."

The doctor nodded. "Yeah, it's tricked out for fancy shooting. Just hold on to it. This one is gun-slick and she can make fancy moves."

"I can't believe someone like you, a respected healer, could be involved in something like this," I said.

"Life's a bitch, ain't it?" Lawson smiled.

I hadn't heard the doctor sneak up behind me and guessed he'd been hiding in one of the tents, and his next statement confirmed my suspicions.

"I could have killed you anytime, but I wanted you

to take care of that diseased lunatic first. Then I realized Schramm's hole wasn't deep enough for the two of you. Seemed like a lot of hard work to dig all that wet dirt myself, so little lady, I'd say you got some shovel work to do."

He motioned with his gun. "Now get down into that pit and start digging, and make it plenty deep. When the museum people come to take away that dinosaur I don't want them to have any unpleasant surprises."

Oh, where is Mr. Wong? I thought desperately. But, my heart sinking, I immediately realized that my employer's great bulk, though a perfect vehicle for his powerful intellect, did not allow for great speed of movement.

Play for time, Chance, I told myself. *Spin this out.*

"How did someone like you get involved in this, Doctor?" I asked, using Lawson's title, playing to his vanity.

The little man smiled. "Dr. Hamilton and I are very much in love. After this is all over, we'll leave Crow Creek forever. And good riddance, I say. What the hell did the town ever give me?"

"But how did you first meet? Was it here at the dig?"

Hurry, Mr. Wong! Please hurry!

"Charity came to my surgery when she first arrived in Montana. She had a cold and I treated her for it. Later we became lovers."

"Then came pillow talk and she told you of her plan to get rid of Dr. Grant."

"Yes, and as I'm sure you've already guessed, I told her about Chick Modell, a man we could use."

"That's why you wanted Mr. Wong to drop this case. You'd used Modell to do your killing and you needed to protect him."

"Close, little lady, but no cigar. Two years ago Modell raped and murdered young Jenny Pearson. I knew that because I did the autopsy and found traces of the syphilis bacterium *Treponema pallidum* in sperm I took from her body. Modell was a banker, he was rich, so I began to—"

"Blackmail him," I finished it for him.

Lawson shrugged. "That's such a harsh, ugly word for it. Let's just say I borrowed money that I didn't ever have to pay back."

"But when I came to you with the full bottles of mercury, you realized Modell was not using the treatment you prescribed and was both dangerous and mentally unstable."

Lawson nodded. "That's when I knew I was playing a very dangerous game, and that Charity and I would have to get rid of him as soon as he killed that idiot Jeremiah Schramm. As it happened, Miss Lee, you did our work for us."

"How convenient for you," I said bitterly.

"Yes," the doctor said. "Yes it was."

He motioned with his gun toward the pit. "Now get down there and start digging. This is the second time I've told you. There won't be a third."

Charity Hamilton put her hand on the small of my back and pushed me toward the pit. I jumped into it and took the shovel from Schramm's dead hand.

"Do you know that this woman is a lesbian?" I asked, looking up into Lawson's cold blue eyes. "She has no interest in you as a lover. She's using you."

Lawson shrugged. "Hell, I know that. Charity can have all the females she wants. At my age I'll be happy to enjoy whatever is left over for me."

"Enough talk," Charity said. "Dig that grave, bitch, and make it quick."

I sank the shovel into the wet earth and threw dirt onto the parapet. Beside me, ugly in death, Schramm's open, sightless eyes were turned to the gray sky. A little beyond his body, the pathetic bones of Mrs. Pagan and her gaudy lover gleamed white and farther away the terrible dinosaur crouched, silent and watchful, rain running down the side of its skull—crocodile tears for my coming demise.

"Dig faster," Charity spat at me. "We don't have all day."

I shoveled another load of dirt, then another.

"Too slow, Tom," Charity said. "Kill her, then dig the damned hole yourself."

"Hard work," the doctor observed.

They were both looking at me, their eyes without feeling, devoid of mercy.

"Kill her, I said."

Lawson sighed. "Okay, but you'll have to help me bury the body."

He raised his Colt.

"Chaaarge!"

Mr. Wong ran from behind the tent closest to the pit, his great belly leading the way like the ram on a Roman trireme, his stubby legs gallantly doing their best to keep up.

Lawson turned, his Colt coming round fast, but my employer, his tiny dancer's feet fairly skipping over the wet grass, rammed him with his mighty stomach, knocking the man backward into the pit.

The little doctor attempted to get up, his gun in his white-knuckled fist, but as he came to his feet I screamed "Kiai!" and delivered a crashing round-house kick to his ribcage. Lawson yelped in pain and went down, his gun flying out of his hand.

Gasping, the little doctor tried to get on his feet while at the same time scrabbling around for his Colt. But I took up a karate fighting stance and said quietly: "Make a move toward that gun and I'll kill you. This is the first time I've told you. There won't be a second."

"Damn you!" Lawson said, sinking back to the ground. "Damn you to hell."

I glanced up at Charity who was frantically pulling back the hammer of my Colt. But my employer was too fast for her. His dragon-headed cane whacked down hard on the woman's wrist and she squealed and dropped the gun.

Satisfied, Mr. Wong went into a little display, lifting his feet high as he strutted toward the parapet, his head magnificently bobbing back and forth. He extended a hand to me.

"Once again, Chester Wong has solved the case and arrived in the nick of time to apprehend the felons," he said, rather pompously I thought. As I joined him on the edge of the pit, he pointed his cane at Charity, who was clutching her wrist, cursing me, Mr. Wong, and all God's creation.

"Chance," he ordered, "arrest that vile and murderous creature."

TWENTY-FOUR

We rode into Crow Creek just as night was falling. Including Modell's big American stud—which wasn't wounded too badly, poor thing, but had only been grazed by my errant bullet—and the doctor's mount, there had been three horses at the dinosaur dig. We put Lawson and Charity Hamilton—securely bound hand and foot—on two of them, while Mr. Wong and I rode the stud.

Alas, much time had been wasted in getting my portly employer onto the back of his mount, the animal standing about seventeen hands high and of a somewhat hypersensitive disposition. But faced with the choice of either riding or walking, Mr. Wong had reluctantly opted for the former and had obtained the services of a nearby rock as a mounting platform.

Unfortunately, every time the brilliant detective stuck out his short and stubby leg to board the beast, it took a sly step to the side, leaving my employer in the embarrassing position of standing on one leg while the other was cocked in the air. Inevitably, unable to recover his precarious balance, he fell over. This happened at least six or seven times, and each time Mr. Wong rose slowly to his feet and took me to task, rather irritably blaming me for failing to keep the recalcitrant equine still.

"I can't believe I've solved this most difficult case, brought the wrongdoers to justice, and freed an innocent man from the gallows," he said, "only to be killed at the moment of my triumph by a fall from a rock."

But finally, with much coaxing of the stud, Mr. Wong succeeded in getting up on the horse, though his seat on the flat English saddle was most uncertain and he looked very tippy indeed. Only when I got up behind him, the horse prancing around in small circles, annoyed by our combined weight, was I able to stabilize my employer and at the same time urge our mount forward.

The town was knee-deep in mustard-colored water as we arrived, the swollen creek having at last overflowed its banks. We splashed toward the saloon, since I believed Heath Wilson the saloon owner was now the most substantial and influential citizen in town and should hear our story before we spoke to Sheriff Havenick's taciturn deputy.

The oil lamps were lit on the walls of the buildings lining the boardwalks. The rain still fell steadily and at first there seemed to be few people abroad, but as we rode closer to the saloon, a small, curious crowd gathered, gawping at Charity Hamilton and their respected doctor bound hand and foot to the backs of their horses.

"Save me!" Lawson appealed to the crowd, turning in the saddle toward them. "I'm an innocent man being kidnapped and railroaded by these Orientals."

There was a murmur of angry disapproval from the crowd, which was growing in number, and I recalled how volatile and unpredictably violent these small Western cow towns could be.

"Let our doctor go, damn you!" said a voice from the crowd.

And another added: "String them Chinks up!"

I had retrieved my oilskins, though I was soaking wet underneath, and held my Colt ready in my right hand.

The crowd, which now numbered about thirty men and a few women and was getting increasingly worked up, kept pace with us along the boardwalk as we splashed toward the saloon.

"Save me, fellow citizens!" Lawson cried piteously. "Don't let them do this to me."

Another angry growl went up from the crowd and Mr. Wong turned his head around and said softly: "Chance, this really looks ugly."

One little banty rooster in a porkpie hat and striped silk vest stepped to the edge of the boardwalk and tried to lift Lawson from the saddle.

I drew the Colt from under my oilskins and pointed it at him. "Mister," I said coldly, "you better step back or I'll blow a hole in you."

The rooster suddenly went green around the gills, dropped his hands from Lawson and faded back into the crowd. I guess he realized I was somewhat on edge, ready for anything, and my temper was somewhat uncertain.

When we reached the saloon, the word of our coming had gone ahead of us because Wilson stood on the boardwalk, a shotgun in his hands. His bartender, a competent-looking older man, was off to his right. He, too, held a shotgun.

"What's going on here?" Wilson asked gruffly. His hair was freshly combed, his mustache neatly trimmed as his business day was just beginning.

"Heath, for God's sake save us!" Lawson wailed.

But the saloonkeeper ignored him, saying only: "Now you just sit quiet there, Doc. I want to hear what these people have to say."

I dismounted and then helped Mr. Wong off the horse and onto the boardwalk. Then, as the crowd gathered round, silent and hostile, I told Wilson the events of the day, sparing none of the details of the house of horrors where the man they knew as Ben Cranwell had lived. I told Wilson, but loud enough so the others could hear, how Cranwell, identified by Matt Jerrell as the gunman and train robber Chick Modell, had killed both Sheriff Havenick and Jeremiah Schramm and how I had evidence to prove he had murdered Jenny Pearson and Dr. Victoria Grant. Pushing my sou'ester hat up from my eyes, I described the events at the pit and how both Dr. Lawson and Charity Hamilton had used Modell for their own evil purposes.

When I'd finished talking, the crowd began to murmur among themselves, a few believing what I'd said, most finding the story too monstrous to believe.

Wilson stood in silence for a few moments, rocking back and forth on his heels, then he turned to an urchin who was standing close by. "Boy," he said, "go get the deputy and bring him right here." The boy fled, and Wilson turned to me and said: "I'm going to call a meeting of the old vigilante committee. We'll hold a hearing right now and get to the bottom of this."

He lifted his head and looked over the crowd. "Some of you boys get a wagon and bring those bodies in. There's enough of them, sounds like."

A few men left to do the saloon owner's bidding and Mr. Wong and I followed Wilson into the saloon. Lawson and Charity were freed of their bonds and followed, the woman looking over at me with both hatred and a gleam of triumph in her eyes.

She knew the crowd was with her, and probably Wilson himself, and she seemed confident she'd walk out of the saloon a free woman.

As for me, I realized with a sinking feeling that she could be right.

I stripped off my clammy oilskins, aware of dozens of pairs of male eyes going right to the front of the peasant blouse where it plastered wetly against my breasts, but I didn't care. I was tired and I just wanted this whole thing over with. I sat at a table near the bar, Wilson watching me, his eyes shrewd and calculating.

The deputy arrived, as humorless and morose as ever, and half a dozen other men filed into the saloon and took their places alongside Wilson. They were all townsmen, heavily armed and unsmiling, their grim faces revealing nothing. These men had to be all that was left of the infamous Crow Creek vigilantes.

Wilson strolled over to Lawson and Charity and had a brief conference, the two accomplices repeatedly pointing in my direction as they animatedly affirmed their innocence and my guilt, not only for arresting them on false evidence but for being of Chinese descent and therefore not to be trusted by any decent Caucasian.

Some tables had been hastily pushed together and

the vigilante committee took their places behind them, Wilson, because of his status as the town's leading citizen, was seated in the middle.

As the crowd elbowed their way into the saloon, a vigilante banged on the table with the butt of a Colt. "This hearing is now called to order," he said, "regarding the guilt or innocence of Ben Cranwell, banker, deceased, and the defendants Thomas J. Lawson, MD and Charity Hamilton, PhD. The honorable Heath Wilson presiding."

Mr. Wong rose to his feet, spluttering in indignation. "Sir, I object! My assistant and I are not on trial here. I have established the guilt of all parties beyond a shadow of a doubt."

"Sit down, fat man!" someone behind us shouted, and my employer, red-faced and angry, raised his cane and brandished it in a most threatening manner as he looked around the crowded saloon for the culprit.

"Mr. Wong, control yourself," Wilson said loudly. "Remember, we have a dead man lying in the back of the saloon." He leaned on his elbows and added in a quieter tone: "This is not a trial, sir. It's a hearing to determine if the circuit judge should be sent for, and, indeed, if Brad Hudson should be hanged tomorrow at dawn or freed."

"Shame!" someone in the crowd yelled, and someone else—I suspected the little banty rooster in the porkpie hat—cried: "Huzzah!"

"Order! Order!" roared Wilson, and gradually the crowd quieted down.

"Now, Miss Lee," Wilson said when order was restored, "let the committee hear your story."

Wearily I rose to my feet, vaguely aware that my nipples were hard and sticking straight out because of the coldness of my blouse and that the lotus tattoo was very prominent against my pale skin. Therefore to say that all eyes were upon me as I once again told of the events that had occurred since Mr. Wong and I had arrived in Crow Creek is not an exaggeration.

I talked for fully fifteen minutes, and when I'd finished Wilson nodded and said: "You may sit down." He was silent for a few moments and then turned to the deputy. "Deputy Scott, you must now do your duty."

The man looked startled and said: "Huh?"

"You will ride at once to Ben Cranwell's home and find this secret room if such exists. Report back here as soon as you possibly can. I now call a recess until your return."

Wilson rose and brushed his mustache with the back of his hand. "Nickel beers and shots until the deputy gets back, boys," he yelled. "Belly up to the bar."

A loud "Huzzah!" rose from the crowd as they elbowed their way to the bar while the deputy, looking grumpy and morose, went to find his horse.

"Chance," said Mr. Wong, rising to his feet, "I'm wasting away from hunger." He pulled up about a quarter inch of loose skin on the back of his hand. "See! Look how much weight I've lost since we arrived in this benighted place."

He then informed me that he would immediately make his way to Ma's Kitchen for a beefsteak sandwich or two, and asked if I'd care to join him.

But I preferred to take advantage of the recess to change out of my wet clothes and made my apologies to my employer. I left the saloon, aware of Charity Hamilton's hostile eyes burning into my back, and quickly walked to the hotel.

The clerk, whom I was now sure had been a paid informant for Chick Modell and had kept the man apprised of the comings and goings of Mr. Wong and I, was not at his post and I hurried upstairs. I lit the oil lamp and found a sadly crumpled shirt at the bottom of my suitcase that I kept only for emergencies and laid it on the bed beside the Dragon Box.

I stripped off the damp peasant blouse and riding skirt and dried myself with the rough hotel towel, rubbing it over my skin until it glowed. I wriggled into my straight black skirt and donned the shirt. It had puffed sleeves, a high neck and was old and frayed at the cuffs, but it was warm and dry and I buttoned it up gratefully.

Blowing out the oil lamp, I found a cheroot and thumbed a match into flame. I sat in my chair by the window, gratefully inhaling the fragrant smoke as the rain battered on the windows and a rising wind rustled restlessly around the eaves of the hotel.

With almost the entire town in the saloon, the street outside was quiet, the light of the oil lamps along the boardwalks illuminating the raking downpour, casting trembling yellow circles on the floodwater.

Across from where I sat, the windows of Crow Creek's false-fronted buildings looked at me with their dark, unreadable eyes, as though the town had withdrawn into itself, standing mute and numb on the prairie, counting its dead and holding its breath, wondering what was about to happen next.

"Let it end," I whispered, my words dropping like

pebbles into the pool of silence that was my room. "Please, just let it end."

I smoked the last of the cheroot and flicked the butt through the open window.

A horseman, his mount plodding slowly through the knee-deep water, raised his head as the smoking butt spiraled through the air, scattering sparks, then hissing into darkness.

By the hunched way he sat his horse, the man could only be the deputy returned, but he did not hurry, letting his exhausted mount pick its own way through the flood.

I left my room, went downstairs and ran through the rain to the saloon, just as the lawman swung out of the saddle and stepped onto the boardwalk.

He glanced at me, his eyes bleak and unwelcoming, and without a word followed me into the saloon.

The deputy didn't wait for the hearing to reconvene. He stood in the middle of the floor, grim and terrible, his hat and slicker dripping rain. Then he said softly, so everyone there had to strain to hear: "It's just like the little Chinee gal said. The room is there . . . it's all there." He looked around the suddenly hushed crowd. "Do you hear what I'm telling you? It's all there."

Long, lank, and stooped, the man strode to the bar. "Gimme a bottle. I'm a temperate man, but this is my night to get drunk."

I looked over at Charity Hamilton. She had also changed clothes. One of the women must have loaned her a dress, a demure cotton affair, high at the neck and printed all over with little blue flowers. Her long hair was pulled back, tied with a blue ribbon at the nape of her neck, and she looked poised, confident, and heartrendingly beautiful.

Lawson by contrast, sat hunched in his chair, gray and old, his haggard face seamed with deep wrinkles, his eyes washed out and lifeless.

How could a man like him, a fine physician and a respected member of the community, have fallen under the evil spell of a woman like Charity Hamilton? I asked myself.

Then I remembered something dear Miss Chastity Charmaine had once told me. "Chance," she said, "one thing the genteel young lady must always remember about men is that a hard cock has no conscience. That is something I've deduced from many years of experience."

Now, recalling the wise words of my dear headmistress, I could only conclude that Dr. Lawson's conscience rose no higher than his crotch.

Heath Wilson left the bar and once again took his place behind the tables. He called the hearing to order, then said to me: "Miss Lee, will Matt Jerrell, foreman of the Rafter H, testify that the man we knew as Ben Cranwell was in fact the desperado Chick Modell?"

"Yes," I said, "if he lives."

Wilson nodded. "Matt Jerrell is a good man and he was a fine Texas Ranger. His word on this matter is enough for me."

Shouts of "Hear! Hear!" rose from the crowd.

"Since Deputy Scott has confirmed your story and personally inspected Modell's house—"

"Damn right I did," the lawman growled from the

bar, his speech already slurred. "An' I wish to hell I hadn't."

Annoyed by this interruption, Wilson gave Scott a hard look then continued: "This, in conjunction with the evidence already presented, to wit, Billy Havenick's map and Modell's belt tip found at a crime scene, brings this hearing to conclude that Chick Modell, alias Ben Cranwell, murdered Dr. Victoria Grant, Sheriff Havenick, Jenny Pearson, and many others as yet unidentified while the balance of his mind was disturbed."

Wilson waved a hand toward the other vigilantes. "I and these other men will also visit the Modell home at first light to confirm Deputy Scott's report. In the meantime"—he turned to the lawman and roared dramatically—"free the innocent rancher Brad Hudson at once!"

"Hear! Hear!" the crowd yelled, as an unsmiling Scott grabbed his bottle off the bar and elbowed his way out the door.

The yelling continued, punctuated with loud cries of "Huzzah! Huzzah!" and "Well done!" as hands reached out to slap the scowling deputy on the back.

They just didn't get it.

It hadn't yet occurred to them, caught up as they were in the excitement of the moment, that Ben Cranwell's bank had been the money engine that powered Crow Creek and without him there would be no future for the town. He had supplied the house mortgages, the loans that had kept the ranchers going through the lean years, paid interest on carefully hoarded savings, and was supplying the money for the church that was yet to be built. Now the rug had been pulled out from under Crow Creek and the town would never recover. It didn't take much to kill a cow town in those days as the tide of modern civilization passed it by, and, without a bank, for there would be no other, Crow Creek was surely doomed.

"Now, young lady," Wilson said to me, after the hubbub had died down, "there is still the matter of your allegations against doctors Lawson and Hamilton." He brushed his mustache with the back of his hand. "Are there any more houses you wish to show us?"

I shook my head as loud retching, punctuated by deathly groans, came from just outside the saloon door. The horrors he'd seen had finally caught up with Deputy Scott and his stomach, urged on by rye whiskey, was signaling its revulsion.

"For Pete's sake somebody see to that man," Wilson ordered impatiently.

He watched in silence as a couple of men reluctantly wandered outside, then he turned to me again and continued: "I need something concrete, young lady. Hard evidence against the two people you've accused."

I had none. There was no hard evidence connecting Charity Hamilton to Chick Modell, nothing that would stand up in a court of law before a Crow Creek jury.

Defeated, and exhausted from the events of the day, including my wild run through the rain, I hung my head and whispered: "Sir, I have no such evidence at this moment."

"Sir!" exclaimed Mr. Wong loudly, rising to his feet. He looked relaxed and almost confident, beefsteak sandwiches having restored his morale to its usual high level. "You have the word of Chester Wong that the accused confessed to their part in the killing of Victoria Grant and would have murdered my assistant had I not intervened and saved the day."

"Evidence?" asked Wilson. "Come now, sir, evidence."

"Surely the word of Wong is evidence enough," declared my employer.

"Not in this case," said Wilson evenly. "All I have is the word of two people against two people, and the accused are very respected professionals well thought of in this community."

As cries of "Hear! Hear!" rang out again, Mr. Wong sputtered his outrage. Wilson ignored him and consulted with the other members of the vigilante committee. I watched him nod in agreement to something, then he banged his fist on the table and hushed the muttering crowd.

"Since no hard evidence has been presented against Dr. Lawson and Dr. Hamilton, " he said, "I would not feel justified in bringing the circuit judge to Crow Creek, since without evidence, there is no case. I therefore rule that they should be allowed to go in peace."

As the crowd cheered wildly, Wilson stood and, though he could barely be heard, declared: "This hearing is now closed."

Charity Hamilton walked up to where I sat. I stood and faced her, seeing the triumph and bitter hatred in her eyes. She leaned toward me, her soft, lush mouth moving like a silken butterfly against my ear, her voice a thin whisper: "You little tramp, did you really think you could win against me?"

"I could have killed you today," I said. "Now I wish I had."

Charity threw back her head and laughed as Lawson stepped beside her and circled her slender waist with his arm. "Boys," he yelled, waving toward the bar, "the drinks are on me!"

The crowd cheered and the piano player struck up "Oh Dem Golden Slippers," and suddenly I felt sick to my stomach.

Mr. Wong stepped beside me and gently patted my shoulder. "Chance," he said, "we have accomplished what we came to Crow Creek to do. Our client's father is a free man and that is all we ever intended."

I looked at him and smiled. "Sir, once again your great intellect goes right to the heart of the matter." I looked around the bar, the flushed and laughing Lawson and Charity the focus of everyone's attention. "I do believe it is time to go home."

TWENTY-FIVE

We were to leave on the noon train, yet, as I dressed that morning in the same clothes I'd worn when I first arrived in Crow Creek, settling my straw boater perfectly straight and level on my piled-up hair, there was much to do before that time.

And the most important of these tasks was to see the Teton Kid decently laid to rest.

The poor young man was placed in his coffin at the saloon, then the hearse carried him down the flooded street to the cemetery.

I hadn't expected it, but around twenty cowboys came in from outlying ranches for the funeral, riding their horses through the knee-deep water in silence. They were for the most part lean, quiet-eyed men, their skins leathery and bronzed from sun and wind, and they came for no other reason than to say farewell to a man many of them hardly knew, but considered one of their own. The cemetery, being on higher ground, was not flooded and the preacher, gray-haired and grim, was already waiting, his Bible held in a gnarled hand pressed close to his breast.

Mr. Wong had not yet breakfasted and was somewhat irritable that morning, but as he approached the grave he went into a little display for the benefit of the cowboys and the few other mourners, lifting his neat feet high and bobbing his sleek head for all to admire.

On the very edge of the cemetery stood a small frame house, the home of the caretaker, a man named Jones who also doubled as town custodian, keeping the street and alleys clean and free of garbage.

There was a good deal of activity at the house, with matronly women coming and going in great haste with towels and buckets of water, and someone whispered to me that Mrs. Jones was about to have her baby, her seventh.

"Poor thing," I said. "I hope everything goes well with her."

Cowboys reverently lifted the Teton Kid's casket from the hearse and laid it at the edge of the grave. The preacher waited in silence, then said: "Ahem," and in a booming, cavernous voice began the doleful and depressing Christian service for the dead.

Ignoring the man, I closed my eyes and whispered a prayer to Lady Kuan Yin the merciful, asking her that she teach the eternal soul of the Teton Kid to balance its karma so that it could fulfill the divine plan by doing loving service in its next life and thus break the circle of birth and death. This I humbly asked, hoping for a favorable reply, since Kuan Yin has vowed to save all the children of God, turning her back on none.

But now that he had a captive audience of wayward cowboys, the preacher was getting himself worked up into a Bible-bashing, fire-and-brimstone frenzy in which the words "hellfire" and "damnation" and "eternal suffering" were being used very frequently.

I caught his eye, giving him a hard look, and his voice faltered—maybe because, like the rest of the townspeople, he was keenly aware that it was I who'd shot the notorious Wild Bunch gunman, Chick Modell—and he concluded his tirade with a hasty and gulping: "Amen."

The cowboys lowered the casket into the damp earth, under the headstone I'd ordered. It was plain enough, just a rectangular piece of marble with the words:

THE TETON KID
1888–1908
A
GALLANT
KNIGHT

But I hoped this simple sentiment was enough to do justice to the memory of that valorous and noble soul.

Bending, I picked up a handful of earth and scattered it on the Kid's coffin, and right at that moment Mrs. Jones' baby came into the world with a loud and outraged cry.

"Thank you, Lady Kuan Yin," I whispered, looking up at a blue sky now cleared of rain clouds. In that sweet instant I knew she was telling me that the Teton Kid would soon be reborn, as this child had just been, so that he could again seek the path to divine enlightenment.

The sun was now bright in the sky and in the distance the mountains were sharply defined, the fir and aspen on their slopes a vivid green after so much rain. The air smelled of grass and pine and it felt good to be young and strong and alive.

"He was a brave youth," said Mr. Wong, laying his hand on my shoulder. "And I believe we've given him a fine send-off."

I nodded, too overcome to speak.

"Now," continued my employer, "we must breakfast to keep up our strength for the long journey ahead."

"Sir," I said, humbly lowering my eyes to the ground, "we have yet another sad task. We must speak to Mrs. Havenick and offer our condolences."

"A shrewish woman," observed Mr. Wong. "She won't thank us, you know."

"Nevertheless, sir, I feel it is our duty."

My employer sighed and consulted his watch. "Oh, very well. We have time enough, I suppose."

When I knocked on the door of the sheriff's home, Mrs. Havenick herself answered, standing on her own two feet with the aid of a cane. She wore a black traveling dress and a matching bonnet.

"Come in," she said, her eyes blank, showing neither friendliness nor hostility.

The woman ushered us into the parlor where she sat primly on the edge of a chair, her still hands folded in her lap.

"You were with him when he died," she said. "Did he suffer?"

"No," I replied. "It was very quick."

Mrs. Havenick nodded. "I'm glad. Glad for him. It's not good to suffer at the moment of death."

"You are leaving, ma'am?" asked Mr. Wong.

"Yes. Billy and I are taking Burt home to Texas. We had not truly lived as man and wife for years, but I will not see him laid to rest in foreign soil."

There was a drawn-out, awkward silence.

Then Mr. Wong rose and gave the widow a little bow. "I wish to offer you my sincere condolences, ma'am."

Mrs. Havenick graciously inclined her head. "Thank you for coming. It was most considerate." She got to her feet and walked toward the door and my employer and I followed at a respectful distance.

Once on the porch, the widow placed the tips of her fingers on my arm.

"If you hadn't come to Crow Creek, my husband would still be alive."

There was no bitterness in her voice. It was just a statement of fact.

"Yes," I said. "I'm so sorry."

"Better for a man like Burt to die with a gun in his hand. Better that than to grow old and feeble and sick and have nothing left but memories, fading away like images on a yellowed photograph." She touched the corner of her left eye with her gloved finger. "That is my fate."

"I'm so sorry," I said again, finding no other words.

Mrs. Havenick smiled faintly. "So am I."

I had no appetite for breakfast and contented myself with coffee. Mr. Wong availed himself of steak and eggs and anxiously kept watch on the kitchen until the smoking platter was set before him.

But he had no sooner started eating than the door

opened and Brad Hudson walked in, Angela at his side.

The rancher looked ten years younger. He was freshly shaved and his hair was combed and he wore a beaming smile. "Mr. Wong," he said, thrusting out his hand, "thank you, thank you for everything."

My employer could not give one of his fine displays sitting down, but he did bob his head this way and that and waved his hand in a most expressive manner.

"It was nothing," he declared. "A simple matter of criminal detection skills combined with a superior intellect."

"God bless you, Chester Wong," Angela said. "You saved my father's life. I'll never forget you for that. Now I know why you are called the world's greatest detective."

"Indeed," said my employer. "From Scotland Yard to the meanest precinct station in Calcutta, from Buenos Aires to Berlin, Nome to Nanking, the name of Wong is known and respected by the law and much feared by the criminal classes."

"How," I asked, before my excitable employer got too overheated, "is Matt?"

Angela smiled happily. "He's recovering well. He badly wants to get out of bed, but I've told him next week will be time enough. By then he'll be strong enough to stand on his own two feet for our wedding. I just wish you and Mr. Wong could attend."

"Alas, dear lady," returned my employer, "duty calls. There are many other cases waiting to be solved by Wong, and felons and low persons brought to justice."

"Mr. Wong," said Brad Hudson, "I guess you know money's been tight around here recently."

"Ah yes," said my mentor. "There is the little matter of my fee."

Hudson nodded, grinning. "As soon as I get back to the Rafter H we're going to cut you out fifty of the finest beef cattle this side of the Brazos. They will be there waiting for you, any time you want 'em." He slapped Mr. Wong on the back. "Can you beat it? You, the most famous private eye in the world, and you're now my partner in the cattle business."

My employer smiled weakly. "That sounds wonderful."

"Fifty of the best head, mind," the rancher said. "No yearlings or culls. I'm talking the best Hereford steers I have." Hudson held up his hand. "No, don't thank me. I can't do any less for the man who saved my life."

Mr. Wong's face was stricken, but he managed another sickly smile.

"I'm sure hoping things get better from now on, an' I reckon they will," Hudson said. "For one thing, now I've got the best claim to that big lizard up in the hills."

"Please, Mr. Hudson," I said, fear knifing at me. "Leave the dinosaur alone. It's taken too many lives already. It just lies there in its pit, grinning to itself as people die around it. It's a thing of evil. Have nothing to do with it."

Hudson laughed. "It's just a pile of bones, is all. An' they say it could be worth ten thousand dollars. Nothing evil about that, little lady."

"Please, just bury the thing and let it guard the hills for the Indians. That is maybe why it is there."

"Some Flathead superstition ain't gonna keep me away from that money," Hudson said, his grin slipping. "The big chicken is mine, no matter what that Charity Hamilton gal says."

I let it go. I'd said what I believed, and could do no more.

Angela Hudson leaned over the table and kissed Mr. Wong on his smooth cheek. "God bless you, you brilliant, brave man," she said, "God bless you."

After the Hudsons had gone, my employer held his head in his hands. "Chance," he groaned miserably, "this case has been a financial disaster. What am I to do? What . . . am . . . I . . . to . . . do?"

"Sir," I said humbly, "you could eat those steers."

Mr. Wong's head snapped up, a delighted smile on his moon face. "But of course! Why didn't I think of that? Meat can be frozen. Hudson could pack the odd steer to me just about anywhere in the world."

"Fifty steers is a lot of meat," I pointed out.

But Mr. Wong shoveled a chunk of steak into his mouth, looked down his nose at me and sniffed: "I have a large appetite."

After we'd eaten, we stood on the boardwalk outside the restaurant and my employer consulted his watch. "Two hours until train time," he said, "and then we can be free of Crow Creek forever."

"Not quite, sir," I said.

"Whatever do you mean, child?"

I inclined my head down the street and Mr. Wong turned in that direction, only to blanch in horror as a sad and melancholy procession made its way toward us.

A huge carthorse, a stern and bearded farmer on its back, was pulling the Model T along the flooded street by means of a stout rope. The little car was shot full of holes, its windshield shattered, and from the bent front wheel came a gloomy little squeak with every revolution.

The farmer stopped his mount as he came opposite us. "By the look of ye, you've got to be Chester Wong, the detective," he said.

My employer allowed that this was indeed the case.

"The vigilante committee tole me to drag this here auto-mobile into town, said you'd know where it was a-goin'."

"Alas," said Mr. Wong in great agitation, "I'd forgotten all about that accursed machine."

"An' did ye fergit where it's goin'?" the farmer asked suspiciously, spitting a stream of tobacco juice into the water.

"No," groaned my employer, "that I haven't forgotten." He waved a hand up the street. "Do you know Spinster Rhodes' house?"

"Reckon I do," the farmer replied.

"Then haul it up there and I'll follow."

"Cost you two dollars, for me bringing this thing in to town, I mean."

Mr. Wong sighed. "I'll pay you when I get there."

The farmer left the Ford in front of Miss Rhodes' house, and my employer and I climbed the stairs to the porch and knocked on the door.

The plump lady answered almost immediately,

looked over Mr. Wong's shoulder at her shot-up car, gave a little cry, lifted her pinafore over her face, and fainted—rather prettily I thought—right into my employer's arms.

Mr. Wong lowered the woman gently to the floor and, in a state of great agitation, chaffed her fat little hand.

"Speak to me, dear lady," he wailed. "I assure you, all will be well."

Miss Rhodes slowly came round, beheld her car a second time, cried out in anguish, lifted her pinafore over her face, and promptly fainted again.

"Oh dear," said my employer in great distress, "I fear she'll never recover, but will faint and go on fainting forever."

But when the spinster stirred a third time, she lifted a corner of her pinafore from a bright blue eye that stared balefully at Mr. Wong. "This," she declared in a strong enough voice, "will cost you a bundle."

And indeed it did.

My employer was still dolefully counting the cost as we made our way back to the hotel to pick up our luggage.

"We must get to the train station at all possible speed," he said. "If I stay an hour longer in Crow Creek than I have to, I'll be quite bankrupt."

Once again loaded down with our luggage I struggled after Mr. Wong as he forged ahead toward the station, as always carrying only his cane.

"Hurry, child," he said, turning to me in irritation, "stop gawping and dawdling."

This time there was no gallant young Teton Kid to help me across the street and I had to wade through the flood, following my employer who had his patent leather pumps in his hand and his pants rolled up to his knees.

I did what I could to lift my tight black skirt above the water, but to no avail and by the time we reached the station platform, it was flapping wetly around my legs.

Mr. Wong slipped on his socks, shoes, and spats, consulted his watch and declared: "Now we can do nothing but wait."

We'd been standing there for only a few minutes, hopefully looking down the tracks as people do when waiting for a train, when there was a commotion in the street and the sound of many horses splashing through the floodwater.

"Holla," said Mr. Wong, "what goes on here?"

A party of heavily armed horsemen, Heath Wilson in the lead, trotted past the station, mud and water flying in all directions from the high-stepping hooves of their mounts.

Mr. Wong hastily made his way to the edge of the platform and waved his stick in the air. "I say, Wilson, over here!"

The saloon owner nodded and swung his horse around, riding close to where my employer stood.

"What goes on here?" asked Mr. Wong.

"You mean you haven't heard?"

"Heard what?"

"Doc Lawson and Charity Hamilton are dead."

Mr. Wong took a step backward in amazement. "Dead? But . . . but how can that be?"

Wilson shrugged. "They went back up there to the hill last night. Couple of cowboys hunting strays found their bodies. They was all shot to pieces but laid out nice and neat at the bottom of the pit with pebbles on their eyes."

"But who—"

"Flatheads most like. There was moccasin tracks all over the place."

So it was Ghost Bear. His threat hadn't been an empty one after all. He didn't want Charity to take his sacred dragon away and he killed her to keep it and with her Lawson.

"We're going after them Indians," Wilson said, waving a hand toward his grimly determined posse. "But if you ask me, they're halfway to Canada by now."

"Mr. Wilson," I said urgently, "Brad Hudson plans to claim the dinosaur and sell it. Please convince him otherwise. It will bring him nothing but grief as it's done to so many already."

Wilson shook his head. "Not much chance of that, little lady. Them cowboys say the skeleton is gone. I don't know how they did it, because those bones must have been heavy, but the Flatheads dug it up and carried it off somewheres. I reckon they buried it at a secret place in the hills where Brad Hudson will never find it, or anybody else for that matter."

"That is for the best," I said. "The Indians believe the Great Spirit appointed the dragon to guard their sacred hills."

Wilson took off his battered Stetson and wiped the band with his fingers. "Don't know nothing about that," he said, settling the hat back on his head. "But it's gone for sure."

The saloon owner studied Mr. Wong and myself

closely for a few moments, then said: "You know, I don't know the right or wrong of this thing. If what you two said in the saloon last night is true, then the doc and his woman were guilty of terrible crimes and got what they deserved. If they wasn't, then they're two more innocent people killed for no reason, and there's already been enough killing in Crow Creek."

He nodded toward the tracks. "My advice to both of you is to get on that train and never come back here. Trouble sure seems to follow you."

He lifted his hand in farewell then splashed through the water toward his waiting companions.

TWENTY-SIX

I looked out the carriage window as the Montana landscape flashed past, the flat prairie stretching as far as the eye could see until it merged with the hazy blue sky.

It was here, in the olden days, that the Flathead and Pend d'Oreilles and later the Nez Percé, Shoshone, and the horseless Sheepeaters had come to hunt buffalo. All had shared a common fate as they were driven from their lands by white settlement, the tribes reduced by war, disease, alcohol, and the destruction of their culture.

Now the silent land seemed empty and the only monuments that marked the passing of the Redman were the buffalo wallows. The shallow depressions dotting the plains were long overgrown by grass, but they waited with timeless patience for the vast, dusty and bellowing herds that would never return.

I must admit these thoughts were somewhat gloomy, but I had plenty of reason to be in a blue funk since Mr. Wong had told me earlier that the Case of the Silver Arrowhead, as he called it, had been ruinously expensive and that we must cut corners in future.

"Your clothing allowance will have to be reduced, I'm afraid," warned my employer, smoothing the fine material of his suit coat over his great belly. "These are hard times, Chance, we must all be prepared to make sacrifices."

I looked away from the window as voices were raised in animated talk at the other end of the carriage, and beside me Mr. Wong roused from a doze.

Three men, smart and well groomed in immaculate black broadcloth with the look of wealthy entrepreneurs about them, were talking to the conductor who gestured excitedly in our direction. Seeing my employer awake and alert, the men approached us, and the oldest of the three, a distinguished-looking old gentleman with snow-white hair and a huge, misshapen nose, stuck out his hand. "My name is John Pierpont Morgan, and this is my railroad. You, sir, by your intelligent forehead and grave demeanor, must be the famous detective Mr. Chester Wong."

"At your service, sir," replied Mr. Wong, beaming. He went into a little display, bobbing his head while he preened himself, pulling down the cuffs of his immaculate white shirt under his suit coat and making a great show of his fine manners.

"And this pretty young lady?"

"My assistant, sir, Miss Last Chance Lee." My employer sighed and waved a negligent hand in my direction. "She rendered me some small assistance during my recent and most perplexing case."

At this pretty and unexpected compliment, I lowered my eyes modestly to my lap and felt my cheeks burn.

"Indeed, sir," said J.P. Morgan, "your fame is al-

ready spreading. We hear"—at this point he introduced his associates, both rich and powerful men—
"that you saved an innocent rancher from the very
shadow of the gallows."

"Most succinctly stated, sir," declared my employer. "Though I must confess even my considerable
powers of deduction were severely put to the test, for
the villain of the piece was a clever and slippery cus-
tomer."

"Precisely," said J.P. Morgan, "and that is why we
stand before you now. Can I prevail upon you, sir, to
put aside your usual modesty and relate to us the
story of your latest case, one that must surely rival
any undertaken by even the great Sherlock Holmes?"

"Why of course, sir," quoth Mr. Wong, pleased by
this comparison, "and thankee. Please be seated"—he
directed Mr. Morgan to the seat facing our own—"and
I will tell you of the Case of the Silver Arrowhead, a
tale that will go down in criminal history as both my
greatest triumph and my greatest trial."

Once Mr. Morgan was settled, my employer
steepled his fingers and said: "It all began three days
ago, when I first beheld the miserable town of Crow
Creek . . ."

Mr. Wong—his Irish half made him an excellent
and colorful speaker—kept his audience enthralled
for more than two hours. And after his story was done
each man jumped to his feet and enthusiastically
shook his hand with many a "Oh, well done, sir!" and
loud "Huzzah!"

"Now, Mr. Wong," declared the obviously delighted J.P. Morgan, "you must come to my private car

and join me for lunch. My chef tells me he has an excellent saddle of lamb and a rare sirloin of beef."

My employer raised his hand, a horrified look on his round face. "Pray you, sir, not a morsel. Not so much as a crumb. This case, as you are now aware, has left me with little appetite for anything but rest."

"Ah," said Mr. Morgan, "I understand. Perhaps some other time."

"Still," said Mr. Wong hastily, rising to his feet, "perhaps I could partake of a little something. I fear I have a long journey ahead and might force down just a soupçon to keep up my strength."

Mr. Wong and I were then ushered politely toward his private car by Mr. Morgan and the others, but I'd quite forgotten the Dragon Box. In my haste to follow my employer I'd left it on my seat and now I rushed back to get it.

Mr. Wong and the other gentlemen, all being of a substantial size, stood like immovable rocks in the jolting, swaying carriage, but I, being small and light, was thrown this way and that as I hurried to rejoin them.

Mr. Wong turned and looked at me in considerable irritation. "Come, child," he said, "and stop gawping out of the windows like a rube." He shook his head at me. "My, how you dawdle."

HISTORICAL NOTE

Over the years, paleontologists discovered some of the world's most impressive and important dinosaur fossils in Montana, including the first Tyrannosaurus skeleton, found north of the town of Jordan in 1908—the year in which *The Silver Arrowhead* is set.

Between 1870 and 1897, Edward Drinker Cope touched off what's been called the Great Dinosaur Gold Rush in Montana. Cope hired teams of collectors to excavate dinosaur bones in a race to be the first to describe the many new species being found almost daily.

Recently, finds in the Judith Basin and the Bear Paw Mountains, especially along the Rocky Mountain front of the Two Medicine Formation, have made the state a major attraction for paleontologists.

Jack Horner and his associates at Montana State University's Museum of the Rockies made startling discoveries in the eroded hills near Choteau, including fossils of baby dinosaurs and colonies of large, duck-billed herbivores.

In the summer of 1990, Horner excavated Sue, the most complete Tyrannosaurus skeleton ever found in North America.

By 1908, cow towns like Crow Creek, which had long served the needs of cowboys and cattlemen, were doomed, like the dinosaur, to extinction.

In 1907 the editor of *The Montana Churchman* wrote: "That time [the cowboy era] has gone forever. Already in her westward march, Civilization has planted her feet firmly on this territory." Cow towns with their jangling saloons, false-fronted stores, and shacks for the girls on the line were replaced by farming communities that looked exactly like what they tried to be—transplanted Midwestern villages.

Strange thing about a ghost cow town: It doesn't tumble down and rot when all the cowboys are gone. Rather, the clapboard buildings start to take on the color of the surrounding landscape and the town just slowly fades away until the night when the rising moon pushes aside a cloud and looks for his old friend . . . and finds only emptiness and the sighing wind.

SIGNET

Charles G. West

Medicine Creek   0-451-19955-3

The white-born, Cheyenne-raised warrior Little Wolf has left
the warpath behind to create a prosperous life with his wife
Rain Song. But when a renegade army slaughters his tribe
and takes Rain Song captive, Little Wolf's dreams for peace
are overrun by the need for bloody vengeance.

Mountain Hawk   0-451-20215-5

Mountain man Trace McCall must rescue his beloved from a
kidnapper without getting caught in a growing conflict
between white homesteaders and Indians.

Son of the Hawk   0-451-20457-3

When a war party of renegade Sioux slaughters his Shoshoni
tribe, the young brave White Eagle has no choice but to
venture into the world of the white man to find mountain
man Trace McCall—the father he never knew.

To order call: 1-800-788-6262

SIGNET HISTORICAL FICTION   (0451)

RALPH COTTON

"Gun-smoked, blood-stained, gritty believability...
Ralph Cotton writes the sort of story we all hope
to find within us."—Terry Johnston

"Authentic Old West detail."—*Wild West Magazine*

HANGMAN'S CHOICE   20143-4
They gunned down his father in cold blood. They are his
most elusive enemies, the outlaws known as *Los
Pistoleros*. And they're still at large. But Federal Deputy
Hart will not give up the chase...Until they hang.

DEVIL'S DUE   20394-1
The second book in Cotton's "Dead or Alive" series. The
Los Pistoleros gang were the most vicious outlaws
around—but Hart and Roth thought they had them under
control...Until the jailbreak.

Also Available:
MISERY EXPRESS   19999-5
BADLANDS   19495-0
BORDER DOGS   19815-8

To order call: 1-800-788-6262

S306